J. Grant Wilson

Biographical Sketches of Illinois Officers

engaged in the War against the Rebellion of 1861

J. Grant Wilson

Biographical Sketches of Illinois Officers
engaged in the War against the Rebellion of 1861

ISBN/EAN: 9783741124976

Manufactured in Europe, USA, Canada, Australia, Japa

Cover: Foto ©Raphael Reischuk / pixelio.de

Manufactured and distributed by brebook publishing software
(www.brebook.com)

J. Grant Wilson

Biographical Sketches of Illinois Officers

PRICE FIFTY CENTS.

BIOGRAPHICAL SKETCHES

OF

ILLINOIS OFFICERS

ENGAGED IN THE WAR AGAINST THE

REBELLION OF 1861.

BAKER—CHICAGO

BY JAS. GRANT WILSON.

CHICAGO:
JAMES BARNET, 189 LAKE STREET.
1862.

OF

ILLINOIS OFFICERS

ENGAGED IN THE WAR

AGAINST THE REBELLION OF 1861.

BY JAMES GRANT WILSON.

Vixere fortes ante Agamemnona
Multi: sed omnes illacrimabiles
Urguentur ignotique longa
Nocte, carent quia vate sac.

ILLUSTRATED WITH PORTRAITS.

CHICAGO:
JAMES BARNET, 189 LAKE STREET.
1862.

GOV. YATES.

THIS VOLUME

OF

BIOGRAPHICAL SKETCHES OF THE LEADERS OF REGIMENTS,

OF WHOM ILLINOIS IS SO JUSTLY PROUD,

IS RESPECTFULLY DEDICATED TO

F. J. T.

Each soldier's name
Shall shine untarnished on the rolls of fame,
And stand the example of each distant age,
And add new lustre to the historic page.

DAVID HUMPHREYS.

———

En avant! Marchons
Contre leur canons!
A travers le fer, le feu des battaillons
Courons a la victoire!

CASIMIR DE LA VIGNE.

———

Sound the clarion, fill the fife,
To all the sensual world proclaim—
One crowded hour of glorious life
Is worth an age without a name.

SIR WALTER SCOTT.

———

To the hero, when his sword
Has won the battle of the free,
Death's voice sounds like a prophet's word;
And in its hollow tones are heard
The thanks of millions yet to be.

FITZ-GREENE HALLECK.

———

Let fame that all hunt after in their lives,
Live register'd upon our brazen tombs,
And then grace us in the disgrace of death;
When spite of cormorant devouring Time,
Th' endeavor of this present breath may buy
That honour, which shall bate his scythe's keen edge,
And make us heirs of all eternity.

WILLIAM SHAKSPERE.

Patriots have toiled, and in their country's cause
Bled nobly; and their deeds, as they deserve,
Receive proud recompense. We give in charge
Their names to the sweet lyre. The historic Muse,
Proud of the treasure, marches with it down
To latest times; and Sculpture, in her turn,
Gives bond in stone and ever-during brass
To guard them, and to immortalize her trust.

WILLIAM COWPER.

———

——— O courage! there he comes;
What ray of honor round about him looms!
O, what new beams from his bright eyes do glance!
O princely port! presageful countenance
Of hap at hand! He doth not nicely prank
In clinquant pomp, as some of meanest rank,
But armed in steel; that bright habiliment
Is his rich valor's sole rich ornament.

JOSHUA SYLVESTER.

———

Like the desolating locust cloud,
The spoilers blight the plains,
And the blaze of Freedom's sun they shroud
With carnage, blood and chains;
Like the rush of the mountain cataract,
The patriot warriors shall bear them back.

How manhood spurns at the name of slave,
When roused from slavery's dream;
How nerved the arm that wields each glaive
With vengeance in its gleam,
While thickly the autocrat's savage hordes
Are sinking beneath their chivalrous swords!

WILLIAM WILSON.

CONTENTS.

APPENDIX.

LIST OF PORTRAITS.

BIOGRAPHICAL SKETCHES

OF

ILLINOIS OFFICERS.

GOV. YATES.

WHEN the story of the War against the Rebellion of 1861 passes into History, the records of the soldiers of Illinois will prove to be as rich in deeds of daring and heroism as any page in the annals of the Revolution, and their names will live in the affectionate remembrance of their countrymen "to the last syllable of recorded time." What loyal dweller therein can look abroad over the faithful States, and not feel a flush of pride, that he can at least claim ILLINOIS as the home of his adoption, if not the place of his birth, content to share her fortunes and the fame of her noble sons who, with

"Nerves of steel and hearts of oak,"

have driven back the enemy on every battle-field where they have met. She has furnished for the war five Major Generals, seventeen Brigadier Generals, and one hundred and fifty-four Colonels of the regular and volunteer service, many of whom won their positions by gallantry on the battle-fields of MILL SPRING, BELMONT, WILSON'S CREEK, PEA RIDGE, NEW MADRID, DONELSON, ISLAND No. 10, SHILOH, IUKA, CORINTH and the HATCHIE. Prominent among the heroes of the day, stands our noble Governor and Commander-in-Chief, RICHARD YATES, who, although he has visited the tented field only to carry aid and words of cheer to our sick and wounded, has acted well his part, and by his untiring and patriotic efforts, has contributed no less

to the glory and renown of ILLINOIS than the chieftains who have led her invincible legions "amid sheeted fire and flame." With their names, his will stand high upon her roll of honor of "brave men and worthy patriots, dear to God, and famous to all ages."

RICHARD YATES was born in Warsaw, Gallatin county, Kentucky, January 18th, 1815. In 1831, his father removed with his family to Illinois, and settled in Springfield. The old gentleman and others of the family still reside in Sangamon county, and are highly esteemed in social life, and as successful and upright men of business. During the time that Richard went to the schools in that city, John Calhoun, over whom he was in maturer life elected to Congress, was one of his teachers. After leaving school, he retired to Island Grove, in Sangamon county, where he engaged for a short time in industrial pursuits. He then went to Jacksonville, entered the college there, and became, in 1837, the first graduate of that ably-conducted institution. Yielding to the advice of Gov. Duncan, and other friends, who saw in his fine abilities the promise of great usefulness, he determined to make Jacksonville his residence, and there commenced the study of the law in the office of Col. John J. Hardin. It was not long before he was admitted to the bar, and at once entered upon extensive and successful practice in his profession. He found time, however, to engage frequently in the great political discussions of the time, to which he was often invited, and from which, as an ardent Whig and passionate admirer of the principles and illustrious life of Henry Clay, he could not withhold himself. He soon became one of the leading champions of the Whig policy, and in 1842, being nominated by his party for the State Legislature, he was triumphantly elected. This was a remarkable success, Morgan county being at that time largely Democratic, and Mr. Yates being the only Whig chosen. Morgan county was then entitled to four representatives, and Mr. Yates took his seat (the youngest member, if I mistake not, of the House) with three Democratic colleagues. He nobly sustained himself, and at the expiration of his term, in 1844, was re-elected by a largely increased majority, and carried with him to the succeeding sessions of the Legislature three Whig colleagues. In 1848, Morgan county being entitled to only two representatives, he was again chosen by a still increased majority. His course in the Legislature evinced great judgment, firmness and ability, and his constituents in Jacksonville were much indebted to his tact and management for those legislative favors for which they are so grateful.

Such was the character for firmness, energy, capacity and eloquence which Mr. Yates had established in and out of the Legislature, and such was his unbounded popularity, that in 1850, a convention of the Whig party of his district, which then extended from Morgan and Sangamon counties north to Lasalle, nominated him by acclamation for Congress. This convention was presided over by Hon. Francis Arenz, of Cass, that able and gallant German citizen, who, though now deceased, will always be remembered with love and honor by those who knew him. The Democratic candidate was Major Thomas L. Harris, of Menard, who, two years before, had been elected to Congress from the same district over another Whig competitor, and who, in addition to great ability, enjoyed the well earned reputation of an officer of a brave Illinois regiment, which in the war with Mexico had greatly distinguished itself in the battle of Cerro Gordo.

The contest between these two young men will long be remembered by the people of that district, the candidates speaking in almost every precinct of the district. The result of a most active and persevering canvass, by the friends of both parties, was Mr. Yates' election by a triumphant majority. Entering upon his Congressional duties, the youngest member, it is believed, of the House of Representatives, and the only Whig representative from Illinois, before the end of the first session, by his able speeches in defence of Western interests, in favor of rivers and harbors, and of the Homestead bill, and by his prompt and indefatigable attention to the business of his constituents in Congress and in the Departments, a vast amount of which, coming from all parts of the State, devolved upon him as being the only Whig member from Illinois, he had secured a high position in Congress, and acquired such strength at home, that he began to be considered invincible. It was during the first or second session of this Congress that he secured, what no representative before or since has done, an appropriation of thirty thousand dollars for the improvement of the Illinois river.

In the meantime, the Legislature of Illinois had redistricted the State, and Mr. Yates was thrown into a new district, composed mostly of new counties, and overwhelmingly Democratic. The Democratic party nominated, as its candidate, John Calhoun, Esq., then regarded as the ablest and most popular man of his party in the district. The Whig convention nominated Mr. Yates. His friends looked upon success as almost hopeless. Mr. Yates, however, entered upon the canvass with characteristic ardor, and a determination to win, and he was again chosen by a large majority.

It was during his second term that the great question of the repeal of the Missouri Compromise came before Congress. Mr. Yates, although a Southern man, and representing for the most part a constituency coming from slave States, did not hesitate. He was among the first to denounce the measure as subversive of the national tranquility and reviving the troublous sectional agitation which had been calmed by the patriotic self-devotion of Clay and Webster: and his eloquent speech on the subject was pronounced by the Republican press throughout the country a masterly effort, and secured for him a national reputation. I quote a single paragraph from this speech, to show how truly and graphically he prophetically predicted the consequences which have followed that disturbing and unstatesmanlike measure:

"This will be no party measure. The great enormity of its introduction into our national councils is, that it tends to make two parties, divided not as heretofore, but by geographical lines,—a Northern party and a Southern party. This is the most fearful aspect of the case. This is what Washington, in his Farewell Address, warned his countrymen to guard against and discountenance. Who can foresee the malignity and bitterness of the strife which is to ensue? Who can foretell its termination?"

In 1854, Mr. Yates was again brought forward as a candidate for re-election against Major Harris, whom he had formerly beaten among a different constituency. In consequence of his course on the Nebraska bill, and his strong denunciations of the author of that measure, his opponents resolved to defeat him at all hazards. Well knowing that the district was in itself largely Democratic, they looked also to the character of the constituency, most of whom, coming from slave States, might well be supposed to have prejudices that might be appealed to with profit. The contest that ensued is, perhaps, one of the most memorable in the political history of the State. Mr. Yates, for his course on the Nebraska bill, was assailed by his opponents and by the author of that bill as an abolitionist—and in the end he was defeated but by a meagre majority of two hundred votes, in a district which, at the previous election, had given Pierce a majority of near two thousand over Gen. Scott.

Mr. Yates having retired for a time from the political arena, and given up the practice of law, was elected, in 1855, President of the Tonica and Petersburgh Railroad, and presided over the affairs of the company with signal ability, until his election, in November, 1860, to the gubernatorial chair. In January, 1861, he was sworn in as Governor of the State of Illinois. No man has done more to hold up the hands of the President since the land has been plunged into "battle and murder" by this unholy rebellion, than Richard Yates.

When the services of the sons of Illinois were called for at the breaking out of the Mexican war, nearly ten thousand answered the summons, though but four regiments were accepted; and nobly did they maintain the honor of Illinois in the severest battles of Taylor's and Scott's campaigns. HARDIN and BISSELL are indelibly associated with the glorious victory of Buena Vista, and the names of BAKER, HARRIS and SHIELDS will be cherished so long as the memory of Cerro Gordo lives in the hearts of their countrymen.

When the echo of the first gun fired at Sumter reached the Prairie State, her citizens sprang to arms with the same alacrity which they exhibited sixteen years before. Under the first call of the President, thirteen regiments of cavalry and sixty-six of infantry took the field; five regiments obeyed the call for three months men, while sixty-eight regiments flew to arms under the last summons: a grand total of two artillery regiments, eighteen cavalry, and one hundred and thirty-four infantry, making, with six batteries of artillery, and several companies and battalions of cavalry—a force of about one hundred and sixty thousand men! being ten full regiments in excess of her quota under all calls by the general Government, and she has done this without resorting to the draft in a single county or township. Much of this glorious record is due to the ability and energy of our noble Governor.

Soon after the President's last requisition, Gov. Yates issued the following proclamation to the people of Illinois, and also sent the letter herewith appended to the President:

Under a late requisition of the President, I am called upon to furnish, at the earliest practical period, nine regiments of Infantry, for three years' service, being a part of the quota of the State, under the call of the President for three hundred thousand men. An order of Adjutant General Fuller, this day published, will give the details as to the mode of raising the troops, subsistence, transportation, places of rendezvous, etc.

The war has now arrived at the most critical point. A series of splendid successes has crowned our arms. The enemy has been driven from Tennessee, Missouri and Kentucky, from Arkansas, Louisiana and Texas, and from the sea-coast at almost all points. The Mississippi has been opened from Cairo to the Gulf. The Potomac has been opened from Washington to the Chesapeake. Beaten, broken, demoralized, bankrupt and scattered, the insurgents have fled before our victorious legions, leaving us a large area of conquered territory, and almost innumerable posts in the enemy's country to garrison with our troops.

The rebels, whose leaders are bold and sagacious, and with whom it is neck or nothing as to the rebellion, have, with the energy of desperation, resolved to cast all upon the hazard of a single battle; and while weak at every other point, they have, by the evacuation of Corinth, and by the rapid concentration of their scattered forces at Richmond, brought together a great and powerful army, far superior in numbers to that of our own at the same point.

With consummate skill and generalship they have planned so as not only to defend their own capital, but also, should they be successful in driving back McClellan, to take ours, and raise the rebel flag upon the capitol at Washington, with the expectation that so great a conquest would reanimate the South, revive their fading fortunes, and then secure them the immediate co-operation of the two great powers of Europe—England and France.

This is their last great stake. The desperation with which they have fought has developed the depth, intensity and recklessness of their designs. Their mode of warfare is the most malignant, desperate and savage. Thus we are brought to the very crisis of the rebellion, and all our hopes, and the hopes of this great country, hang upon the issue.

It is for this reason that the President telegraphs me in a private dispatch, "Time is everything. Please act in view of this."

Illinoisans! In view of the crisis, when the battles soon to be fought will be decisive; when the alliance with foreign powers is not only sought, but confidently relied upon by the rebels; and when our own brave volunteers contending against unequal numbers stretch out their hands for help, I cannot doubt the response you will give. Indeed, I am most happy to state, that in response to the active measures already taken, every mail brings me the glad tidings of the rapid enrollment of our volunteers in the nine regiments which are forming.

Covered all over with glory, with a name honored throughout the earth—shining with the lustre of the great achievements of her sons on almost every field, Illinois will not now hold back and tarnish the fame she has so nobly earned. To the timid who suppose that the State will not now respond, I say "take courage." They vastly underrate the patriotism and courage of the men of Illinois.

But I repeat, time is everything. Defeat now would prolong the war for years. Also remember that every argument of public necessity, of patriotism, every emotion of humanity appeals to the people to turn out in overwhelming demonstration, so that the rebellion may be speedily crushed, and an end put to this desolating war. Remember the words of Douglas, that the "shortest road to peace is the most stupendous preparation for war."

The crisis is such that every man must feel that the success of our cause depends upon himself, and not upon his neighbor. Whatever his position, his wealth, his rank or condition, he must be ready to devote ALL to the service of the country. Let all, old and young, contribute, work, speak, and in every possible mode further the work of the speedy enrollment of our forces. Let not only every man, but every woman be a soldier, if not to fight, yet to cheer and encourage, and to provide comforts and relief for the sick and the wounded. The public as yet know but little how much the country is indebted to the noble women of our State for their assistance to our soldiers in the field. All along the path of our army, upon the banks of our rivers, filling our steamboats and ambulances, in the tent of the soldier far from his home, I have witnessed the bright traces of woman's enduring love and benevolence. When the war shall have closed and its history shall be written, the labors of our Sanitary Associations and Aid Societies will present pages as bright as the loftiest heroism of the camp and field. Let all loyal men and women persevere in the good work.

Illinoisans! Look at the issue and do not falter. Your all is at stake. What are your beautiful prairies, comfortable mansions and rich harvests—what is even life worth, if your government is lost? Better that the desolation of pestilence and famine should sweep over the State, than that the glorious work of our fathers should now forever fail. Look out upon your country with a government so free, institutions so noble, boundaries so broad—a beautiful sisterhood of States so prosperous and happy, and resolve afresh that as your fathers gave it you, you will hand it down to your children, a glorious inheritance of liberty and union for their enjoyment forever. For seven long years our fathers endured, suffered and fought to build up the fair fabric of American freedom. The precious boon purchased by patriot blood and treasure was committed to us for enjoyment, and to be transmitted to our posterity with the most solemn injunctions that man has the power to lay on man. By the grace of God, we will be faithful to the trust! And if need be, for seven years to come will we struggle to maintain a perfect Union, a government of one people, in one nation, under one Constitution.

The coming of the brave boys of Illinois will be hailed on the banks of the Potomac and James rivers with shouts of welcome. During my recent visit East, I felt my heart to leap with exultant delight at the praise of Illinois heard from every lip. You will be hailed as the brothers of the men who have faced the storm of battle and gloriously triumphed at Donelson, Pea Ridge, Shiloh, and other memorable fields.

Go then, and doubt not the result. We are sure to triumph. The God of liberty, justice and humanity is on our side.

Your all and your children's all—all that is worth living or dying for, is at stake. Then rally once again for the old flag, for our country, union and liberty. RICHARD YATES.

EXECUTIVE DEPARTMENT,
SPRINGFIELD, ILL., July 11th, 1862.

PRESIDENT LINCOLN, *Washington, D. C.:*

The crisis of the war and our national existence is upon us. The time has come for the adoption of more decisive measures. Greater vigor and earnestness must be infused into our military movements. Blows must be struck at the vital parts of the rebellion. The Government should employ every available means compatible with the rules of warfare to subject the traitors. Summon to the standard of the Republic all men willing to fight for the Union. Let loyalty, and that alone, be the dividing line between the nation and its foes. Generals should not be permitted to fritter away the sinews of our brave men in guarding the property of traitors, and in driving back into their hands loyal blacks, who offer us their labor, and seek shelter beneath the Federal flag. Shall we sit supinely by, and see the war sweep off the youth and strength of the land, and refuse aid from that class of men, who are at least worthy foes of traitors and the murderers of our Government and of our children?

Our armies should be directed to forage on the enemy, and to cease paying traitors and their abettors exorbitant exactions for food needed by the sick or hungry soldier. Mild and conciliatory means have been tried in vain to recall the rebels to their allegiance. The conservative policy has utterly failed to reduce traitors to obedience and to restore the supremacy of the laws. They have, by means of sweeping conscriptions, gathered in countless hordes, and threaten to bent back and overwhelm the armies of the Union. With blood and treason in their hearts, they flaunt the black flag of rebellion in the face of the Government, and threaten to butcher our brave and loyal armies with foreign bayonets. They arm negroes and merciless savages in their behalf.

Mr. Lincoln, the crisis demands greater and sterner measures. Proclaim anew the good old motto of the Republic, "Liberty and Union, now and forever, one and inseparable," and accept the services of *all loyal men*, and it will be in your power to stamp armies out of the earth—irresistible armies that will bear our banners to certain victory.

In any event, Illinois, already alive with beat of drum and resounding with the tramp of new recruits, will respond to your call. Adopt this policy and she will leap like a flaming giant into the fight.

This policy for the conduct of the war will render foreign intervention impossible, and the arms of the Republic invincible. It will bring the conflict to a speedy close, and secure peace on a permanent basis. RICHARD YATES.

On Sept. 15th, the Governor issued another proclamation to the people of Illinois, in regard to organizing an additional force of twenty regiments to be ready for any emergency that might arise. It is rich in words fitly spoken—"apples of gold in pictures of silver." About the same time, in answer to a letter regarding arrests for treason in Illinois, he says:

"My influence shall be given at all times to protect every citizen in the full enjoyment of his constitutional rights. If consulted, I should under no circumstances recommend arrests, except in clear cases of treasonable words or acts against the Government. I regard the question of arrests of this nature as a very tender and delicate one; yet on the other hand, it is my full conviction that no man who is a traitor to his country, or who by word or deed, would give aid and comfort to the enemies of the Government, should be permitted to breathe the free air of Illinois. Let every such man be the scorn of all good and loyal citizens; let him leave the State, which his presence disgraces. Justice to the brave men who are periling their all for the Government, as well as the memory of our dead, who have gloriously given up their lives for their country, requires that *no sympathizer with treason should be suffered to live in Illinois.*"

Not long since, Gov. Yates received a letter from Oskaloosa, Ill., wherein the writer complained that traitors in his town had cut down the American flag, and asking what ought to be done in the premises. The Governor promptly wrote him, and I give a portion of a reply that ought to be historic: "You say," writes the Governor, "that the pole which floated the stars and stripes on the 4th of July, was cut down by secessionists, and that at a pic-nic which you are to have, it is threatened that the flag shall be taken down, and you ask me whether you would be justifiable in defending the flag with fire-arms? I am astonished at this question. As much so as if you were to ask me whether you would have a right to defend your property against robbers or your life against murderers. You ask me what you shall do? I reply, do not raise the American flag merely to provoke your secession neighbors—do not be on the aggressive, but whenever you raise it on your own soil, or on the public property of the State or county, or at any public celebration, from honest love to that flag, and patriotic devotion to the country which it symbolizes, and any traitor dares to lay his unhallowed hand upon it to tear it down, shoot him down as you would a dog, and *I will pardon you for the offence.*"

12

GEN. GRANT.

Among the most prominent actors in what has been so well called this "fearfully glorious present," stands Major General ULYSSES S. GRANT, the hero of Fort Donelson and the bloody battle-field of Shiloh, and at present in command of the army of Tennessee. He was born at Mount Pleasant, Clermont co., Ohio, April 22, 1822, and entered the West Point Academy from his native State at the age of seventeen, receiving his appointment as cadet from the late Gen. Thomas L. Hamer, of Ohio. He graduated with honors, June 30, 1843, in the same class with Generals French, Franklin, Hamilton, Quimby, Peck, Reynolds, and others in the Union service, and Generals Hardee and Ripley, now serving in the Confederate army; and was attached as brevet 2d Lieutenant to 'the 4th Infantry. He was promoted 2d Lieutenant at Corpus Christi in Sept., 1845. He served through the Mexican campaign, under General Taylor at Palo Alto, Resaca de la Palma and Monterey, and under Gen. Scott from Vera Cruz to the city of Mexico; and was twice promoted for his bravery on the battle-field. He was Regimental Quartermaster from April 1, 1847; and when he resigned from the service, July 31, 1854, he was a full Captain in the 4th Infantry. After his resignation, he settled in St. Louis co., Missouri, and continued to reside there until 1859, when he moved to Galena, Illinois, and entered into the leather trade, in partnership with his father. When the echo of the first gun fired at Fort Sumter reached him, he hastened to Springfield, and offered his services to Gov. Yates, and was appointed Colonel of the 21st Regiment of Illinois Volunteers. He served with his regiment until promoted a Brigadier General, with commission and rank from May 17, 1861. He was engaged as Col. and acting Brigadier General in several of the contests in Southeastern Missouri, and his course as commander of that district received the commendation of his superior officers. Among his other praiseworthy acts, was the occupation of Paducah, and stoppage of communication and supplies to the rebels, via the Tennessee and Cumberland rivers. At 11 o'clock, Sept. 6th, Gen. Grant, with two regiments of infantry, one company of artillery, and two gunboats, took possession of the town. He found secession flags flying in different parts of the city, in expectation of greeting the arrival of the Southern army, which was reported three thousand eight hundred strong, sixteen miles distant. The loyal citizens tore down the secession flags on the arrival of the national troops. Gen. Grant took possession of the telegraph office, railroad depot, and the marine hospital, and issued the following proclamation:

"I have come among you not as an enemy, but as your fellow-citizen. Not to maltreat or annoy you, but to respect and enforce the rights of all loyal citizens. An enemy, in rebellion against our common Government, has taken possession of, and planted its guns on the soil of Kentucky, and fired upon you. Columbus and Hickman are in his hands. He is moving upon your city. I am here to defend you against this enemy, to assist the authority and sovereignty of your Government. I have nothing to do with opinions, and shall deal only with armed rebellion and its aiders and abettors. You can pursue your usual avocations without fear. The strong arm of the Government is here to protect its friends and punish its enemies. Whenever it is manifest that you are able to defend yourselves and maintain the authority of the Government and protect the rights of loyal citizens, I shall withdraw the forces under my command."

While in command of the District of Cairo, Gen. Grant learned that the rebels at Columbus were about to send out a strong force to cut off an expedition that had been sent into Missouri, and he at once determined to make an attack upon them at Belmont, nearly opposite to Columbus. On the night of Nov. 6, a strong force, under his command, left Cairo on steamers, the gunboats Tyler and Lexington accompanying, and landed the morning following at Lucas Bend, on the west side of the Mississippi, three miles above Columbus. The troops were formed into line of battle, and for two and a half miles up to the camp of the enemy at Belmont, through the woods, the ground was hotly contested, but the rebels were driven back, and their camp totally destroyed. Gen. Grant finding that the enemy were crossing from the Kentucky shore and threatening his rear, gave the order to return to the boats, when our army was confronted by several thousand fresh troops sent from Columbus. Another terrible engagement ensued, in which

GEN. GRANT.

every regiment suffered severely before reaching the boats. The troops all displayed the greatest bravery. The following is Gen. Grant's official report:

CAIRO, Nov. 12, 1861.

On the evening of the 6th inst., I left this place with two thousand eight hundred and fifty men of all arms, to make a reconnoissance toward Columbus. The object of the expedition was to prevent the enemy from sending out reinforcements to Price's army in Missouri, and also from cutting off columns that I had been directed to send out from this place and Cape Girardeau, in pursuit of Jeff.Thompson. Knowing that Columbus was strongly garrisoned, I asked Gen. Smith, commanding at Paducah, Ky., to make demonstrations in the same direction. He did so by ordering a small force to Mayfield and another in the direction of Columbus, not to approach nearer, however, than twelve or fifteen miles. I also sent a small force on the Kentucky side with orders not to approach nearer than Ellicott's Mills, some twelve miles from Columbus. The expedition under my immediate command was stopped about nine miles below here on the Kentucky shore, and remained until morning. All this served to distract the enemy, and led him to think he was to be attacked in his strongly fortified position. At daylight, we proceeded down the river to a point just out of range of the rebel guns, and debarked on the Missouri shore. From here the troops were marched by flank for about one mile toward Belmont, and then drawn up in line of battle, a battalion also having been left as a reserve near the transports. Two companies from each regiment, five skeletons in number, were then thrown out as skirmishers, to ascertain the position of the enemy. It was but a few moments before we met him, and a general engagement ensued.

The balance of my forces, with the exception of the reserve, was then thrown forward—all as skirmishers—and the enemy driven foot by foot, and from tree to tree, back to their encampment on the river bank, a distance of two miles. Here they had strengthened their position by felling the timber for several hundred yards around their camp, and making a sort of abatis. Our men charged through this, driving the enemy over the bank into their transports in quick time, leaving us in possession of every thing not exceedingly portable. Belmont is on low ground, and every foot of it is commanded by the guns on the opposite shore, and of course could not be held for a single hour after the enemy became aware of the withdrawal of their troops. Having no wagons, I could not move any of the captured property: consequently, I gave orders for its destruction. Their tents, blankets, etc., were set on fire, and we retired, taking their artillery with us, two pieces being drawn by hand; and one other, drawn by an inefficient team, we spiked and left in the woods, bringing the two only to this place. Before getting fairly under way, the enemy made his

appearance again, and attempted to surround us. Our troops were not in the least discouraged, but charged on the enemy again and defeated him. Our loss was about 84 killed, 150 wounded—many of them slightly—and about an equal number missing. Nearly all the missing were from the Iowa regiment, who behaved with great gallantry, and suffered more severely than any other of the troops.

I have not been able to put in the reports from sub-commands, but will forward them as soon as received. All the troops behaved with gallantry, much of which is attributed to the coolness and presence of mind of the officers, particularly of the colonels. Gen. McClernand was in the midst of danger throughout the engagement, and displayed both coolness and judgment. His horse was three times shot. My horse was also shot under me. To my staff, Capts. Rawlins, Logan, and Hilyer, volunteer aids, and to Capts. Hatch and Graham, I am much indebted for the assistance they gave. Col. Webster, acting chief engineer, also accompanied me, and displayed highly soldier-like qualities. Col. Dougherty, of the Twenty-second Illinois Volunteers, was three times wounded and taken prisoner.

The Seventh Iowa regiment had their Lieut. Colonel killed, and the Colonel and Major were severely wounded. The reports to be forwarded will detail more fully the particulars of our loss. Surgeon Brinton was in the field during the entire engagement, and displayed great ability and efficiency in providing for the wounded and organizing the medical corps.

The gunboats Tyler and Lexington, Capts. Walker and Stemble, U. S. N., commanding, conveyed the expedition and rendered most efficient service. Immediately upon our landing they engaged the enemy's batteries, and protected our transports throughout.

I am sir, very respectfully, your obedient servant,

U. S. GRANT,
Brig. Gen. Commanding.

In January, 1862, Gen. Grant being still in command at Cairo, turned his attention to operations on the Cumberland and Tennessee rivers, and obtained permission from the War Department to move up those rivers, and to act in concert with the gunboats. Early in February, our forces moved up the Tennessee. At the capture of Fort Henry, Feb. 6, 1862, General Grant commanded the land forces, acting in concert with the gunboats, under command of Flag-Officer (now Admiral) Foote. From Fort Henry, he proceeded, on the 12th, with his army, to invest Fort Donelson, on the Cumberland river. The attack began on the morning of the 13th, and was continued on the 14th and 15th, the troops being exposed for four nights without shelter during the most inclement weather known in that latitude. On the morning of the 16th, the rebel commander, Gen. Buckner, sent in a flag of truce, proposing an armistice, and appointment of commissioners to settle terms of capitulation, to which Gen. Grant replied that "no terms other than unconditional and immediate surrender can be accepted;" and added, "I propose to move immediately on your works." The post was at once surrendered. Gen. Grant made the following report to Gen. Halleck, dated Fort Donelson, Feb. 16, 1862:

"I am pleased to announce to you the unconditional surrender, this morning, of Fort Donelson, with twelve to fifteen thousand prisoners, at least forty pieces of artillery, and a large amount of stores, horses, mules, and other public property.

"I left Fort Henry on the twelfth inst., with a force of about fifteen thousand men, divided into two divisions, under the command of Generals McClernand and Smith. Six regiments were sent around by water the day before, convoyed by a gunboat, or rather started one day later than one of the gunboats, with instructions not to pass it.

"The troops made the march in good order, the head of the column arriving within two miles of the Fort at twelve o'clock M. At this point the enemy's pickets were met and driven in.

"The fortifications of the enemy were from this point gradually approached and surrounded, with occasional skirmishing on the line. The following day, owing to the non-arrival of the gunboats and re-enforcements sent by water, no attack was made; but the investment was extended on the flanks of the enemy, and drawn closer to his works, with skirmishing all day. The evening of the thirteenth, the gunboats and re-enforcements arrived. On the fourteenth, a gallant attack was made by Flag Officer Foote upon the enemy's works with his fleet. The engagement lasted probably one hour and a half, and bid fair to result favorably to the cause of the Union, when two unlucky shots disabled two of the armored gunboats, so that they were carried back by the current. The remaining two were very much disabled also, having received a number of heavy shots about the pilot-house and other parts of the vessels. After these mishaps, I concluded to make the investment of Fort Donelson as perfect as possible, and partially fortify and await repairs to the gunboats. This plan was frustrated, however, by the enemy making a most vigorous attack upon our right wing, commanded by Gen. J. A. McClernand, with a portion of the force under Gen. L. Wallace. The enemy were repelled after a closely contested battle of several hours, in which our loss was heavy. The officers, and particularly field officers, suffered out of proportion. I have not the means yet of de-

termining our loss even approximately, but it cannot fall far short of one thousand two hundred killed, wounded and missing. Of the latter, I understand through Gen. Buckner, about two hundred and fifty were taken prisoners. I shall retain enough of the enemy to exchange for them, as they were immediately shipped off, and not left for recapture.

"About the close of this action, the ammunition in the cartridge-boxes gave out, which, with the loss of many of the field officers, produced great confusion in the ranks. Seeing that the enemy did not take advantage of this fact, I ordered a charge upon the left—enemy's right—with the division under Gen. C. F. Smith, which was most brilliantly executed, and gave to our arms full assurance of victory. The battle lasted until dark, giving us possession of part of their entrenchments. An attack was ordered upon their other flank, after the charge by Gen. Smith was commenced, by the divisions under Gens. McClernand and Wallace, which, notwithstanding the hours of exposure to a heavy fire in the fore part of the day, was gallantly made, and the enemy further repulsed. At the points thus gained, night having come on, all the troops encamped for the night, feeling that a complete victory would crown their labors at an early hour in the morning. This morning, at a very early hour, Gen. S. B. Buckner sent a message to our camp under a flag of truce, proposing an armistice, etc. A copy of the correspondence which ensued is herewith accompanied.

"I cannot mention individuals who specially distinguished themselves, but leave that to division and brigade officers, whose reports will be forwarded as soon as received. To division commanders, however, Generals McClernand, Smith and Wallace, I must do the justice to say that each of them were with their commands in the midst of danger, and were always ready to execute all orders, no matter what the exposure to themselves."

For his ability and gallantry displayed at the capture of Fort Donelson, Gen. Grant was promoted to a Major General, his commission being dated Feb. 16—the day of its surrender to our forces.

The occupation of Savannah by Gen. Grant was made about the middle of March, and Sherman's division pushed on to Pittsburgh Landing. Gradually his whole army advanced to Shiloh, to await the arrival of Buell's divisions before assailing the enemy, under Johnston and Beauregard, entrenched at Corinth. Sherman's division had the extreme advance left wing, supported by Gen. Prentiss; McClernand held the centre; Wallace, of Illinois (commanding Gen. Smith's forces), held the right; Hurlbut's brigades forming the reserve. Gen. Wallace, of Indiana, was stationed with his division at Crump's Landing, forming the extreme right wing of Grant's army. This was the position of our army on the morning of Sunday, April 6th, when the enemy made the attack. The following is Gen. Grant's official report of the engagement, made to Gen. Halleck:

"It becomes my duty again to report another battle fought between two great armies, one contending for the maintenance of the best government ever devised, the other, for its destruction. It is pleasant to record the success of the army contending for the former principle.

"On Sunday morning our pickets were driven in by the enemy. Immediately the five divisions stationed at this place were drawn up in line of battle, ready to meet them. The battle soon waxed warm on the left and centre, varying at times to all parts of the line.

"The most continuous firing of musketry and artillery ever heard on the continent was kept up until nightfall, the enemy having forced the entire line to fall back nearly half way from their camps to the landing. At a late hour in the afternoon, a desperate effort was made by the enemy to turn our left, and get possession of the landing, transports, etc. This point was guarded by the gunboats Tyler and Lexington, Captains Gwinn and Shirk, U. S. N., commanding, four 29-pounder Parrot guns, and a battery of rifled guns. As there is a deep and impassable ravine for artillery or cavalry, and very difficult for infantry, at this point, no troops were stationed here except the necessary artillerists, and a small infantry force for their support. Just at this moment the advance of Major General Buell's column (a part of the division of Gen. Nelson) arrived, the two Generals named both being present. An advance was immediately made upon the point of attack, and the enemy soon driven back. In this repulse, much is due to the presence of the gunboats Tyler and Lexington, and their able commanders, Captains Gwinn and Shirk. During the night, the divisions under Generals Crittenden and McCook arrived.

"Gen. Lew. Wallace, at Crump's Landing, six miles below, was ordered at an early hour in the morning to hold his division in readiness to move in any direction to which it might be ordered. At about 11 o'clock, the order was delivered to move it up to Pittsburgh, but owing to its being led by a circuitous route, did not arrive in time to take part in Sunday's action. During the night all was quiet, and feeling that a great moral advantage would be gained by becoming the attacking party, an advance was ordered as soon as day dawned. The result was a gradual repulse of the enemy at all points of the line, from morning until probably 5 o'clock in the afternoon, when it became evident the enemy was retreating.

"Before the close of the action, the advance of Gen. T. J. Wood's division arrived, in time to take part in the action. My force was too much fatigued from two days' hard fighting, and exposed in the open air to a drenching rain during the intervening night, to pursue immediately. Night closed in cloudy and with heavy rain, making the roads impracticable for artillery by the next morning. Gen. Sherman, however, followed the enemy, finding that the main part of the army had retreated in good order. Hospitals of the enemy's wounded were found all along the road, as far as pursuit was made. Dead bodies of the enemy and many graves were also found. I enclose herewith the report of Gen. Sherman, which will explain more fully the result of the pursuit. Of the part taken by each separate command, I cannot take special notice in this report, but will do so more fully when reports of division commanders are handed in.

"General Buell, coming on the field with a distinct army, long under his command, and which did such efficient service, commanded by himself in person on the field, will be much better able to notice those of his command who particularly distinguished themselves, than I possibly can.

"I feel it a duty, however, to a gallant and able officer, Brigadier General W. T. Sherman, to make a special mention. He not only was with his command during the entire of the two days' action, but displayed great judgment and skill in the management of his men. Although severely wounded in the hand the first day, his place was never vacant. He was again wounded, and had three horses killed under him.

"In making this mention of a gallant officer, no disparagement is intended to the other division commanders, Major Generals John A. McClernand and Lew. Wallace, and Brigadier Generals S. A. Hurlbut, B. M. Prentiss and W. H. L. Wallace, all of whom maintained their places with credit to themselves and the cause.

"Gen. Prentiss was taken prisoner in the first day's action, and Gen. W. H. L. Wallace severely, probably mortally wounded. His Assistant Adjutant General, Captain William McMichael, is missing—probably taken prisoner.

"My personal staff are all deserving of particular mention, they having been engaged during the entire two days in carrying orders to every part of the field. It consists of Col. J. D. Webster, chief of Staff; Lieut. Col. J. B. McPherson, chief engineer; assisted by Lieutenants W. L. B. Jenny and Wm. Kossac, Capt. J. A. Rawlings, A. A. General W. S. Hillyer, W. R. Rawley and C. B. Lagow, aides-de-camp, Col. G. G. Pride, volunteer aid, and Capt. J. P. Hawkins, chief commissary, who accompanied me upon the field.

"The medical department, under direction of Surgeon Hewitt, medical director, showed great energy in providing for the wounded, and in getting them from the field, regardless of danger.

"Col. Webster was placed in special charge of all the artillery, and was constantly upon the field. He displayed, as always heretofore, both skill and bravery. At least in one instance he was the means of placing an entire regiment in a position of doing most valuable service, and where it would not have been but for his exertions.

"Lieut. Col. McPherson, attached to my staff as chief of engineers, deserves more than a passing notice for his activity and courage. The grounds beyond our camps for miles have been reconnoitered by him, and plats carefully prepared under his supervision, giving accurate information of the nature of approaches to our lines. During the two days' battle he was constantly in the saddle, leading troops as they arrived to points where their services were required. During the engagement he had one horse shot under him.

"The country will have to mourn the loss of many brave men who fell at the battle of Pittsburgh, or Shiloh, more properly. The exact loss in killed and wounded will be known in a day or two; at present I can only give it approximately at 1500 killed and 3500 wounded.

"The loss of artillery was great, many pieces being disabled by the enemy's shots, and some losing all their horses and many men. There were probably not less than two hundred horses killed.

"The loss of the enemy, in killed and left upon the field, was greater than ours. In wounded, the estimate cannot be made, as many of them must have been sent to Corinth and other points."

A later official report of Gen. Grant gives the number of killed as 1614; wounded, 7721; missing, 3963; making a total of 13,508 killed, wounded and missing, in that terrific two days' engagement. As to the enemy's loss, no authentic data is available, but it is supposed to have been much greater than ours.

An important victory was gained by Gen. Grant over the rebels at Iuka, Miss., Sept. 19th and 20th. The following is his official report, dated from field of battle:

"Gen. Rosecrans, with Stanley's and Hamilton's divisions, and Misener's Cavalry, attacked Price south of this village about two hours before dark yesterday, and had a sharp fight until night closed in. Gen. Ord was to the north with an armed force of about 5000 men, and had some skirmishing with the rebel pickets. This morning the fight was renewed

by Gen. Rosecrans, who was nearest to the town, but it was found that the enemy had been evacuating during the night, going south. Gens. Hamilton and Stanley, with cavalry, are in full pursuit. This will, no doubt, break up the enemy, and possibly force them to abandon much of their artillery. The loss on either side, in killed and wounded, is from 400 to 500. The enemy's loss in arms, tents, etc., will be large. We have about 250 prisoners. I have trustworthy intelligence that it was Price's intention to move over east of the Tennessee. In this he has been thwarted. Among the enemy's loss are Gen. Little, killed, and Gen. Whitford, wounded. I cannot speak too highly of the energy and skill displayed by Gen. Rosecrans in the attack, and of the endurance of the troops. Gen. Ord's command showed untiring zeal, but the direction taken by the enemy prevented them from taking the active part they desired. Price's force was about 18,000."

In a later dispatch, dated 22d, Gen. Grant says: "Our loss was over-estimated, and the rebel loss was under-estimated. We found 261 of them dead upon the field, while our loss in killed was less than 100."

Another desperate battle was fought by Gen. Grant's troops at Corinth, Oct. 4, in which the rebels, under Price, Van Dorn and Lovell, were most signally repulsed, and sustained a heavy loss in killed, wounded and prisoners. On the 6th, another severe engagement with the enemy on the banks of the Hatchie terminated in their being completely routed, and retreating after throwing away their baggage and commissary stores. The rebel loss, in killed, wounded and prisoners, was very great.

Gen. Grant has been constantly in the field during the whole campaign, and is now (Oct. 16th) in command of the army of Tennessee, with his headquarters at Jackson. Neither he nor the noble army which he has so long commanded, and which, I am proud to record, are chiefly Illinoisans,—and many are the victor-wreaths they have won,—have ever yet met with defeat, and but twice fallen back, and in those cases, when outnumbered nearly two to one, fell back with their faces to the foe. Illinois can claim for Gen. Ulysses S. Grant, without fear of contradiction, the proud distinction of being the most successful General that the war against the rebellion of 1861 has yet developed in our Union armies.

GEN. PAINE.

ELEAZER A. PAINE was born in Geauga county, Ohio, Sept. 10, 1815. Was appointed a cadet to the United States Military Academy in June, 1835, and graduated in June, 1839. Among his classmates were Major Generals Halleck and Ord, and Brigadier Generals Canby, Hunt and Stevens. After graduating, he was appointed 2d Lieutenant in the First Infantry, Gen. Taylor's old regiment, and served on Taylor's staff during the war in Florida. Resigned his commission in 1840, and commenced the study of law. In 1844, he began the practice of his profession, in Ohio, which he continued until the fall of 1848, when he removed to Monmouth, Warren county, Illinois, where his family still reside. Here Mr. Paine practiced law successfully until the breaking out of the rebellion, when he received an appointment on the Governor's staff. In April, 1861, he was elected Colonel of the 9th Regiment Volunteers, and Sept. 3d was promoted to Brigadier General.

When Gen. Grant proceeded up the Tennessee, to invest Fort Henry, Gen. Paine was placed in command of Cairo and its dependencies, which embraced Bird's Point and Fort Holt, on the Kentucky shore, Mound City, above Cairo, on the Ohio river, and a portion of Missouri. In the performance of his numerous duties while in command at Cairo, Gen. Paine proved himself to be an able officer, and by his rare combination of administrative and executive ability and military knowledge and skill, placed everything within his command upon a successful military footing. On the 12th of march, he was assigned to the command of the 1st division of the army of the Mississippi, under Gen. Pope, and on the next day participated in the battle of New Madrid, where, at the head of his division, by his cool and intrepid conduct, he contributed largely to the eminent success of our arms in that important engagement, which resulted in the defeat of the rebels at that place, and the abandonment of their forts, batteries, arms, ammunition and stores, all of which fell into our hands, the rebels narrowly escaping in the darkness, by the aid of their transports, protected by their gunboats.

After the battle at New Madrid, Gen. Paine labored diligently to promote the efficiency of

his command, and by giving it a more thorough organization, and perfecting its discipline, became deservedly popular with his officers and men.

At the taking of Island No. 10, Gen. Paine, with his division, consisting of two brigades, the 1st, commanded by Col. Morgan, of the 10th Illinois, and the 2d, commanded by Col. Cumming, of the 51st Illinois, occupied the advance, and bore so conspicuous and distinguished a part in that glorious achievement, by his rapid and vigorous pursuit of the enemy, and with his division driving a rebel force larger than his own from three different positions, where they attempted to make a stand before reaching Tiptonville, as to capture, at the latter place, the whole rebel force, of over six thousand men, including two Generals and several Colonels, with all their arms, stores, cannon, etc., before any other division of Gen. Pope's army came up. The success of the army of the Mississippi at New Madrid, at Island No. 10, which had so long defied and kept in check the Federal gunboats, and at Tiptonville, resulted in the capture, at these places and the shore batteries, of over one hundred cannon, ten thousand stand of arms, a large quantity of ammunition, army wagons, horses, mules and military stores, from the rebels, which sent a thrill of joy throughout the loyal States, and won for Gen. Paine the universal praise of both army and people, which he so justly merited, for the bold and skillful manner with which he had conducted and directed his command in these brilliant achievements.

The army of the Mississippi, including Gen. Paine and his command, soon after proceeded down the Mississippi to Fort Pillow, and were about to invest that place, when they were ordered up the Tennessee to join Gen. Halleck. Here Gen. Paine, with his division, was again placed in the advance, and participated in all the skirmishes in the march upon Corinth. At the battle of Farmington, the bold advance made by Gen. Paine, the stern manner in which he resisted the attack of the vastly superior force which the rebels hurled upon his command, and the skillful manner in which he eluded the overwhelming force sent

2

against him, so completely foiled the designs of the enemy, as to hasten the evacuation of Corinth by the rebels, and leave the Federal army undisputed masters of that strongly fortified place.

In person, Gen. Paine is tall, has a fine, commanding appearance, is affable in conversation, is possessed of good judgment, is an able tactician, cool and decisive in action. He is held in high esteem in the army, has the entire confidence of his command, and has in all respects shown himself an able and efficient commanding officer.

GEN. McARTHUR.

Brigadier General JOHN McARTHUR was born in the parish of Erskine, Renfrewshire, Scotland, November 17, 1826. His father, John McArthur, was the blacksmith for Lord Blantyre. On reaching the common age for youths to attend school, he was sent there, and it appears displayed so much aptitude in learning his tasks as to attract the attention of the parish minister, who wished to educate him for the ministry. This project did not please the boy, who was very fond of working among the tools in his father's shop, and when his mother, a worthy woman, tempted his vanity by asking him "if he would not like to be called the *Rev. John McArthur?*" his predilections asserted their sway, and he answered, "No, I would rather be—JOCK, THE SMITH." He accordingly entered his father's shop, where he remained until the age of twenty-three, when he determined to seek a wider field of usefulness on the broad prairies of Illinois. In due time he arrived at Chicago, and found employment as foreman of boiler-making in Cobb's foundry. In 1852, he formed a copartnership with his brother-in-law, Carlyle Mason, occupying a shop on West Randolph street, as blacksmiths and boiler-makers—where, begrimmed with dust and smoke, he laid the foundation of a more active and distinguished career. His success in business exceeded his expectations. It grew with the growth of his adopted city, and, although he suffered in the reverses of 1857, like other business men, he held his ground manfully, never retreating before a fancied disaster, but working his way through difficulties with a stout heart and steady purpose. The cares of his household and business did not prevent his entering the ranks of our citizen soldiery, in which he always evinced a deep interest. On the formation of the Chicago Highland Guard, he was elected its First Lieutenant, and soon after was elected Captain. When the war broke out, Captain McArthur quickly arranged his business matters, and went forth at his country's call. He was elected Lieutenant Colonel of the Washington Independent Regiment (of which the Highland Guard formed a part). A few weeks later he was elected Colonel of the 12th Regiment Illinois Volunteers. When the troubles commenced in Kentucky, Col. McArthur with his regiment was stationed for several months at Paducah, and from there was ordered to Fort Henry. At Fort Donelson he was acting Brigadier, and in the fierce conflict displayed such intrepidity, coolness and daring, as to win his General's commission. He was next engaged on the field of Shiloh, where, on the first day, he was wounded by a ball passing through his foot, which disabled him for above a month. At the expiration of this time, he again joined his brigade in the army of the Tennessee under Major General Grant, and is now in command of a division comprising eleven regiments.

GEN. MCARTHUR.

GEN. PRENTISS.

GEN. PRENTISS.

Brigadier General BENJAMIN F. PRENTISS was born on the 23d day of November, 1819, at Belleville, Wood county, Virginia. In 1835, he, with his father, Henry L. Prentiss, removed from Virginia to Missouri, and whilst residing there, and before becoming of age, he commanded a company raised during the Mormon troubles in that State.

In 1841, Gen. Prentiss, with his father's family, removed from Missouri to Quincy, Adams county, Illinois, where Gen. Prentiss has since resided. There he supported and educated himself by working at his trade, which is that of a rope maker.

In 1844, the troubles between the authorities of Illinois and the Mormons, then under the leadership of Joe Smith, commenced. Prentiss at that time was First Lieutenant of the Quincy Rifles, then and for some time afterwards under the command of Capt. (now Brigadier General) James D. Morgan. He, with his Captain and company, went to Hancock county, where the Mormons were, and again, in 1845, did good service in keeping peace and preserving order. He was retained for several months in Hancock county, on duty with his company during the continuance of the Mormon difficulties.

At the commencement of the Mexican war, he was among the first to volunteer, with his old Captain, James D. Morgan, and many of the former Quincy Rifles, and join the 1st Regiment Illinois Volunteers, under Col. Hardin. When the regiment was organized, he was appointed by Col. Hardin, Adjutant, and did duty as such with his regiment until they arrived at Monclova, when he was elected Captain of a company in the same regiment, which he commanded until its term of service expired. He was succeeded as Adjutant by William H. L. Wallace, who lost his life at Shiloh, fighting side by side with Prentiss, who was ever his warm friend. James D. Morgan and Prentiss were posted at Saltillo at the time of the battle of Buena Vista, and under orders from Gen. Taylor held that post against a greatly superior force of the enemy. The two companies under command of Morgan (who was the ranking Captain) and Prentiss (who was his junior), were regarded as among the best drilled and most efficient of the volunteer companies in Gen. Taylor's column in the Mexican war.

After the termination of the war, Capt. Prentiss returned to Quincy, and followed his business as a rope maker for several years, when he commenced business as a forwarding and commission merchant, which he continued until the breaking out of the rebellion. The news of the fall of Sumter reached Quincy on Sunday morning, and the next Sunday, Prentiss, with two hundred brave men, composed in part of the Quincy Rifles, which he reorganized, were on their way to Cairo, Ill. He was elected Colonel of the 7th Regiment, and as soon as a brigade could be got together, he was elected, by a large majority, Brigadier General of the Illinois troops, in service under the three months call. His old commander and friend, James D. Morgan, who was Lieut. Colonel of his regiment, became Colonel upon Prentiss becoming Brigadier General. Morgan could have been Colonel of another regiment at the same time Prentiss was made Colonel, but he preferred to serve under Prentiss, and wished afterwards, when he became Colonel, to be assigned to Prentiss' brigade.

When the three months service ceased. Gen. Prentiss was appointed Brigadier General of Volunteers, by the President, for the war. During the three months service he was in command at Cairo. After that service ended, and almost as soon as he was appointed for the war, he was ordered into Southern Missouri, and there fitted out and conducted a large expedition from Pilot Knob, through Southern Missouri. Being relieved by Gen. Grant at Cape Girardeau, he was ordered to North Missouri, where, with a small command, he kept the secessionists and traitors of that region perfectly quiet, the only period since the rebellion commenced that quiet and peace have been thoroughly preserved there, except for a short time whilst Col. John Glover, who succeeded him, was in command. A short time before the battle of Shiloh, Gen. Prentiss was relieved from duty in North Missouri, and ordered to report to Maj. Gen. Grant, which he did at once at Pittsburgh Landing, where he arrived only two or three days before the battle. Gen. Prentiss was at once ordered to the front, and regiments assigned to his command, composed of good men, but they were mostly new troops, very few of whom had ever been under fire. Prentiss' command was not surprised on Sunday morning, April 6th, as has been erroneously stated, but, on the contrary, was in line of battle early in the morning, and fought, almost on their own ground, from nine o'clock in the morning until half-past four in the evening, when, being unsupported and almost surrounded by overwhelming numbers of the enemy, he was compelled to surrender.

In the thick underbrush where they made their last stand, with McClernand's division on the left and Hurlbut's on the right, almost every shrub and bush was struck by bullets, and no spot on the field exhibited evidences of more desperate fighting, excepting the "Battalion Drill Ground." The last time Gen. Prentiss met Gen. Hurlbut, he asked him, "Can you hold your line?" and was answered, "I think I can." Not long after, Hurlbut sent a messenger to inform him that he was forced back, but he was probably killed, as the message was never received. About the same time, McClernand was forced back, and Prentiss, without knowing that his supports were gone, held his position. The enemy, both on his right and left, were nearly half a mile in his rear before he discovered it, and his capture was inevitable.

In 1860, Gen. Prentiss was the candidate of the Republican party for Congress, in the Fifth Congressional District, in Illinois, but the district being largely Democratic, he was defeated by his competitor, William A. Richardson. Gen. Prentiss is an active, energetic man, always ready for any emergency, and perfectly temperate in his habits, having never drank any spirituous liquors. His personal courage is undoubted. He does not know what fear is. The writer has seen his courage tried in many modes, and he has always proved himself to be cool and prepared for whatever may occur, and equal to the occasion. Should he be exchanged, he will be found, as ever amongst the foremost, fighting for his government and the country he loves so well.

COL. ROBERTS.

Col. GEORGE W. ROBERTS is a native of Westchester county, Penn., where he was born, October 2, 1833. After the necessary preparation, he entered the sophomore class at Yale College, and graduated in 1857. Adopting the law as his profession, he studied in his native county, where he was admitted to the bar, and continued to practice until the spring of 1859, when he removed to Chicago. There, while in the successful exercise of his profession, he determined to enter the army, and in company with David Stuart, began recruiting for the 42d Regiment Illinois Volunteers. On the 22d of July, he received his commission as Major of the regiment, and on the 17th of September was elected Lieut. Colonel. Upon the death of Col. Webb, Dec. 24, 1861, he was elected Colonel. With his regiment Col. Roberts took part in the well known march of Gen. Fremont to Springfield, after which the 42d went into quarters at Smithtown, Mo. After the fall of Fort Donelson, the Colonel proceeded with his regiment to Fort Holt, near Cairo, where he held command of the post, at that time garrisoned by the 42d Illinois, 8th Ohio, and a battery of the 2d Illinois artillery. From there Col. Roberts was ordered to Columbus, after its evacuation by the enemy, and next proceeded to Island No. 10, where he performed most valuable service during a night expedition, in spiking a number of guns. The regiment was next ordered to Fort Pillow, and from there accompanied Gen. Pope up the Tennessee, and took part in the engagement at Farmington. At the time of the evacuation of Corinth by the rebels, Col. Roberts had command of Palmer's brigade.

GEN. BUFORD.

GEN. BUFORD.

The subject of this sketch, Brigadier General NAPOLEON B. BUFORD, was born on the 13th of January, 1807, in Woodford county, Kentucky. His father was Col. John Buford, a popular, patriotic and generous man, who was greatly esteemed, and filled many important public stations worthily. He was seven years a member of the Legislature in Kentucky, and four years a Senator of Illinois. His mother was Nancy Hickman of Bourbon county, Kentucky.

In the year 1823, at the age of 16, Napoleon B. Buford was appointed a cadet, by the influence of Col. Richard M. Johnson, whose notice he had attracted while at school near his residence, and graduated at the West Point Military Academy with distinguished honor, in 1827, when he was commissioned a Lieutenant of Artillery. While in the army, which was for the period of eight years, he was a diligent student and an active officer. First stationed at the School of Practice at Fortress Monroe, it was here he commenced to employ his leisure in the study of law, and by the invitation of Col. Richard M. Johnson, he visited Washington, and was introduced by him to all the cabinet officers of the President, John Quincy Adams. In the delightful family of Mr. Wirt, the Attorney-General, he made the acquaintance, which has since ripened into a warm friendship, of the Hon. S. P. Chase, now Secretary of the Treasury, then a law-student of Mr. Wirt, and a cherished member of his family.

Lieutenant Buford was next, on the requisition of the Governor of Kentucky, detailed as a Topographical Engineer, and made the first surveys of the Kentucky river, which led afterwards to its being converted into a noble canal, by a system of locks and dams. The following winter, at the instance of Mr. Bates, now Attorney-General, but then Member of Congress from Missouri, he was sent by the Secretary of War to survey the Des Moines and Rock Island rapids of the Mississippi river, which he executed with ability.

In 1830, Lieut. Buford joined his regiment at Eastport, Maine, and with his regular garrison duties, resumed his legal studies. Gen. Scott granted him a leave of absence in 1831

that he might enter the Law School of Harvard University, then presided over by Judge Story of the Supreme Court. It was at this time he became acquainted with his present wife, Miss Mary Ann Greenwood, of Newburyport, Mass., a lady of rare merit, whose virtues have always shone brightly; who has always been beloved, but perhaps never so much as by the noble officers and men of the 27th Regt. Ill. Volunteers after the battle of Belmont, who were the witnesses of her ministrations to the wounded, and for a period of months, to her pious deportment. They were not married until after a separation of 27 years, and if we were permitted to tell the story of their pure intercourse, sweet remembrances, useful lives, and happy union, our short biography would grow into a romance, illustrating the adage, that "Truth is stranger than fiction."

In 1833, Lieut. Buford was appointed one of the assistant Professors of Natural and Experimental Philosophy at West Point, the duties of which occupied him until 1835, when called by his native State as one of her Civil Engineers, he resigned his commission in the army, and was engaged in the public improvements of Kentucky, until 1842. During most of this time he was the resident Engineer of the Licking river slack-water navigation, and made his winter residence in Cincinnati. There he again enjoyed the society of the Hon. S. P. Chase, and also of Judge Burnet, Judge McLean, Bishop McIlvaine (who was his Professor at West Point), Hon. Larz. Anderson, Prof. (now Maj. General) Mitchell, Prof. Parker, Prof. Gross, Dr. Lyman Beecher, and others ever to be remembered.

In 1843, Mr. Buford removed from Cincinnati to Rock Island, Illinois, his present home, where he engaged actively in business. He was a merchant, iron-founder and banker successively. The monuments of his industry still adorn the beautiful city of Rock Island. He was one of the originators of the Chicago and Rock Island Railroad; for several years one of its directors, and subsequently President of the Rock Island and Peoria Railroad.

The breaking out of the rebellion was ruinous to his banking business, as he had $200,-000 invested in State bonds, which lost half of their market value on the fall of Fort Sumter. Bred a soldier, he felt it his duty to volunteer in the service of his country, but the prostration of his credit, by the fall of the bonds, made it imperative that he should, in person, settle up his business, and liquidate his obligations, by the delivering of his large real and personal estate; and faithfully did he do it. At the time of the battle of Bull's Run he was at Washington asking for a commission in the regular army. The Secretary of War referred him to his own State. He offered his services to Gov. Yates, and before he could get an answer, Gov. Dennison, of Ohio, unsolicited, offered him a Colonel's commission. He preferred his own State, Illinois, and as soon as ten companies were mustered into the service at Camp Butler, Gov. Yates, on the 10th of August, 1861, commissioned him Colonel of the 27th Regt. Illinois Volunteers, which he marched to Cairo, and in a very short time he had it in a thorough state of discipline.

On the 7th of November, 1861, occurred the battle of Belmont. In this bloody contest, the 27th Regiment bore a distinguished and an honorable part. It was first in the action; it was the last out. It captured the enemy's camp, tore down the rebel flag, secured 75 prisoners of war, burned up his tents, killed the horses and drove off the gunners from Watson's New Orleans Battery, and with the loss of 13 killed and 42 wounded, secured a complete victory on the right of the line. When the centre and left of our line was overborne with overwhelming numbers, which had been landed from Columbus during the engagement, the 27th Regiment, led by its Colonel, retired by the same route it had entered into the field, securing its prisoners and its honor. When it came in sight of the river, the transports and gunboats were steaming far up on their way to Cairo, all thinking the gallant 27th was cut off, but they marched steadily forward, and at nightfall a transport and gunboat had been halted for them, 12 miles from the battle-field, and from their barracks the next morning they emerged fresh and vigorous. They were now veterans!

Before this battle, strict discipline, the necessity for which it was difficult for newly enlisted volunteers to comprehend, had made Col. Buford unpopular with a part of his command, but those who most complained of the Colonel before the battle, were most sincere in their praises after it was over.

In the month of February, 1862, at the request of Commodore Foote, Col. Buford was given the command of the troops that should accompany the Flotilla, and with the gunboats he made two reconnoisances near Columbus, but no attack was made. General Halleck's masterly movement up the Tennessee, and the glorious victories of Fort Henry and Fort Donelson, had made it evident that Columbus must be evacuated. On the 4th of March he took possession of that strongly fortified position, which had been plundered and evacuated by the rebels, but still leaving immense ordnance stores, which he secured.

On the 14th of March the Flotilla moved down to attack Island No. 10, attended by Col. Buford, with three regiments of infantry, one field battery of artillery, one siege battery, and one company of cavalry. On arriving, the water overflowed the banks so as to render land operations almost impossible. The gunboats took up their position, the mortar boats lashed to the shore, and Col. Buford, from the 14th of March to the 8th of April, maintained a strong guard to cover the mortar boats, and daily made reconnoisances, the first of which was to send a communication by the hands of his Adjutant, across the peninsula, by the route the canal was afterwards cut, to announce to General Pope his arrival. The bombardment continued twenty-four days, during all of which time the enemy maintained a post at Union City, 15 miles south of Hickman, and made several demonstrations on Columbus and Hickman.

If the enemy had been permitted to establish himself at any point on the Mississippi river stronger than Col. Buford's command, and he at Humboldt 86 miles by railroad south of Hickman, had five times as large a force, it would have led to the most ruinous consequences. Col. Buford had already weakened his force at Island No. 10, by stationing four companies of infantry, three companies of cavalry, and one company of artillery at Hickman.

To secure his position, it was indispensable that the post of the enemy at Union City should be broken up. Col. Buford was equal to the occasion. On the 30th of March he left

Island No. 10, with his own regiment, the 27th Illinois, the 15th Wisconsin, Col. Heg, and suddenly landed at Hickman. He summoned Lieut. Col. Hogg, with his three companies of cavalry, and one company of artillery, and pushed out for Union City at 3 p. m., capturing and detaining every person he encountered on the road. He proceeded 10 miles before it became too dark to go further. He bivouacked 4 miles from Union City, and secured all the people in the four nearest farms. He marched again at dawn, passing six farms, populous with masters and slaves, detaining all as he went, and got within a quarter of a mile of the enemy before he was discovered. His line of battle was formed, his cavalry charged, his artillery opened fire, and the enemy, consisting of 1400 infantry and cavalry, under the command of Cols. Pickett and Jackson, abandoned their camp and ran in all directions. He burned both camps, one of tents, the other huts, destroyed all their commissary and ordnance stores, captured 3 flags, 15 prisoners, 110 horses and mules, 12 wagons, 200 stand of arms, and returned in triumph to the Flotilla before sunset, his troops marching 30 miles in 24 hours. The post was never re-established.

On his return to the Flotilla, he was congratulated by Commodore Foote and all the officers of the Navy. The Assistant Secretary of War, Col. T. A. Scott, was present, and telegraphed the successful result of the enterprise, and was answered the same day, April 1st—"The President has nominated Colonel Buford of Illinois, a Brigadier General," and he was confirmed a few days after by the Senate.

On the night of the 7th of April, Island No. 10 was surrendered to Commodore Foote, who immediately turned it over to General Buford, who took possession of it before dawn. The works on the main shore were evacuated the same day, and the troops had all surrendered to Gen. Pope. The whole enemy's forces, 100 cannon, with 100 rounds of ammunition for each gun, 5 steamboats and 2 wharf boats filled with stores, were captured.

General Buford was then attached to the Army of the Mississippi; the troops and the Flotilla went down to attack Fort Pillow; the overflow left no foothold for the troops; and Gen. Halleck ordered the army to join him

at Pittsburg Landing, which they did on the 24th of April.

Since that time General Buford has commanded one of the brigades that invested Corinth, and since its evacuation has led his troops in the pursuit of the enemy to Booneville and Ripley.

On the 11th of July, 1862, on the invitation of the officers of the 27th Regiment, General N. B. Buford, accompanied by the regimental commanders of his brigade, Col. Sanborn, 4th Minnesota, Col. Boomer, 26th Missouri, Col. Alexander, 59th Indiana, Col. Eddy, 48th Indiana, and Lieut. Col. Matthias, of the 5th Iowa, went to the headquarters of the 27th Regiment, at their camp on Clear Creek, near Corinth, where they were received by Col. Harrington, and the officers of the regiment.

Lieut. Stout, having been selected to make the presentation, said :

General Buford: The commissioned officers of the 27th Regiment desire to present you a slight testimonial of the great regard they entertain for their former commander. To their kind partiality am I indebted for the honor of being selected to make the presentation; and while I highly appreciate the favor conferred, I have to regret that their choice did not fall upon one more competent to represent them.

Sir, it has been the good fortune of most of the officers of this regiment to have participated with you in some of those stirring scenes which have transpired since this accursed rebellion was inaugurated. The part the regiment bore on those trying occasions it is unnecessary to enumerate here—it is a portion of the history of our common country, and as such will ever find a prominent place in its pages! I trust, however, it will not be considered inappropriate if I should particularly allude to one of those occasions well calculated to "try men's souls." Sir, I refer to the bloody field of Belmont. It was *there* that the confidence in the soldierly qualities of our commander culminated, and we felt proud of our noble leader! And from that time until the present I am happy to state, that nothing has occurred calculated to impair the great respect created on that memorable day! On the contrary—and the officers here present will guarantee the truth of my assertion—if I were to go among the *men* of the 27th Regiment, and say to them:—"*Forward boys! Buford leads the column!*" there would be none wanting to constitute a "forlorn hope," or "storm the deadly breach!" In the course of events it became necessary for you to leave us, to assume the arduous duties of a more important command, and while we regretted the separation, we consoled ourselves with the reflection, to you it was a "reward of merit," and for the country's good! But, sir, we have not forgotten the *pain* it gave you to separate from your *old* regiment, and your farewell words still linger in our ears. We feel that we are greatly your debtors. For chiefly to your energy and perseverance is this regiment under obligations for the enviable position it holds among the justly celebrated volunteers of Illinois. As a slight indication of our regard, we present you this beautiful sword and these epaulettes. Sir, the sword is the most fitting testimonial a warrior can receive. And we have the confidence to believe that yours will only be used in the sacred cause of "truth and justice," and that it will *never* be laid aside so long as an armed foe to our "starry flag" exists upon our soil. Of these "epaulettes" I will only say, "may their stars increase in number." Accept these "our gifts," and may we, before another year is numbered with the mighty past, witness on the American continent the rise of a "Napoleon," whose military genius shall astonish the world anew; who will bring peace to this distracted land and confer additional lustre upon a name already famous in the world's history.

A sword, belt, sash, a pair of epaulettes, field glass and a pair of spurs were then presented to General Buford, who received them from the hands of the officers, and then replied as follows:

Lieutenant Stout, and Gentlemen of the 27th Regiment of Illinois Volunteers: I am deeply sensible of the honor you do me in presenting me these beautiful and valuable testimonials of your approbation and regard. I accept them with heartfelt pleasure, and shall treasure them as long as I may live, and transmit them to my children as an heirloom.

Educated by my country, I belong to her. When this unnatural rebellion broke out, I tendered my services to her, and was exceedingly fortunate in being assigned to the command of the 27th Regiment of Illinois Volunteers. For nearly one year my name and my fame were connected with yours, and happy have I been in the connection. Your deeds have shed undying honor on your names, reflected honor which has fallen upon me. Our connection was honorable. It was only severed by my promotion, and not until you had, by your good conduct and valor, won an imperishable name, and the pen of history had honorably connected you with Belmont, Union City, and Island No. 10; and upon your banner I hope to see these names inscribed. You have won them, and a grateful country will award them to you.

The love of glory is the inspiration of a soldier. To me glory and virtue are synonymous terms. You were not surprised that I accepted a promotion in the service of our common country. But it has not separated us. You are all personally dear to me. We will continue together in the honorable service of our glorious Union, until its banner floats over all the States, the Constitution re-established, and peace restored. We shall then retire to our homes, where I shall always dearly cherish the sweet memories connected with the 27th Regiment.

To you, Lieutenant Stout, I must make my acknowledgements for the flattering terms in which you have been pleased to make this presentation. You overrate my merits; but warm hearts always overflow. To you, to the officers, and to the men of the gallant 27th, I again express my heartfelt acknowledgements.

COL. TRUE.

The subject of this sketch, Col. JAMES M. TRUE, was born in Scott county, Ky., on the 14th of October, 1823. His father moved to Coles county, Illinois, during the fall of 1834. Young True's early days were spent on a farm, with very limited educational facilities. At the age of nineteen, he engaged in business for himself, attending school most of the first year after he left home. He settled on a farm, and continued to follow the occupation of a farmer until 1850, when he went into the dry goods business, in Charleston, Ill., at which place he remained until August, 1855. He then removed to Mattoon, Ill., continuing the same business. At the breaking out of the rebellion, he took an active part in making up the first companies from his section of the country. He entered the service on the 2d day of August, 1861, as Captain of Co. E, in the 38th Regiment Illinois Volunteers. He went with that regiment into Southeastern Missouri, participated in the battle of Fredericktown, on the 21st of October. On the 1st day of December last, he received the appointment of Colonel of the 62d Regiment Illinois Volunteers, from the Governor. Since that time he has been with his regiment, drilling and disciplining it, until it is now one of the best in the service.

During the life of the old Whig party, Col. True was a zealous Clay Whig, and since the organization of the Republican party, he has been a prominent member of that party in his county.

COL. MULLIGAN.

Col. JAMES A. MULLIGAN, the hero of Lexington, was born in Utica, N. Y., on the 25th of June, 1830, of Irish parents, and is devotedly attached to the land of his parentage. He removed to Chicago in the fall of 1836, graduated at the University of St. Mary's of the Lake, in June, 1850, being its first graduate, and receiving the degree of Master of Arts. During the same year he entered the law office of Judge Dickey, remaining there one year, when he accompanied Stevens, the traveler, in his exploring expedition through South America. Returning to Chicago in 1852, he entered the law office of J. Y. Scammon, with whom he remained a few months. He then studied three years with Arnold, Larned & Lay. During this time he edited a weekly Catholic paper, called the *Western Tablet*. In November, 1855, he was admitted to the bar. From that time until the breaking out of the war, he practiced at the Chicago bar, if we except the winter of '58, when he held an appointment in the Indian Bureau, under Buchanan, which he resigned to come home and stump the State for Judge Douglas. He was connected with the Chicago Shields Guard, of which he was for some time commandant. In October, 1858, he was married by the Rt. Rev. Bishop Duggan, to Miss Marian Nugent, an accomplished lady of Chicago. Immediately after the fall of Sumter, a meeting was held at North Market Hall, Chicago, having for its object the organization of an Irish regiment. Three days afterwards the regiment was tendered, *full*, by the Colonel to Gov. Yates. It was the first regiment offered as a body from Illinois, and the first Irish organization in the Northwest. The Governor refused it. Col. Mulligan, who had been elected Major, went on to Washington, tendered the regiment to the President direct, and it was accepted by the Secretary of War. Col. Mulligan returning, the regiment was rapidly organized, meeting, however, with considerable delay in the Quartermaster's Department.

The Irish Brigade were mustered into the service on the 15th of June, 1861. Col. Mulligan was elected Colonel without a dissenting vote. The regiment left Chicago on the 15th of July, 1861, 1064 strong. They went to Quincy; from there started down the Mississippi to St. Louis. Remaining there a day, they went to Jefferson City, and on the first day of September, left for Lexington, with orders to cut their way through. They reached their destination in safety, on the 9th of September. Col. Mulligan immediately took command of the post, which consisted of the 14th Missouri, 1st Illinois cavalry, five pieces of artillery, and the Brigade—in all about three thousand. On the 10th, the Colonel was informed of the approach of Price on Lexington, and immediately commenced fortifying. On the evening of the 11th the engagement opened by Gen. Price, with 28,000 men. At early dawn, on the 12th, the engagement recommenced. The siege continued nine days, and on Friday, the 20th of September, the garrison was surrendered. The officers and men were parolled. Col. Mulligan determinedly refused the parole, and was held by the rebel General as a prisoner of war, but treated with every courtesy. On the 25th of November he was exchanged for Gen. Frost, of Camp Jackson. Returning to Chicago, Col. Mulligan immediately commenced reorganizing his regiment. An order was, however, received from Gen. Halleck, mustering the men and officers out of service. The Colonel then, at the request of his officers, repaired to Washington, where he was warmly received by the President, who proffered him a brigade, which he refused, because his regiment would thus be thrown out of service. Gen. McClellan, in a general order, considered the Irish Brigade as "continuously in the service from the date of their original muster in." The Colonel then made a short tour through the Eastern States, lecturing for different benevolent purposes.

The regiment was reorganized, and stationed at Camp Douglas, guarding the rebel prisoners, Col. Mulligan having command of the post. On the 16th of June, 1862, the Irish Brigade left Chicago, and are now at New Creek, Va., on the line of the Baltimore and Ohio Railroad (the Middle Department). Col. Mulligan has command of the post, consisting of four infantry regiments, a battery, and a company of cavalry.

COL. CARLIN.

WILLIAM P. CARLIN was born on a farm in Greene county, Illinois, on the 34th of November, 1829. His father, William Carlin, then a farmer, was for many years subsequent to his birth, Clerk of the County and Circuit Court of Greene county. He was the youngest brother of Thomas Carlin, once Governor of Illinois. In 1846, at the age of sixteen, young Carlin entered the U. S. Military Academy at West Point, where he graduated in 1850. Receiving an appointment as brevet 2d Lieutenant in the 6th U. S. Infantry, he joined his company, then at Fort Snelling, Minnesota Territory, where he remained till promoted, April 15th, 1851, to a Second Lieutenancy. This change took him to Fort Ripley, Minn., 125 miles above Snelling, where he served till October, 1854. His regiment was then ordered to Jefferson Barracks, Mo., to recruit, preparatory to going to California. But the massacre of Lieut. Grattan and his command, near Fort Laramie, and the generally disturbed condition of Indian affairs on the western plains, changed its destination. His regiment formed a part of the Sioux Expedition, under Gen. Harney, and Lieut. Carlin marched in the spring of 1855 to Fort Laramie, N. T. In the summer of '55, he commanded a detachment of infantry and a battery of prairie howitzers, on an expedition, under Capt. C. S. Lovell, to Fort Pierce, on the Missouri river. The march was 325 miles to Fort Pierce, and the same distance returning—thus they marched 650 miles on that expedition. On his return, Lieut. Carlin was stationed on the Black Hills, guarding a government sawmill, till November, when he received command of his company, D, 6th Infantry, in consequence of the Captain's absence. On the 3d of March, 1855, he had been promoted to a First Lieutenancy. During the winter of '55-6, he was stationed at Fort Laramie, and till July, 1856, when he was ordered to Platte River Bridge, 125 miles west of Laramie, to protect the emigration to and from California. Returning in September to Laramie, he was appointed Assistant Quartermaster and Acting Assistant Commissary of Subsistence, at the post, in addition to the command of his company.

In 1857, Lieut. Carlin joined the expedition of Col. (now Gen.) Sumner, against the Cheyenne Indians, then hostile to our people. As that was an Indian expedition, its history has never been written. They had but one fight, July 30th, on Solomon's Peak, Kansas river. The Indians were routed, and never afterwards seen by our troops, till a treaty of peace had been made. When this expedition was ordered, Lieut. Carlin had a leave of absence, but relinquished it for the sake of joining the expedition. After marching over the plains for four months—three weeks of which time living on buffalo meat and poor beef, without bread, coffee, pepper, salt, or anything but the meats mentioned, they were ordered to Salt Lake City. They had then marched over 500 miles after the Indians. The order was, however, countermanded, and they were sent into Kansas, to preserve order at the October elections. Reaching Fort Leavenworth in October, Lieut. Carlin availed himself of the leave of absence referred to. But four weeks before his leave of absence expired, he was ordered to return to his regiment, which was then under orders to march to Salt Lake, to the relief of Gen. A. S. Johnston, commanding the Utah Expedition. At Leavenworth he was appointed Regimental Commissary, and acted in that capacity till the arrival of the regiment at Fort Bridger, late in July. Their route was through Bridger's Pass, south of the old emigrant route, until then untracked and untravelled, except by a few trappers and Indians. At Medicine Bow river, Lieut. Carlin was sent forward with the engineer company and a detachment of infantry, to open the road, build bridges, etc. For nearly a hundred miles they had to construct their road and to build many bridges, the timbers for which were necessarily hauled a great distance. On arriving at Bridger, and finding that their services were not required—the rebel Mormons having accepted the pardon of President Buchanan—they received orders to continue their march to California. After a long and dreary march, the detachment arrived at Benecia, California, Nov. 15th. They had been delayed three weeks at Bridger, for want of supplies, and experienced perhaps

COL. CARLIN.

ten days' delay in consequence of having to build the road. Including these delays, their march from Fort Leavenworth, Kansas, to Benecia, Cal., a distance of 2,250 miles, occupied just five months. They had little time to rest at Benecia. In December, Lieut. Carlin's company was ordered to march to the head of Russian river, into the Indian country, about 100 miles north of Benecia. After remaining there, endeavoring to preserve peace between the whites and Indians, for nine months, Lieut. C. was assigned to the command of Fort Bragg, in Mendocino county, directly on the Pacific coast. There he remained for nine months more—without the society of any other officer, and with but two or three companionable citizens within a day's ride. In May, 1860, he was detailed for general recruiting service, and embarked for New York, where he arrived June 13th, 1860. He was assigned to the station of Buffalo, N. Y., and entered upon the duties on the 1st of July, 1860, remaining there during the whole of the exciting political campaign, but taking no part therein. On the first call of President Lincoln for troops, Lieut. Carlin received the unanimous vote of the officers of the 74th N. Y. S. M., at Buffalo, for the position of Lieut. Colonel. The regiment was then under orders for Washington—which orders were, however, countermanded. Subsequently, the Secretary of War authorized him to raise a regiment of cavalry in western New York, but this authority having been sought by other parties, against his wishes and without his knowledge, he declined to act under it. He had resolved, if he entered the volunteer service, to serve with those from his own State, preferring that if ever he achieved a desirable reputation, it should be in connection with the sons of his native State. Finally, on the 15th of August, 1861, Governor Yates tendered him the Colonelcy of a regiment, which was immediately accepted. Gov. Kirkwood, of Iowa, at the same time tendered him the Lieutenant Colonelcy of an Iowa regiment, which, of course, he felt compelled to decline. Col. Carlin joined his regiment, the 38th Illinois Volunteers, at Camp Butler, September 7th, 1862. On the 19th of the same month, he was ordered by Maj. Gen. Fremont, then commanding Department of the Missouri, to Ironton, Mo. Arriving there on the 21st of

September, he assumed command of all the forces there, by virtue of senior commission. From this time forward, he has been constantly engaged in the war. On the 21st of October, 1861, very early in the morning, Col. Carlin entered Fredericktown, with the 21st, 33d and 38th Illinois volunteers, the 8th Wisconsin volunteers, Capt. Mauter's battery, 1st Missouri light artillery, and about 400 of the 1st Indiana cavalry. When they marched from Pilot Knob, on the 20th of October, at 3 o'clock, he had precise information as to the whereabouts of Jeff. Thompson and his forces, and had based all his plans on the expectation that he would remain where he was for a few hours longer; and so he would, but for the unfortunate occurrence now to be related. Col. J. B. Plummer was marching from Cape Girardeau, to find Thompson, and unfortunately sent a despatch by one of his Sergeants, for the commanding officer at Pilot Knob. This despatch bearer went directly along the main road leading to Thompson's camp, and was, of course, arrested by the rebel picket. The despatch was delivered to Thompson, and he immediately availed himself of the information it contained, and started on his retreat, marching twelve miles on the afternoon and night of the 20th. Early next day, thinking his seizure of the despatch would prevent the arrival of any force from Pilot Knob, Thompson made a move with the view of cutting off Plummer, and routing him. But in finding the latter, he found it necessary to return to the vicinity of Fredericktown, where Col. Carlin's force was now united with Plummer's. The result of the fight, and Col. Carlin's gallantry during the engagement, is well known.

On the succession of Gen. Halleck to the command of the Department, he appointed Col. C. to the command of the District of South-East Missouri, which he retained till the column of Gen. Steele was organized for the purpose of marching through Arkansas. He commanded the 1st brigade of that column. On their march southward, the advance guard of his brigade, under Col. Hall Wilson, 5th Illinois cavalry, attacked and routed a force of 150 rebels, strongly posted on Current river, opposite Doniphan. This occurred on the 1st of April, 1862. About the 20th of April, his brigade occupied Pocahontas, Ark., till recently a rebel stronghold. Early in

May, his brigade being several days in advance, entered Jacksonport, Ark. It was here that the infantry regiments of the brigade, the 21st and 38th Illinois volunteers, received orders to go to Corinth, by forced marches, via Cape Girardeau, Mo. Col. Carlin received the order at 9 o'clock P. M., on the 9th of May. On the 10th of May his brigade marched twenty miles. On the 20th of May, they arrived at Cape Girardeau, having been delayed one and a half days in ferrying Black and Current rivers—thus marching, in very hot weather, 212 miles in nine and a half days. His brave soldiers were eager to participate in the expected battle at Corinth. On the 24th of May the brigade reached Hamburg, Tenn., and on the 26th joined Gen. Pope's army, at Farmington. On the 28th, 29th and 30th of May, the brigade occupied the trenches on the extreme left of our position, while demonstrations were being made in front of Corinth. They participated in the march of Gen. Pope's army, in the rear of the retreating rebels, to Boonville, Miss. Since then Col. Carlin has served in the army of the Mississippi, commanded by Brigadier General Rosecranz, and now commands the 2d brigade, 4th division.

COL. CAMERON.

DANIEL CAMERON, JR., commanding the 65th (Scotch) Regt. Ill. Volunteers, now in service in the valley of the Shenandoah, was born in the town of Berwick-upon-Tweed, Scotland, on the 13th of April, 1828, and is consequently in the thirty-fifth year of his age. Though a borderer by birth, Col. Cameron is of Highland extraction (the family coming originally from Breadalbane, Perthshire), and is a lineal descendant of Cameron of Lochiel, who fell on the ever-memorable field of Culloden. After receiving a good English education, he was placed in his father's office, where he remained until he acquired, by practical experience, a thorough knowledge of the "art preservative of arts," which proved so beneficial to him in after-life. Like most of the people of that good old town (for the world does not seem to whir there as it does here), he pursued the even tenor of his way, no event transpiring worthy of record, till the spring of 1851, when, in company with his family, he resolved to seek a more extended field of action—one which offered greater inducements to the industrious and enterprising than the little town of Berwick. Naturally he turned to the prairies of the West, and after completing the necessary arrangements, sailed from Greenock on the 21st of May, and arrived in New York, July 3d, where, after spending a short time in visiting old friends, he resumed his journey, and finally settled near the village of Wheeling, in the northern part of the State of Illinois.

Naturally of an ardent and ambitious temperament, and failing to appreciate the inducements or seclusion of a country life, he came to Chicago in the spring of 1854—then in the zenith of her attractions—and shortly afterwards became connected with the *Courant* newspaper—which was merged into the *Young America*, and subsequently into the *Chicago Daily Times*, which latter journal obtained such an extended reputation from its being edited by the trenchant pen of James W. Sheahan, and being acknowledged as the home organ of the Hon. Stephen A. Douglas ; and was one of the proprietors of that journal during the eventful campaigns of 1855, '56 and '58. In 1859 he disposed of his interest to Mr. Price, ex-postmaster of Chicago, and again took up his residence in the country, in the hope of recruiting his health, which had been failing for some time.

In the spring of the following year he recommenced business in Chicago—and shortly afterwards resumed the business management of the *Times* (which had again changed hands), which position he retained until it was purchased by William F. Storey, late of the Detroit *Free Press.*

In politics, it is almost unnecessary to state that Col. Cameron is, or rather was (for I do not know how recent events may have changed his opinions , an ardent Democrat, and the firm, unwavering supporter of Stephen A. Douglas. He took a prominent part in every Democratic convention held in Chicago since 1855, and was for two years a member of the Executive Committee of Cook county.

Shortly after the President issued his call for 300,000 troops, and when the glorious 79th Highland Regiment of New York had vindicated the valor of Scotchmen on more than one well contested battle-field, the question was asked, why should Illinois lag? The subject once broached was put to a practical test, and after encountering difficulties which would have dampened the ardor of those less determined, he received special permission from the War Department and from Gov. Yates, to raise a regiment of infantry, to be known as the Scotch Illinois.

There is one feature in connection with the raising of this corps which is worthy of notice and commendation: no false or exaggerated inducements were held out. The truth was simply and plainly stated; thus avoiding a prolific source of recrimination and mutiny. And although the season was deemed inaus-

picious, and fears entertained of its success, yet, with the energetic co-operation of his brother officers, he succeeded in raising a body of men of which any State or commander might be proud. After doing garrison duty for several months at Camp Douglas, in guarding the Fort Donelson prisoners, the regiment left Chicago, amid the "God-speed" of thousands, on the 24th of June, en route for Harper's Ferry, which was afterwards changed to Martinsburg, Va., where they are at present stationed, and which is the headquarters of the commissary department of the army of the Shenandoah. The regiment is, however, under the immediate command of Major Gen. Wool, stationed at Annapolis, to which point they expect daily to be ordered.

Although the 65th has seen but little active service, we believe that when the hour of trial comes, it will not be found wanting, and will prove that Scottish valor has not degenerated by being transplanted to the prairie soil of Illinois—for

"High, high are their hopes, for their chieftain has said,
That whatever men dare they can do."

COL. OZBURN.

Lindsay Ozburn was born May 19, 1824, in Jackson county, Illinois, and until the age of eighteen spent his life upon a farm, without having received during that period any educational advantages. In 1842, he left home to enter the employment of a person engaged in the Indian trade, and for nearly two years young Ozburn was trafficking among the Indians of Arkansas. At the expiration of this time he was taken seriously ill, and as soon as he recovered sufficiently to travel, he returned to the home of his childhood, and was elected Deputy Sheriff of the county. At the breaking out of the Mexican war, Mr. Ozburn volunteered in an Illinois regiment, and was appointed First Sergeant of the company. He served throughout the war with distinction, and at its close returned to his native county, and engaged in the lumber trade. This business he continued with success until 1850, when he entered the well

known "Dowdall Flour Mills," which he carried on until the breaking out of the rebellion, filling during the period of ten years, including 1861, several responsible county offices with great credit to himself and advantage to the public. When the call for volunteers was made by the President, Mr. Ozburn at once enlisted as a private in the 31st Illinois Regiment, Col. John A. Logan, and was soon promoted to Regimental Quartermaster, in which position he served until Col. Logan's promotion to a Brigade Generalship, when Quartermaster Ozburn was unanimously elected to the vacant Colonelcy, and by Gov. Yates was appointed, April 1st, 1862, to the command of the 31st. Col. Ozburn has been actively engaged in the field ever since, with his regiment, which now forms a part of the 1st Brigade of the 1st Division of the army of the Mississippi.

COL. BRAYMAN.

MASON BRAYMAN was born in Buffalo, N.Y., May 23, 1813. His early life was spent on a farm, and his education limited to what could be learned in the district school. With David M. Day, of the Buffalo *Journal*, he began the trade of printer, and in the second year was made foreman of the office. He soon after commenced the study of the law, with Sheldon Smith, an attorney of high character and commanding ability, who died young. At twenty years of age, Mr. Brayman became editor of the Buffalo *Bulletin*, a Democratic paper, supporting Gen. Jackson; at twenty-two was admitted to the bar, and the year following married Miss Mary Williams, of Chatauque county, N. Y.

In 1837, Mr. Brayman removed to the West, where he practiced law, and become the editor of the Louisville *Advertiser*. In March, 1842, he removed to Springfield, Illinois, where he practiced at the bar. In 1845, he revised the statute laws of Illinois, under the appointment of Gov. Ford, and approved by the Legislature, which Murray McConnel facetiously called the "Bray-minical code." In 1846, Mr. Brayman was appointed by the Governor a special commissioner and attorney for the State, to prosecute offenders and restore the peace and happiness disturbed by the "Mormon War," aided by a military force.

On the organization of the Illinois Central R. R. Co., in March, 1851, he was, in conjunction with the late Gov. Bissell, selected attorney and solicitor. Col. Bissell being a member of Congress, and in feeble health, Mr. Brayman was charged with the chief labor of organizing the operations of the Company in Illinois, its legal business, right of way, the protection of its lands, the securing of depot grounds, etc., his office and residence being in Chicago. He resigned in 1856.

He soon after engaged in efforts to secure the construction of the Cairo and Fulton Railroad, in Missouri and Arkansas, a line reaching from Cairo to the Texas boundary, connecting south and west to Galveston and the Pacific—donated lands, 1,750,000 acres. He was President of both companies, and largely interested. The project was successful, until the beginning of the present troubles, which brought ruin, of course, upon the enterprise, and dissipated the prospect of the "Southern route to the Pacific."

In August, 1861, Mr. Brayman was commissioned by Gov. Yates Major of the 29th Regiment, forming part of Gen. McClernand's original brigade, and was appointed Chief of Staff and Assistant Adjutant General, which position his business experience and executive ability eminently fitted him for. Nov. 7, 1861, Major Brayman shared in the desperate battle of Belmont. Feb. 13, 14 and 15, 1862, he was constantly engaged and exposed throughout the contest at Fort Donelson. He was present at the battle of Shiloh, and encountered danger to an unusual degree during the whole two days. His horse was shot, as he galloped forward to rescue Major Stewart, who was wounded near the enemy. At one time, when the enemy were advancing to take two of our batteries, the supporting regiments faltered, and Major Brayman seized the flag of one of them, which lay on the ground, unfurled, and bore it up and down the front, and rallied them again, passing repeatedly through the enemy's volleys, but escaped unhurt.

April 15th, Major Brayman took command of the 29th regiment, *vice* J. S. Reardon, resigned. Col. Brayman entered service in feeble health, notwithstanding which he has performed most severe labor, in the office and field, transacting the business of the command, and been present at every march and battle. Col. Brayman is an old line Democrat, of the "Hard-Shell" species, and has supported every Democratic ticket and every Democratic President from Jackson down (what an immeasurable distance *down!*) to James Buchanan. He is unconquerably devoted to the Union, and has an abiding faith that *all will yet be well,* believing God to be just, and his providences wisely directed. He has entire confidence in the ability, integrity and sagacity of Abraham Lincoln, and in this crisis prefers him above any living man.

N. B.—The able editor, successful lawyer, and gallant Colonel, expects to be a Democrat again, when the war is over.

COL. BRAYMAN.

COL. CHETLAIN.

Augustus L. Chetlain was born in St. Louis, Mo., on the 26th day of December, 1824. His parents, who are still living, are French Swiss, and emigrated to this country but one year before his birth. As early as 1826, his family moved to Galena, Ill., where they have resided ever since. He received an English education, and at the age of twenty left his father's farm, to make his way in the world. In 1850, he engaged in mercantile business, and prosecuted it successfully for nine years, when he disposed of his interest, and spent the succeeding year traveling on the continent of Europe. Taking an active part in the political campaign of 1860, he strongly and earnestly advocated the election of Mr. Lincoln to the Presidency.

The first gun from Sumter drew him, with thousands of others, to the ranks. As a great whirlwind attracts and gathers together a multitude of things, so were gathered and heaped in disorder, in the camps at Springfield, the thousands who rallied to the support of our flag; and from among the multitude of applicants—for even a private position—he was selected as Lieut. Colonel (with Gen. John McArthur as Colonel) of one of the six regiments accepted from Illinois by the Government. Three months passed, and the old 12th was mustered out of the service. In the reorganization for three years, he was again elected a Lieut. Colonel, the men feeling that they could not do better. At this time the regiment was quartered at Cairo. In September, by order of Gen. Grant, it moved, with the 9th Illinois, on Paducah, Ky., and not a moment too soon was this move made, for already were a body of rebels moving toward the same point. Here he was one of the few who gave their support to Gen. C. F. Smith, when assailed by the press.

About the close of September, Col. Chetlain, with a portion of his regiment, was ordered by Gen. C. F. Smith (then in command at Paducah) to Smithland, Ky., to hold and fortify the place. Here he threw up fortifications that won for him the praise of our best engineers. He continued in command of that military post four months, his troops increasing the meanwhile to some 1500 men. Relieved in the command at Smithfield by Gen. Low. Wallace, he returned to Paducah in time to take part in the attack on Fort Henry, his regiment forming part of Gen. Smith's division, which occupied the heights opposite, known as Fort Hindman. Crossing the river in transports, they took their line of march for Fort Donelson. The disappointment in not sharing the fight but rendered himself and command the more anxious to reach the foe. In this memorable struggle, on the morning of Saturday, the 15th of February, he, with the balance of Gen. McArthur's brigade, held the extreme right of the line, and kept in check for hours the overwhelming force under Gen. Floyd, who were endeavoring to cut their way out. At Shiloh he was again at the head of his regiment, having arisen from a sick bed to lead it. Its losses, especially in the last battle, were very heavy. His regiment testifies to his ability. A better drilled and disciplined regiment is rarely met with. In military matters he proves a just leader. Always approachable, he concedes to all their rights, yet enforcing a strict obedience. Never overstepping his limits, he never shrinks from a duty. In action he is with his men cool and cautious, yet never turning back while there is a chance for success. In address and appearance, a perfect gentleman. Thoroughly conversant with society, overflowing with anecdotes, he ever proves himself an agreeable and pleasing companion. On the 21st of April he was commissioned Colonel of the 12th Regiment, which is still with Maj. Gen. Grant's army, and took an active part in the siege of Corinth, Miss.

COL. BARNES.

MYRON S. BARNES, Colonel of the 37th Regiment Illinois Volunteers, was born in Bangor, Franklin county, N. Y., March 4th, 1825. He received a liberal education, and during his studies learned the "art preservative of arts" —and became a printer. At the age of sixteen he became editor and proprietor of a weekly newspaper, and continued in that business until the war between the United States and Mexico broke out, in 1846, when he laid down the pen, and replaced it with a musket, and served twelve months in the late Col. Wm. H. Bissell's 2d Illinois Regiment. He was at the battle of Buena Vista—received a wound, and at the end of the war was honorably discharged. On his return, he resumed his old profession, and purchased the Southport (now Kenosha, Wis.) American. He continued there until the fall of 1849, when he removed to Central New York, and shortly after became the editor and proprietor of the Independent Watchman, at Ithica, N. Y., where he remained till 1856. The paper was a temperance Whig paper, and then a temperance (Maine Law) Republican paper. Mr. Barnes represented the 27th Congressional District of New York in the Philadelphia Republican Convention, which nominated Fremont, and after the defeat of Fremont, in 1856, he removed to Chicago, and became the senior editor of the Chicago Daily Ledger, At a later date he removed to Rock Island county, and was at the time of the breaking out of the rebellion, editor of the Rock Island Daily Register.

In conjunction with Julius White, of Chicago, now a Brigadier General, he raised the 37th Regiment Illinois Volunteers, formerly known as the Fremont Rifle Regiment. The regiment was recruited in Rock Island, Cook, Lake, La Salle, Stark and Vermilion counties, and is said to be one of the best disciplined in the field. On entering Missouri, he was ordered to take command of the post of Boonville, and had allotted to him the counties of Cooper, Saline and Howard, three of the most intense rebel counties in the State. During his administration, he took a large number of prisoners, and inaugurated peace and quietude in that section. He administered the oath of allegiance to over five hundred persons, and took bonds of secession sympathisers to the amount of $500,000.

On the 24th of January, 1862, he was ordered to join his regiment, and take command at the Samine river, near Otterville, and the next day left for Arkansas, and had command of the regiment from that time till after the battle of Pea Ridge, and led it two days in the battles of Louisburgh and Elkhorn Tavern, commonly called Pea Ridge. After the battle, the regiment went to Cassville, and Col. Barnes became the commandant of that post, and for a long time had command of the troops in Southwest Missouri. While in command of the post at Cassville, many expeditions were sent into the country, and a large number of prisoners were taken. The oath of allegiance was administered to over seven hundred persons, and bonds taken in sums of one and ten thousand dollars from over two hundred.

On the 1st of August, Gen. Brown sent out a force of cavalry and infantry under command of Col. Barnes, with five days' rations, to scout the country in the neighborhood of Ozark and Forsythe, Mo. On the morning of the 3d an attack was made upon a rebel band under Col. Lawther, several killed, thirty horses, fifty guns, and seventy saddles captured, besides some very important documents among the rebel Colonel's baggage. The expedition was a most successful one, and reflects great credit upon the commanding officer, Col. Barnes. The regiment is now stationed at Springfield, Mo. An effort has been made to have the 37th sent to Richmond, Va., by petition of all the officers and Gen. White, but the movement has been opposed by Gen. Brown, who commands that district, and the military authorities at St. Louis, on the ground that the regiment is needed in Missouri.

COL. BARNES.

COL. RANSOM.

Col. Thomas E. G. Ransom, 11th Illinois Infantry, was born Nov. 29th, 1834, at Norwich, Vermont. In 1846, he entered the primary class of Norwich University—a military college, under the charge of his father, T. B. Ransom, then a Major General of Militia of the State of Vermont. His father was afterwards appointed Colonel of the 9th U. S. Infantry, and was killed in Mexico, at the battle of Chapultapec, Sept. 15th, 1847. During the Mexican war, young Ransom was taught engineering, under tuition of his cousin, B. F. Marsh, on the Rutland and Burlington Railroad. After his father's death, he returned to the military school—the Norwich University, a famous academy, and a rival of West Point, founded by Capt. A. Partridge, in 1820, and still in a flourishing condition—and continued there until the spring of 1851. In 1851, he removed to Peru, La Salle county, Illinois, to enter upon the practice of his profession of an Engineer. In 1854, he embarked in the real estate business, with his uncle, under the firm of Gilson & Ransom. In December, 1855, the firm removed to Chicago, and became largely engaged in land operations, under the firm name of A. J. Galloway & Co. After this, and on the death of Gilson, Ransom removed to Fayette county, and while engaged in trade, acted as agent there for the Ill. Central Railroad Company. He was there when the war broke out, and immediately raised a company in Fayette county, and arrived at Camp Yates, April 24th, 1861. The company was organized into the 11th Illinois Regiment, and on an election for field officers, he was elected Major. The regiment was ordered at once to Villa Ridge, near Cairo, and there remained in camp of instruction until June, when they were ordered to Bird's Point, Mo.

On July 30th, the regiment was mustered out of the three months service, and those who wished were mustered into the three years service. On an election of the men, Major Ransom was unanimously elected Lieut. Colonel. Col. Wallace (afterwards General, and killed at Shiloh) was most of the time commanding either the post or a brigade, and thus the command and instruction of the 11th

devolved entirely upon the young Lieut. Colonel, who brought them into that perfect condition of discipline and drill which has since covered them with glory. About August 23d he led his regiment against a large force of rebels under Major Hunter, concentrated at Charleston, Mo. Fifty horses and men were taken, and from twelve to fifteen killed on the rebel side. The Federal loss was three killed and fifteen wounded. Col. Ransom was wounded in the shoulder by a mounted rebel, who pretended to surrender, but fired upon him as he approached to take his arms. After receiving the bullet in his right shoulder, Col. Ransom fired upon the traitor, and killed him instantly, taking from him a beautiful cream colored horse, now in Chicago, and rejoicing in the name of "Secesh."

At Donelson the conduct of Col. Ransom was meritorious, as was also that of all the officers and men of the 11th. Col. Ransom commanded, Col. Wallace acting as Brigadier, and was again shot in the shoulder, but would not leave the field until the fight was ended. His clothes were pierced with six or eight bullet holes, and a horse was killed under him. Fatigue, cold and prolonged exposure did their work. A long sickness followed; but he would not leave his regiment, and when they moved from place to place, he was carried in an ambulance, determined to cling to the brave boys who had fought with him. For his bravery, skill and gallantry at Donelson, Lieut. Col. Ransom was promoted to the Colonelcy of his loved 11th.

At Shiloh he led the regiment through the thickest of that bloody fight, and though wounded in the head early in the engagement, remained with his command through the day. He assisted Gen. McClernand in rallying an Ohio regiment that was falling back on his right, and forced them to move forward with his own troops upon a rebel battery. In the official report of this battle, Gen. McClernand spoke of Col. Ransom, at a critical moment, "performing prodigies of valor, though reeling in his saddle and streaming with blood from a serious wound." The following evidence of the gallant conduct of the 11th is taken from a private letter, written by Capt. Waddell, of Company E. He says:

"It was nearly half a mile from our encampment to the position where the enemy had attacked us. The order for 'double quick' was given, and we were soon on the field of action. We had not to wait long, for soon in front of us was seen—not three hundred yards distant—the enemy, five regiments deep, advancing steadily. It was a glorious but a terrible sight. The order was, 'The whites of their eyes, boys, and then give it to them,' and the 11th was again engaged. Never, *never* in my life have I seen, or in the annals of history have I read of such a death-struggle.

"Our men fought well at Fort Donelson, but never did they fight as they fought on the 6th of April. The enemy were repulsed; they stood for a moment seemingly thunderstruck, and then broke their ranks and started to fly. The officers rallied them, and then, under a most galling fire, commenced retrieving their lost ground. Our regiment being badly cut up—Col. Ransom shot in the head (not mortally), Capt. Carter dead, Capt. Coats mortally wounded, five or six of our Lieutenants down, and no reserve coming to our assistance—the order was given to fall back. We gradually, but obstinately, fell back. We were soon cheered by the assistance of several regiments coming up, who filed in our front, and we were

for a time relieved. We fell back—and what a sight! Not one hundred men remained in the 11th! It was an awful sight to look at that little band, besmeared with blood and dirt, with their trusty guns in their hands, looking along the line to see how many of their beloved companions were left to them. It was a sight I never wish to see again. But there was little time to lose, and no time to complain. Gen. McClernand came up, and asked if that was all that was left of the 11th. 'Yes,' was the reply. 'Well, my men,' he said, 'we must win this day, or *all* will be lost. Will you try it again?' 'We will, General,' was the response. The boys called on *me* to lead them. I formed the regiment (or company, as it was) on the left of the 70th Ohio regiment, and was again ordered to take our position in front. Ten minutes' time and we were again engaged."

For his conduct in this battle, he was recommended by Gens. Grant and McClernand for promotion to a Brigadier General. In June he was placed upon the staff of Gen. McClernand, as chief of staff and Inspector General of the army of the Tennessee. At the present writing, August 25th, Col. Ransom is in command of the District of Cairo.

COL. ELLIS.

EDWARD F. W. ELLIS was born in Wilton, Maine, April 15th, 1819. At the age of nineteen he emigrated to Ohio, where he studied law and was admitted to the bar when 22 years of age. In 1845 he was married to Miss Lucy A. Dobyns, by whom he had four children. In the spring of 1849 he went to California, engaged there in the mercantile business, was burned out in six months, losing all he had, and leaving him some $5,000 in debt. He then commenced practising law with great success, and in the fall of 1851 was elected to the Legislature. He there vehemently opposed slavery, and was highly lauded for his efforts. In the spring of 1852 he returned to Ohio, and in the fall of 1854 removed with his family to Rockford, Illinois, where he has since resided. Soon after removing to Rockford, he engaged in the banking business with Mr. Chas. Spaf-

ford and Dr. D. G. Clark, and continued connected with them, under the firm name of Spafford, Clark & Ellis, most of the time since.

Very soon after the attack on Sumter, he was instrumental in organizing a company in Rockford, which elected him Captain, and assumed the name of the Ellis Rifles. The company became connected with the 15th Illinois Regiment at its organization in June, 1861, and Capt. Ellis was elected Lieutenant Colonel of the regiment. Most of the time, however, he acted as Colonel of the regiment (Colonel Turner acting Brigadier), and was in command at the battle at Shiloh, in which he was killed while bravely leading on his men.

Illinois will cherish the name and memory of Ellis with that of Baker, and Ellsworth, and Raith, and Wallace, and other of her sons, who have fallen in defence of their country.

COL. BAKER

COL. BAKER.

EDWARD D. BAKER, the most illustrious victim from Illinois of the terrible struggle against the rebellion, was of English birth, but came to this country when five years of age, and settled with his father's family, who were Quakers, in the city of Philadelphia. In a few years the parent died, and left Edward and a younger brother relationless and unprovided, in a strange land. The eldest boy obtained employment as a weaver in a small establishment in South street, and devoted for a time a portion of his earnings to the support of the younger, at the same time gradually instructing him in the business of weaving, that he might, in time, support himself. Possessed of an ardent imagination, he naturally took a deep interest in reading, and his taste being stimulated by the allurements of romance, enlarged, until it embraced the whole range of sober as well as of illusive literature.

Edward, whose mind had dwelt upon the marvels of the West, determined to seek its broad, inviting platform for his future. He accordingly communicated his resolution to his brother, and the young adventurers, with packs upon their shoulders, strong staffs in their hands, and stout, hopeful hearts within their bosoms, set their faces towards the Alleghanies. On foot they undertook their ascent, and on foot they crossed ; and so they trudged along, through broad intervening States, until they found themselves in that portion of the far west known as Illinois. Here the young men paused and cast their lot, Edward selecting Springfield, the capital, as his special place of residence. There, in a little while, he was enabled to turn to account the legal reading which he had begun in Philadelphia, and having a happy gift of language to help it into use, he was soon enabled to support himself by the practice of law. He rose rapidly, and ripening with exercise, it was not long before he was among the most popular advocates at the bar of Illinois.

Through his prosperity, he was now enabled to look beyond the narrow circle of the petty spites and griefs in which the mere attorney is required to abuse his mind, and enter the broad field of politics. He embraced the doctrines of the Whig party, and transferred his

eloquence to the forum with such success that he soon won his way to Congress. He occupied his seat in the House of Representatives with dignity and credit, and was fast being recognized as one of the leaders of that body, when the temptations of the Mexican campaign appealed to his ardent and enthusiastic mind, and induced him to abandon civil life and enter the field. He went to Illinois, raised a regiment, the 4th Illinois Volunteers, and at once proceeded to the Rio Grande. A pause in the campaign enabled him to return temporarily to Washington, in order that he might express himself upon the policy of the war, and cast his votes ; but that done, he went back to his command, and followed its fortunes on the line from Vera Cruz to the Mexican capital. All the actions of the hotly contested road to Mexico recognized his valor ; and when Shields fell at the head of his brigade, at Cerro Gordo, it was Col. Baker's distinguished fortune to rise to the command, and to lead the New York regiments through the bloody struggles of that day.

Returning to Illinois in triumph, Col. Baker was again elected to represent his district in Congress, where he served out his term, and in 1852, yielding to certain business views, went for a time to the Isthmus of Panama. The local fever soon drove him home, where, being recruited in health, a new contagion seized his mind, and he turned his steps to the Pacific coast—the new El Dorado of the West. His fame had gone before him, and he was spared any efforts to popularize himself in the new field of labor. He took at once a place in the front rank of the bar of San Francisco, and a large proportion of the heavy cases of the circuit sought the advantage of his extensive legal knowledge and wonderful eloquence. By common consent he was acknowledged to be the most eloquent speaker in California ; but a proof was in reserve, in a circumstance beyond the narrow limits of prosaic eloquence, to create for him the claim of being perhaps the most accomplished orator of the day. Broderick, who had defended California from the doom of slavery, had been taken in the toils by a band of unscrupulous villains, and slain. " They have killed me because I was opposed to the extension of slavery, and a corrupt administration," was the last declaration of the dying Senator; and as the words fell from his lips, they became fire in the heart of the weeping orator, who stood by his side, and closed his eyes.

San Francisco was steeped in gloom at the contemplation of the monstrous deed. All trade and business was stopped; no sound of bustle was heard along her streets; and by common consent, without pageantry or parade, or any sound but the low, measured, muffled throb of the church bells, the dejected people, walking as if they almost held their breaths, gathered in the main square, and formed themselves, like so many shadows, round the bier. At the foot of the coffin, stood the priest; at the head, and so he could gaze on the face of his friend, stood the pale figure of the orator. Both of them, the living and the dead, were self-made men; and the son of the stonecutter, lying in mute grandeur, with a record floating round that coffin which bowed the heads of the surrounding thousands down in mute respect, might have been proud of the tribute which the weaver's apprentice was about to lay upon his breast. For minutes after the vast audience had settled itself to hear his words, the orator did not speak. He did not look in the coffin, but the gaze of his fixed eye was turned within his mind, and the still tears coursed rapidly down his cheek. Then, when the silence was the most intense, his tremulous voice rose like a wail, and with an uninterrupted strain of lofty and patriotic words—only less burning and beautiful than those poured out over the body of the noble Roman, by his friend and follower, Mark Anthony—he so penetrated and possessed the hearts of the sorrowing multitude, that there was scarcely a cheek less moistened than his own. For an hour he held all that vast assemblage as with a spell; and when he finished, by bending over the calm face of the murdered Senator, and stretching his arms forward with an impressive gesture, exclaimed in quivering accents, "Good friend! brave heart! gallant leader! true hero! hail and farewell!" the audience broke forth in a general response of sobs. Rarely has eloquence been more thrilling; never better adapted to the temper of its listeners. The

merit of the eulogy divided public encomium with the virtues of the deceased, and Baker was invested with Broderick's political fortunes. The senatorial field in California being, however, not open to immediate occupation, Col. Baker transferred himself to Oregon, and there the glow of his last effort soon carried him to the highest honors of the State. He was elected Senator for the full term of six years, in 1860, and at the time of his death had enjoyed its honors but two sessions. How he improved the prestige of the place by great arguments in favor of the Constitution, and by withering denunciations of the advocates of treason, is familiar to all. He was the master debater of the war term of Congress.

The capture of Fort Sumter fired his soul anew with military ardor, and on the 20th of April, at the great mass-meeting in Union Park, New York city, he delivered an address which thrilled the souls of all who heard it. The noble patriot then pledged his personal services to his country as a soldier, and closed his speech with these impressive and eloquent words, which were greeted with thunders of applause: "And if, from the far Pacific, a voice feebler than the feeblest murmur upon its shore, may be heard to give you courage and hope in the contest, that voice is yours to-day; and if a man whose hair is gray, who is well-nigh worn out in the battle and toil of life, may pledge himself on such an occasion and in such an audience, let me say, as my last word, that when amid sheeted fire and flames, I saw and led the hosts of New York as they charged in contest upon a foreign soil for the honor of your flag, so again, if Providence shall will, this feeble hand shall draw a sword, never yet dishonored—not to fight for distant honor in a foreign land, but to fight for country, for home, for law, for government, for constitution, for right, for freedom, for humanity, and in the hope that the banner of my country may advance, and wherever that banner waves, there glory may pursue and freedom be established."

The pledge there made was speedily fulfilled. All these honors, and the acknowledged prominence which he had won in the Senate of the United States, was not enough for his active and daring spirit while the country was in arms. He left his seat, and organized the

COL. MORO.

California regiment, which he led to the field. When offered a Brigadier, and even a Major Generalship, he declined both, preferring to be at the head of his own regiment. When he fell, on the bloody field of Ball's Bluff, October 21st, 1861, with the "light of battle" in his features, although acting as a General, he was simply Colonel of the First California Regiment of Volunteers. At the head of eighteen hundred of his own and Col. Deven's Massachusetts Regiment, and three guns, the noble leader fought the rebels, who outnumbered his force four to one, during the whole afternoon. The alternatives were, fight and conquer, surrender, or be captured. The noble band of heroes and their gallant commander understood these terrible alternatives, and nobly did they vindicate their manhood. During all those long hours, from two o'clock P.M. until the early dusk of the evening, the gallant Baker continued the unequal contest, when he fell, pierced by three bullets, and instantly expired. A council of war was called (after the frightful death struggle over his lifeless remains and for them), and it was decided that the only chance of escape was by cutting through the enemy and reaching Edwards' Ferry, which was at once decided upon; but while forming for the desperate encounter, the enemy rushed upon our little band of heroes in overpowering numbers, and the rout was perfect. When the gallant Senator and soldier fell on that disastrous field, he had been nominated for Brigadier General, and had he been spared, would have been unanimously confirmed.

"Death," says Bacon, "openeth the gate to good fame." In this brief biography of Edward D. Baker, it has not been my aim to make him too much a hero. I cannot better leave him than with his own beautiful words, applied to another, and which may be even more truthfully applied to himself: "Good friend! brave heart! gallant leader! true hero! hail and farewell!"

COL. MORO.

Col. FRANCIS MORO was born in the City of New York, Sept. 5, 1824. His father came to the United States with General Lafayette, remaining in this country after the Revolutionary war. He was of the family of General Moreau, and at an advanced age married a Miss Raymond, a member of an old New England family. In 1840, the subject of this brief sketch came to the West, and settled in Cincinnati, where he studied medicine, and practised several years. In 1853, after having resided in the South several years, he removed to Illinois, and married a daughter of Daniel Keen, of Wabash County, where he continued to reside until the breaking out of the present rebellion. Soon after his marriage, Dr. Moro was ordained a minister of the Missionary Baptist Church, and only abandoned the ministry and the practice of medicine to take up arms in defence of his country. In a private note Col. Moro says: "I raised my regiment, the 63d Volunteers, in Southern Illinois, having abandoned peaceful pursuits for the profession of arms, and am now in the field, ready to strike for the defence of the glorious country for which my father fought before me. I am proud my country has honored me with the command of a regiment of which I am not ashamed."

Col. Moro received his commission Dec. 1st, 1861. A portion of the 63d was engaged at Memphis; the Ram fleet, under command of Col. Ellet, being supplied with sharp-shooters from his regiment. Soon after, he was ordered, with 364 men, to Henderson, Mo.; and he is now stationed with the entire regiment at Jackson, Tenn. Col. Moro has brothers in the army, who write their names *Moreau;* but he says: "I, purely American by birth and feeling, have anglicized the spelling—hence the difference. I prize more highly my citizenship in this great country, than I do my relationship to one of the proudest families of the old world."

COL. LOGAN.

Col. John Logan is the eldest son of James Logan, who emigrated from Ireland to this country in 1793, and settled at North Bend, Hamilton county, Ohio, where his son was born, Dec. 30th, 1809. He served under Gen. Harrison during the Indian wars in the North-west, as a First Lieutenant, and afterwards Captain of Ohio troops. In 1815, he removed to the Territory of Missouri, and resided among the Indians for ten years, when he took up his residence in Jackson, Illinois. Here the subject of this sketch had the benefit of a school for nine months, the only instruction he ever received from a teacher. In 1831, Mr. Logan commenced the study of medicine. The following year he volunteered, and served a campaign against Black Hawk. He returned home in the fall, and for the want of means had to give up his study of medicine, and work again at his trade of a carpenter for a support. In 1833, he married Miss Sophia Hall, and settled in Macoupin county, Ill. His wife lived to have two children, who also both died, one before and the other soon after their mother. Being left without a family, he decided to resume the study of medicine, and worked hard at his trade while reviewing and finishing his studies, and preparing for medical lectures. In the winter of 1840-41, he took his first course of lectures, in McDowell's College, St. Louis. In January, 1841, he married Miss Ann E. Banks, of St. Louis. The next summer he attended the Hospital, with Professor McDowell, and in the fall of the same year returned to Chesterfield, Macoupin county, Ill., where he continued in the practice of his profession, with results entirely satisfactory to himself and the public, until 1853, when he removed to Carlinville, the county seat of Macoupin county. He continued the practice until the rebellion commenced, when, believing it to be his duty to do something for the defence of the country, Dr. Logan called a meeting of the citizens of Carlinville and vicinity, for the purpose of adopting some measures for raising volunteers. The meeting appointed him to superintend the raising and organizing of one company. In three days he had, with the aid of Richard Raucet and G. W. Woods, succeeded in raising one hundred and eight men. After

this Dr. Logan set to work in earnest, and raised, by the aid of his many good friends, one company of cavalry, one of artillery, and a regiment of infantry, known as the 32d Illinois, of which he was, by Gov. Yates, appointed Colonel. This regiment was mustered into service December 31, 1861, and marched to Bird's Point, Mo., from thence to Fort Henry, Tenn. Here Col. Logan was placed in command of the post, as senior officer. In the battle of Shiloh, the 6th and 7th of April, this regiment, being the second of the 1st brigade, 4th division, under Gen. Stephen A. Hurlbut, was by that gallant officer led to the field early in the morning, and for six hours was under an unceasing fire from Beauregard's column, composed of the best troops of the rebel army. The 32d Regiment never changed its position during the day, except when, after having driven the enemy from the field before it, the commanding General ordered it to the left, where the battle thickened, and the enemy was moving forward in solid column. Here the regiment being strongly posted by Capt. Long, of Gen. Hurlbut's staff, held its position until every other regiment was compelled to retire, and for the last twenty minutes held the field alone, against three times its own numbers, and only retired when the last cartridge was fired. Their loss in this battle was very severe, in both commissioned officers and men, the color guard being all killed or wounded except two. The number of killed, wounded and missing in the regiment amounted to above two-fifths of those who went into the action. Col. Logan and the Lieut. Colonel were both wounded—the latter mortally—three Captains and five Lieutenants—two mortally—and several officers killed in the action.

In a private letter, Col. Logan says: "I profess to be a christian, and joined the Methodist Episcopal Church at the early age of eighteen, and although an unworthy member, the church has permitted me to live within its bosom until the present time. If I have ever done anything to entitle my name to occupy a place in even the humblest niche of the history of my country, I owe it all to the grace of God, and to Him be all the praise and glory."

COL. LOGAN.

COL. BANE.

Col. MOSES M. BANE was born on the 30th of November, 1825, in Athens county, Ohio. At the age of twelve years, he removed with his parents to the Miami valley, north of Dayton, Ohio. He determined to educate himself to the extent of his limited abilities, his father being unable to aid his efforts but very little. Through his own exertions he received an academical education, and determined to enter the profession of medicine. Bending all his energies toward its accomplishment, he was enabled, by teaching and labor, to procure the means to assist him in the prosecution of his studies. After having studied one year, Mr. Bane went to Columbus, Ohio, and entered the office of Dr. R. L. Howard, Professor of Surgery in Starling Medical College, remaining there until he graduated from that institution, in February, 1849. In October, he married, and removed to Payson, Adams county, Ill., where he at once entered upon the active duties of his profession. In the fall of 1856, he was elected to represent the people of Adams county in the Legislature, and again in 1858, after which he returned to his profession, in which he continued to be engaged until after the breaking out of the rebellion, when he was solicited to take charge of a regiment, to be raised in Adams and adjoining counties. He was commissioned by Gov. Yates on the 20th of August, and went into camp, where the regiment remained but a short time before being ordered into active service, in Missouri. The 50th was subsequently at Fort Henry, suffered severely at Fort Donelson, and finally at Shiloh, where, on the 6th of April, while on duty with his regiment, a ball passed through his right arm, above the elbow, shattering the bone, entered his side, fracturing two ribs, and lodged in his body, where it still remains. Upon examination by the surgeons, the wound in his side was pronounced mortal, and it was several hours before they considered it advisable to amputate his arm, which they did about midnight. For nearly three months Col. Bane lay upon his back, gradually recovering, until the end of July, when he again took command of his regiment, at Corinth, Miss., where it is now stationed.

COL. BELL.

Thomas Bell, the grandfather of the subject of this sketch, came to the United States, from Scotland, before the Revolutionary War, and took an active part as a private soldier in that great struggle for liberty. Col. Bell's father, the Rev. Joseph E. Bell, of Tennessee, served under Gen. Jackson during the war of 1812–14. JOSEPH W. BELL was born in Tennessee in the year 1815. He studied law, and practised in the South until 1855, when he removed to Chicago. After the election of Mr. Lincoln to the Presidency, having taken an active part in that memorable political campaign, Col. Bell received an appointment in the War Department, and accordingly, in the spring of 1861, removed to Washington. After the Federal defeat at Bull Run, he received authority to raise a regiment of cavalry, when he resigned his office, returned to Chicago, and soon organized the 13th Cavalry, which was ordered to join the army of Gen. Curtis. The regiment, in separate battalions, has taken part in two engagements—one at Clear Run Station; the other at Bayou Cache, on the 7th of July. Being ordered by Gen. Curtis to reinforce Col. Hovey, who was then engaging the enemy four miles in advance of them, Col. Bell arrived just as the enemy fled. He was ordered to take command of his 2d battalion, one battalion of the 5th Illinois cavalry, and one regiment of infantry and a light battery, and to pursue the retreating foe. Col. Bell pursued for about five miles, scattering them like chaff, shelling the rebels at every opportunity, till near night, when, by order of Gen. Benton, who had just arrived, they returned to the main battle ground, and encamped with the balance of the army.

COL. KNOBELSDORFF.

CHARLES KNOBELSDORFF, commanding the 44th Regiment Illinois Volunteers, and the 2d Brigade, 5th Division of the Army of the Mississippi, is a graduate of the military school at Culan, kingdom of Prussia. He was born on the 31st day of October, 1827, and is a descendant of an old Prussian military family. He entered the Prussian army as a Lieutenant, in 1846, and when, in 1848, the revolutionary war broke out between the states of Schleswig-Holstein and Denmark, he joined the Schleswig-Holstein army at once, and fought with distinction in most of the battles of that war, as a First Lieutenant and as commander of a company in the 1st and 2d Rifle Battalion. At the battle of Missunde he was severely wounded in his right arm. When the Schleswig-Holstein army was disbanded, through the intervention of the Austrian and Prussian armies, in the spring of 1851, Col. Knobelsdorff, being no longer willing to submit to the rule of despotism, formed at once, at Hamburg, an association of dismissed officers and soldiers of the Schleswig-Holstein army, for the purpose of emigrating to the United States, and he, with hundreds of his comrades, arrived in America in the summer of 1851. He has lived most of the time since at Milwaukee, Wis., and the last two years at Chicago, in which latter city he was in the employ of the Illinois Central Railway Company. (This vast Railway Corporation has furnished to the Union army, from among her officers and employees, three Major Generals—Banks, Burnside and McClellan, one Brigadier General—Turchin, and Colonels Brayman, Ransom, Wyman, and the subject of this sketch, besides a host of officers of lower rank in the 89th, and other Illinois regiments.) Col. K. has always taken a prominent part in the agitation of our national politics, and especially in the promotion of the welfare of the laboring classes. When the southern rebellion broke out, Col. Knobelsdorff organized at once four companies of infantry, as a reserve, in the city of Chicago, and soon after recruited and organized two independent rifle regiments, the 24th and 44th Illinois Volunteers, and went himself into the field with the last named regiment, on the 14th day of September, 1861. His regiment was attached to Gen. Sigel's division, and marched with him in his expedition, under Gen. Fremont, to Springfield, Mo., in the fall of 1861, and the next winter, under Gen. Curtis, marched to Arkansas. Col. Knobelsdorff commanded his regiment during the battle of Pea Ridge, on the 6th, 7th and 8th of March, 1862, and has shown himself a cool, courageous and experienced commander. At the commencement of the battle, on the 8th, two regiments of infantry and a battery of Gen. Davis' division, broke unexpectedly, and retreated in confusion, throwing themselves on Col. Knobelsdorff's regiment, who were covering the right flank of Gen. Sigel's division. Instead of allowing his men to retreat also, he advanced in line of battle, ordered the battery to halt, drove the retreating infantry out of his lines, and in this way saved the honor of the day.

Col. Knobelsdorff is known as an excellent tactician, and as an officer who takes the best care of his men, and is always ready to act and to fight. He commanded for a long time the 1st and 2d brigades of Gen. Sigel's division, and is now commanding the 2d brigade of Gen. Asboth's (the 5th) division, army of the Mississippi.

COL. GREUSEL.

COL. GREUSEL.

The parents of Col. Greusel, with eight children, among whom Nicholas was the seventh child, arrived in the city of New York, June 2d, 1833, when he was at the age of fourteen years. Sergeant N. Greusel, Sen., the father of Nicholas, was one of the brave men who fought under Gen. Murat, and was promoted for bravery on the snow fields of Russia. He took great pains to educate Nicholas in his youth concerning the duties of a soldier. On the 3d of June, calling his family together, he informed them that he had expended all his fortune to bring them to the land of freedom, and he would give them a good dinner, after which each must take his bundle and look up a place for himself, at the same time telling them, if any got sick he would be found at Newburg, on the Hudson river. It was the fortune of Nicholas to fall into the service of Mrs. Nicholas Fish, mother of Hon. Hamilton Fish, late Governor of New York, on 9th street, near St. Mark's Church, then the outskirts of the city, where he remained seven months, when, becoming ashamed of doing housework, he left for Newburg, where he obtained employment from Gen. Belnap, who was largely engaged in the brick business, and worked for him at nineteen dollars per month. After working some time, his father informed him of his intention of removing to Michigan. All his children but one accompanied him, and arrived in the city of Detroit on the 27th day of June, 1835.

Nicholas at once found employment with Messrs. J. Rice & Co., lumber dealers, with whom he remained until the war broke out with Mexico, in 1846. Having held a commission as Lieutenant since 1839, Adjutant of the 1st battalion, and Captain of the Scott Guard, he received the appointment of Captain of Co. G, 1st Regiment Michigan Volunteers, commanded by Col. T. B. W. Stockton, under whom he did good service from Vera Cruz to Orizaba, in Col. Bankhead's brigade, consisting of the following regiments: 1st Alabama, 1st Michigan, one squadron Georgia mounted men, four companies 2d dragoons, and one battery, taken from the steamer Mississippi man-of-war. Peace having been declared, the regiment returned to Detroit, and were mustered out of the service on the 27th day of July, 1848. On the 28th of July, at sunrise, Capt. Greusel was at his post in the lumber yard again.

Stories prejudicial to the officers of the regiment having been circulated while the 1st was en route to Detroit, the soldiers received much sympathy in Chicago, from the citizens, on account of supposed bad treatment, and the Mayor of Chicago went on board of the Oregon, then lying at the foot of Dearborn street, to satisfy himself. Having accosted Capt. Greusel, he asked him how he could neglect his men in the manner represented. The Captain called his company of seventy-two men together, and asked the Mayor and committee if his men looked like being starved to death. The Mayor was much surprised at the splendid appearance of Capt. Greusel's men, and complimented him highly on their good looks and excellent discipline. While at Chicago, the Captain, having saved some three hundred dollars from company rations, purchased new shirts for his entire company, and all necessaries to clean arms and accoutrements, and packed them away, saying nothing to any one about it. On arriving at Lake St. Clair, the Captain called his company together, and ordered a general washing and cleaning up of arms, etc. After coming in sight of Detroit, the rest of the officers commenced to suspect something in the appearance of their own men, and began to enquire how Capt. Greusel got his new clothing, and white belts, and polished shoes. The Captain informed them that there were plenty in Chicago. On arriving in Detroit, Lieut. Col. N. S. Williams, having gone across the country by railroad and stage from Chicago, came on board, and seeing the state of the troops, refused to march them through the streets of Detroit, unless Capt. Greusel's company would take the right of the regiment. This was finally acceded to by the balance of the Captains, Co. D being the second company on the left of the regiment. Arriving on Jefferson avenue, Col. Williams gave the order, "By platoons, into line;" but seeing Co. D platoons longer than the rest of the companies, ordered Capt. Greusel to break into sections, in which shape the regiment marched to the barracks, receiving the cheers and admiration of the citizens. The papers of the next day complimented Capt. Greusel's company as being the best looking as to health, clothing and military discipline in the regiment.

Capt. Greusel was engaged in the lumber trade for two years, held the office of Alderman in the city of Detroit, and afterwards was appointed Inspector General of Lumber for the State of Michigan. In 1857, Capt. Greusel went to Chicago, Ill., where he entered the service of the Chicago, Burlington and Quincy Railroad Company, and remained in their employ until the bombardment of Fort Sumter, April 13th, 1861. On Monday, April 15th, Capt. Greusel enrolled himself as a private of a company in the city of Aurora, and arrived at Springfield on Friday, with one hundred and forty-eight privates, and was elected Captain of the same. On the 24th of April, the first regiment was formed—the 7th. John Cook was elected Colonel, and Captain Greusel, Major. The Major being the only man who had ever done military duty, the task of drilling the regiment devolved on him, and it was said by military men to be the best drilled regiment in the service. There are at this writing fifty-eight commissioned officers who were privates on the 24th of July. After the three months service, Major Greusel was commisioned Lieut. Colonel. On the 20th of August, he was promoted to the Colonelcy of the Fox River Regiment, afterwards called the 36th Regiment Illinois Volunteers. The regiment was ordered to Rolla, Mo., for drill. On the 14th day of January, 1862, it was ordered to march for Lebanon, Mo., where it arrived on the 25th of January. The regiment was brigaded with the 12th, 3d and 17th Missouri Volunteers, Welfley's Missouri and Capt. Hoffman's batteries. Col. Greusel was placed in command, by Brig. Gen. Sigel, in which capacity he followed Gen. Price on his retreat to Batesville, Ark. He was in the masterly retreat of Gen. Sigel to Pea Ridge, and fought bravely during that ever memorable battle, for three successive days. He was highly complimented by Generals Curtis and Sigel, for his coolness and bravery on the field, especially for preventing a stampede, which would have been most disastrous but for the coolness and presence of mind displayed by Col. Greusel.

The regiment received orders, when fifteen miles beyond White River, Ark., to march to Corinth, by forced marches—240 miles distant—which the regiment accomplished in ten days, when they embarked on the steamer Planet, and arrived and joined Gen. Pope's command at the trenches in front of Corinth, two days before the evacuation of that place by Gen. Beauregard. Have since marched to Boonville, and back to Rienzi, where the regiment is now lying. There are now left 1038 men of the 1248 taken into the field in September, 1861.

While on a recent visit to his friends in Detroit, Col. Greusel was tendered a public dinner by his admirers in that city, as a testimonial of their sense of the value of his services at Springfield and Pea Ridge, to which invitation he returned the following reply:

DETROIT, July 16, 1862.

To his Excellency, Gov. Blair, and others:

GENTLEMEN: I have the honor to receive your very flattering invitation to dine with you. Availing myself of a short furlough to recruit my health, I have only come to my old adopted home to spend a fleeting moment with my aged parents. The familiar names of many old friends among your number touch my heart, and recall pleasant recollections of former days. But I prefer to look beyond myself, and appreciate your kindness as a spontaneous demonstration in behalf of the idea of liberty and constitutional free government. If I have followed the beloved flag of the country over sanguinary fields, it is because I have been in pursuit of that idea. God grant it may prevail over the ends of the earth. However happy a convival meeting with my old friends would be, now is not the time for such enjoyment. The crisis demands that every man should do his duty—especially that every *soldier shall be at his post.* When the smiles of peace shall again bless us, I hope to have the pleasure which I must at this time decline.

Yours, respectfully,   N. GREUSEL,
          Col. 36th Reg't Ill. Vol.

COL. HOUGH.

COL. HOUGH.

ROSELLE MARION HOUGH was born in St. Lawrence county, N. Y., in 1819. In 1836, he came west with his father's family, and settled in Bloomingdale, Du Page county, where he spent three years, assisting his father on a farm. In 1844, he went to Chicago, and was employed by Sylvester Marsh, beef and pork packer, after which he entered the service of Messrs. Wadsworth, Dyer & Chapin, as a foreman of their establishment. In 1850, Mr. Hough formed a partnership with his brother, Orrin T. Hough, and Joseph Brown, of Massachusetts, and built the first packing house at Bridgeport, near Chicago. In 1853, the partnership was dissolved, Mr. Brown withdrawing from the firm. When the news of the fall of Fort Sumter reached Chicago, Mr. Hough, leaving his large business, at once threw himself into the good cause, which he aided in various ways, as a private citizen, and as a member of the War Committee. When Gen. Hunter passed through Chicago, en route to Missouri, he met Mr. Hough, at that time Major of the 9th Illinois Cavalry, and offered him a place on his staff, which was accepted. In October, Maj. Hough joined Gen. Hunter, and was placed in charge of the transportation service, in which he rendered valuable and efficient aid. In December, Major Hough returned to Chicago, on leave of absence, and remained until March, 1862, when he accompanied Gen. Hunter to South Carolina, and was present at the taking of Fort Pulaski. Soon after he was detailed to accompany the prisoners of war to New York, and on his arrival there resigned his commission. In June, he was elected Colonel of the 67th Regiment Illinois Volunteers, and is now stationed at Camp Douglas, Chicago, acting in conjunction with Col. Tucker, commandant, as guard over the ten thousand rebel prisoners confined there.

COL. RAITH.

JULIUS RAITH was born in Germany in 1819, and came to this country with his father's family in 1836. They settled in St. Clair county, Illinois. When about 18 years of age, he went to Columbia, Monroe county, where he learned the trade of a millwright, and became an expert in that occupation. On the breaking out of the Mexican war he enlisted in Col. Bissell's regiment, and was commissioned as Captain, winning laurels at Buena Vista and in all the engagements of his regiment, which showed itself to be one of the most gallant and meritorious in that campaign. Soon after Captain Raith's return from Mexico, he married a daughter of Hon. John D. Hughes, of Belleville, taking up his residence in St. Louis, where he remained in the pursuit of his occupation as millwright, until 1860, when he removed to Illinois, and built a large flouring mill in O'Fallon, on the Ohio and Mississippi Railroad, which is still operated in the name of Julius Raith & Co. He constructed some of the best and most noted mills in Missouri and Illinois, and was widely known to millowners and mechanics in the West.

During the summer of 1861, Capt. Raith raised the 43d Regiment, and entered the service as its Colonel in October. At the battle of Shiloh, Col. Raith was in command of the 3d brigade, composed of his own regiment, the 17th, 29th and 49th Illinois. Whilst leading his command, on the first day of the conflict, he was wounded by a minie ball in the leg above the knee. He lay on the battle-field for twenty-four hours, when he was picked up in a feeble and exhausted condition. He was placed on board the steamer Hannibal, and on the way to the Hospital at Mound City, Illinois, suffered the amputation of his leg. He died from tetanus, or lock-jaw, produced by his injuries.

Colonel Raith's wife died in the latter part of 1859, being survived by two sons, one of whom is now ten and the other seven years of age.

COL. WYMAN.

Col. JOHN B. WYMAN is of Welch extraction, his ancestors emigrating to New England at an early day. His great-grandfather, Ross Wyman, lived to the age of ninety-four. His grandfather, Seth Wyman, lived to the age of seventy, and his father, Seth Wyman, Jr., is still living, and reached the age of seventy-three years on July 30th, just past,—all of Shrewsbury, Worcester county, Mass. Col. Wyman's mother was Lucy Baker, daughter of John Baker, also of Shrewsbury.

The subject of this sketch was born in Shrewsbury, on the 12th of July, 1817, and is consequently now forty-five years of age. At the age of eighteen, he was elected a Lieutenant in the Shrewsbury Rifle Company, and on removing to Cincinnati, Ohio, joined the Citizen's Guards, of that city, where he served three years under Capt. (now Major General) O. M. Mitchell. In 1841, he removed to Worcester, Mass., where he joined the Worcester City Guards, and was soon elected a Lieutenant, and served until 1846, when he removed to Springfield, Mass., where he was elected First Lieutenant of the Springfield City Guards, and served two years. In 1848, he was appointed to a position on the New York and New Haven Railroad, his residence being in New York city. There he joined the famous New York Light Guards, in which fine corps he served two years. In 1850, he was appointed Superintendent of the Connecticut River Railroad. In August of the same year, the Springfield Light Guards were reorganized, when Lieut. Wyman was unanimously elected their Captain, in which capacity he served two and a half years. In February, 1853, Capt. Wyman was appointed Assistant Superintendent of the Illinois Central Railroad.

On the 22d day of February, 1854, the Chicago Light Guards were organized, and Capt. Wyman, by unanimous vote, was made commander of this splendid corps of citizen soldiers. After serving as Captain of this company three years, he resigned, but was again elected to the same position in 1858. After leaving the Illinois Central Railroad, he returned to his home, in Amboy, Lee county, Ill., where he engaged in private pursuits, carrying into them the same extraordinary energy that he had always shown in his public labors.

The guns of Sumter awoke Capt. Wyman from his dream of home and rest, and the quiet of civil pursuits, and forced the conviction into his mind that stern war was upon us, and that our country required all of its true hearts and strong arms to beat back and crush the traitorous foe who were striking at the institutions that had given us all liberty and happiness. Capt. Wyman immediately offered his services to the Government, and he was early selected as a man whose energy and decision of character, backed by his experience in military matters, eminently qualified him to command and lead in the campaigns against the rebels. He was commissioned as Colonel of the 13th Infantry Illinois Volunteers, by Gov. Yates, but as his services were needed in the office of the Adjutant General of the State, which place his business talents eminently fitted him for, he did not join his regiment until the 14th of June, 1861.

Col. Wyman, with the 13th, was ordered to Rolla, Mo., by the War Department, and arrived there July 7th, 1861. Rolla being the terminus of the southwestern branch of the Pacific Railroad, it was considered one of the most important posts in Missouri, and the key to the whole south-western part of the State, and, in fact, of the State of Arkansas, also, for at that time the Mississippi river was closed by the rebels, from a little below Cairo to the Gulf. The immense railroad interests, the receiving, distributing and forwarding of vast amounts of Government stores, the rendezvousing of many thousands of troops at different times, the hospital interests, the building and protecting of a fort, and the receiving, guarding and forwarding of many hundreds of prisoners to St. Louis, from time to time, all these, and many other interests, required a man of no ordinary ability to take command of the post, and in selecting Col. Wyman for this position, the Government were not disappointed nor mistaken in their man, for during the eight months that he was commandant of the post, he performed its varied and arduous duties to the entire satisfaction of the Government, and the admiration of all those who were at all acquainted with the difficulties he had to encounter.

Through all the long and tedious marches of over twelve hundred miles, in all weather, and much of the time over the worst possible roads, the men suffering from sickness, fatigue, hunger, thirst, exposure of heat and cold, part of the time many of the men barefooted and almost naked, Col. Wyman ever showed himself the soldier's friend, frequently dismounting to let a lame or sick soldier ride, and by such acts of kindness earning their lasting respect and love, by his warm and active sympathy in all their sufferings.

Col. Wyman married Maria S. Bradley, daughter of Osgood Bradley, Esq., of Worcester, Mass., on the 23d of November, 1843. They have four children, three sons and one daughter. The eldest, Osgood B. Wyman, is with his father in the army, as a private soldier. The next, Henry, is at a military school, preparing for West Point. The two youngest, Lucy and John B. Wyman, Jr., are with their mother, at Amboy, Lee county, Ill.

Col. Wyman is now in command of one of the finest brigades in the south-western army, of which the 13th Illinois is the nucleus, and all eager to follow him against the enemies of our country.

COL. MARSH.

CHARLES CARROLL MARSH, Colonel of the 20th Regiment Illinois Volunteers, was born in Oswego, N. Y., Sept. 17, 1829. In 1853 he removed to Chicago, and the year following was married to Miss Harriet B. Cooley. He had read law for a year, but feeling that the profession was already crowded, he determined to give up the study for other pursuits more congenial to his active, enterprising mind. During his seven years' residence in Chicago, Mr. Marsh was actively engaged in business, and exhibited a deep interest in military matters. He was for some time Captain of the Chicago Light Guard, one of the best disciplined military organizations in the country. He was called from his home at Chicago at a moment's notice, to go to Springfield. Only knowing that the business was of a military kind, and that he could be of some assistance to his State, he did not hesitate an instant, but was astonished on being put in command of Camp Yates, and in a few days had seven thousand men under his command. On being sent to Camp Goodell, in May, 1861, to muster in the 20th Regiment, although an entire stranger to all, yet he had the flattering compliment of being elected to its head by a nearly unanimous vote. In a

private letter written at this time, he says: "I feel in its full force the terrible responsibility that rests upon me. One thousand men under me to look after, care for, and protect; it is no small task, but I have put on the armor, and will bear it to the end, even though that end be my existence. I have endeavored to exercise my authority with discretion and dignity. I feel that God who called me here, did it for some wise purpose, and if my country needs my life, her cause is sacred, and He who has numbered the hairs of my head will not permit me to die in vain."

At Fort Donelson, Col. Marsh greatly distinguished himself, and at the battle of Shiloh he was an acting Brigadier General, having command of the 2d brigade of Gen. McClernand's division, comprising the 11th, 20th, 45th and 48th regiments Illinois Volunteers. His command lost in killed, wounded and missing in the engagement, five hundred and fifty men, rank and file. The 20th is now stationed at Jackson, Tenn., and in August Col. Marsh was away on a twenty days' furlough, being the first absence from his regiment during more than a year's hard service in the field.

GEN. CARR.

Brigadier General EUGENE A. CARR, was born March 20th, 1830, in Erie county, N. Y. His father, Clark M. Carr, removed from New York to Galesburg, Ill., at which place he now resides, and Gen. Carr may be claimed as an Illinoisian, that being the State where his home has been located since the year 1849.

At the age of sixteen, young Carr entered the military academy at West Point; and graduating above the average of his class, was appointed brevet Second Lieutenant in the regiment of mounted riflemen. After a short service at Jefferson Barracks, Mo., he was ordered to proceed to Fort Laramie, and for many years was engaged in prosecuting hostilities with the Indians on the plains of New Mexico, Texas, and the far West.

In a severe skirmish near Diabolo mountain, in the year 1854, Lieut. Carr, advancing with daring alacrity upon a body of Indians, whom, despite serious indisposition, he had pursued for nearly one hundred miles, was severely wounded in the abdomen, by an arrow, the effects of which wound are still of inconvenience to him. Without discontinuing his attack, he still followed the enemy, routing them with great loss. On account of his conduct on this occasion, he was promoted into the 1st Regiment of Cavalry.

In 1857, he was ordered to Kansas, at the time of the Border Ruffian and Free State hostilities, and during the difficulties, being assigned as aid to Gov. Robert J. Walker, was unceasing in his endeavors for the maintenance of order between the conflicting parties. Lieut. Carr accompanied Governor Walker to Washington in the fall of 1857, and in the spring of 1858 served under Col. (now Gen.) Edwin V. Sumner, in the expedition to Utah.

At the outbreak of the present war, Capt. Carr (having again received promotion) was in command at Fort Washita, and cognizant of the treachery of Gen. Twiggs and many minor officers, repeatedly warned the War Department of their traitorous movements; but that office being in the hands of the notorious Floyd, Capt. Carr was unable to obtain their arrest.

Receiving orders, he moved with his command through the Indian nation to Fort Leavenworth, and from thence toward Springfield, Mo., participating in the battle of Wilson's Creek, and covering with his command the retreat of Gen. Sigel.

Reporting at St. Louis to Gen. Fremont, he received permission from the War Department to accept the command of a regiment of volunteer cavalry, two of which were offered him; and after a few weeks in camp, again took the field, at the head of the 3d Regiment Illinois Cavalry, in September, 1861, and has continued constantly in service since that date.

At the desperate battle of Pea Ridge, Ark., where Col. Carr commanded the 4th division of the army of the Southwest, with a force of less than 2500 men, he bore the brunt of the battle, and at Elkhorn Tavern for three days sustained the shock of nearly 20,000 rebels, led by Gen's Price, McCulloch and McIntosh, repulsing them with great slaughter, utterly routing their combined force. The sanguinary fury of this fight may be conceived from the fact that the 4th division lost about 700 men, being more than half the entire loss sustained by Gen. Curtis' army.

Col. Carr was severely wounded in three places on the first day of the battle, but continued in his saddle until victory crowned our arms, and, bearing his shattered wrist in a sling, was ever foremost where danger beckoned.

For his gallant conduct on this occasion, Col. Carr was promoted to a Brigadier Generalship, March 7th, 1862, and still leads his noble division, which forms a part of the army of Gen. Curtis, now in Arkansas.

COL. WEBSTER.

JOSEPH D. WEBSTER, Colonel of the 1st Regiment Illinois Artillery, and chief of Maj. Gen. Grant's staff, was born at Old Hampton, New Hampshire, May 25th, 1811. He was educated at Dartmouth College, and after graduating, adopted the profession of civil engineer. He was appointed to a position in the corps of U. S. Topographical Engineers, and served with distinction through the Mexican war, receiving a Captaincy for meritorious conduct. In 1850, he resigned his commission, since which date he has resided with his family, in Chicago.

Col. Webster accompanied the first body of troops that went from Chicago to Cairo, in April, 1861, and took charge of the fortifications at that place, also at Bird's Point and Fort Holt, and at the same time acted as Paymaster at Cairo. He also, at the request of the late Gen. Charles F. Smith, erected the fortifications at Paducah.

Col. Webster was present at the capture of Fort Henry and Fort Donelson, and made the annexed report in regard to the capture of the last mentioned post:

"The preparations made by the enemy for the defence of this position were very extensive. A complete and accurate survey of the works and vicinity would require more means and time than can now be commanded.

"The water batteries, (upper and lower,) which were intended to subserve the primary object of the position, the control of the river navigation, were well located for the purpose.

"At the lower and principal one were mounted nine pieces—eight thirty-two pounders and a ten-inch columbiad. At the upper, one gun of the extensive form and dimensions for a ten-inch columbiad, but bored as a thirty-two pounder and rifled, and two thirty-two pound carronades. Both these batteries are sunken or excavated in the hillside. In the lower, strong traverses are left between the guns, to secure them against an enfilading fire. The elevation above the water, say thirty feet at the time of the gunboat attack, gave them a fine command of the river, and make the task of attacking them in front an arduous one. The range of the guns in arc were, however, quite limited.

"The main fort was in the rear of these batteries, occupying a high range cloven by a deep gorge opening toward the south. The outworks consisted in the main of what come

to be called rifle-pits—shallow ditches, the earth from which is thrown to the point, affording them a shelter from the fire of the attack.

"Along the front of this extensive line, the trees had been felled, and the brush cut and bent over breast high, making a wide abattis very difficult to pass through. The line run along a ridge, cut through by several ravines running toward the river. The hillside rises by abrupt ascents to a height of perhaps seventy-five or eighty feet.

"Our army approached the place with very little knowledge of its topography. Our first line of battle was formed on the 12th instant, in some open fields opposite the enemy's centre. On the 13th we were established on a line of heights in general parallelism with the enemy's outworks, and extending a distance of over three miles.

"Various elevations and spurs of the hills afforded position for our artillery, from which we annoyed the enemy, but which were not of such commanding character as to enable us to achieve decided results. The ranges were long, and the thick woods prevented clear sight.

"During the next two days our lines were gradually extended to the right and left, our skirmishers thrown out in front, keeping up an active and, as we since learn, an effective fire upon the enemy's outworks. On the 13th, a gallant charge was made against the enemy, and was probably only prevented from being successful by the fall of the Colonel leading it, who was seriously wounded.

"Up to the 15th our operations had been chiefly those of investment, but we had not gained a position from which our artillery could be advantageously used against the main fort. On the 15th, the enemy, seeming to grow uncomfortable under the constricting process, came out of his entrenchments and attacked our right with great force and determination, achieving considerable success in the forenoon. This active movement necessitated active retaliation. On the left wing an attack was ordered on the outworks, and the right was reinforced and ordered to retake the ground lost in the morning. How well both orders were executed need not be stated. On the right our former position was regained and passed, and on the left a successful assault gave us possession of a position within the enemy's lines, and opened the way to a still better one, which nightfall alone prevented us from occupying with our rifled artillery, which would readily have commanded the enemy's main works.

"This repulse from the ground so hardly won in the forenoon, and probably still more our possession of a vantage gained within their lines, induced the enemy to capitulate on the morning of the 16th."

At the battle of Shiloh, Col. Webster rendered most valuable service, and to him has been justly awarded great praise for arresting the progress of the victorious rebels on the afternoon of Sunday, the 6th of April, when our troops were being driven before the enemy towards Pittsburgh Landing.

COL. LOOMIS.

JOHN MASON LOOMIS, one of Chicago's most active military as well as business men, was born at Windsor, Ct., Jan. 5, 1825, and received his education at Westfield, in his native State. At an early age he exhibited a strong *penchant* for the profession of arms, and at the age of eighteen was Captain of a company of militia, in Windsor. Upon the breaking out of the Mexican war, the young Captain's followers were anxious to enlist, and follow his fortunes throughout the campaign. The State's quota was, however, full, and the company was not accepted. About this time, Capt. Loomis left his native town, and for several years followed the sea, making repeated voyages to China. In 1848, he came to the West, settled in Milwaukee, and established himself in the lumber trade. In 1854, he removed to Chicago, continuing in the same business. Capt. Loomis took an active part in organizing the Chicago Light Guard, in 1854, serving as a private until 1859, upon the election of Gen. McClellan, now in command of the army of the Potomac, to the Captaincy of the Guard, when Capt. Loomis was elected First Lieutenant. He afterwards, upon the resignation of Gen. McClellan, commanded this famous company. In the spring of 1861, Capt. Loomis was elected to the command of the Chicago City Guard, an organization which, under his thorough discipline, soon attained great efficiency. In July, 1861, Capt. Loomis was offered the Colonelcy of the 19th Regiment Illinois Volunteers, which he declined; and on the 9th of August was tendered by the Governor command of the 26th Regiment, which he accepted, and at once proceeded to Springfield and placed himself at the head of his regiment. With the 26th, Col. Loomis proceeded to Hannibal, Mo., an important depot for commissary stores, where he had command of the post, and during the autumn and winter following rendered valuable service in guarding the Hannibal and St. Joseph Railroad, and in maintaining order in that section of the State. In February, his command was ordered to New Madrid, and took part in the engagement at that point, and also took an active part in the capture of Island No. 10. By order of Gen. Pope, the colors of the 26th are inscribed with the names of New Madrid and Island No. 10. The regiment next proceeded to Fort Pillow, and from there accompanied Gen. Pope's division up the Tennessee river, and joined Gen. Halleck's army of the Mississippi. Col. Loomis greatly distinguished himself in the battle of Farmington, where, owing to the sickness of Gen. Plummer, he commanded a brigade, and entered Corinth with Gen. Halleck's army. Col. Loomis has been an acting Brigadier General ever since the capture of New Madrid, and at this time has command of the late Gen. Plummer's brigade, at Danville, ten miles south of Corinth.

GEN. WALLACE.

None knew him but to love him,⎱
None named him but to praise.   *Halleck.*

WILLIAM HENRY LAMB WALLACE was born at Urbana, Ohio, on the 8th of July, 1821. In the year 1833, his father's family removed to Illinois, and settled in La Salle county, on the south side of the Illinois river, about four miles south-east of the site of the present city of La Salle. In 1830, the family removed to Mt. Morris, Oglo county. In the winter of 1844–5, young Wallace went to Springfield, the State Capital, to commence the study of law, but concluded to go to Ottawa for that purpose, and accordingly early in 1845 commenced his studies with Judge (now Colonel) T. L. Dickey, in Ottawa. He was admitted to the bar early in 1846, but did not enter upon the practice of his profession until after his return from the Mexican campaign. In 1846, he enlisted as a private in Co. I, 1st Regiment Illinois Volunteers, Col. Hardin, Judge Dickey being the Captain of the company. At Alton, he was chosen Second Lieutenant. At San Antonia, Texas, Adjutant (now General) Ben. M. Prentiss was elected Captain of the company, *vice* Dickey, resigned on account of ill health, and Lieut. Wallace was appointed Adjutant of the regiment. Though engaged in several skirmishes, the only important battle in which the regiment took part was at Buena Vista, where they suffered a heavy loss. Adjutant Wallace rode near the gallant Colonel in the desperate charge in which the latter lost his life. At the expiration of a year, when their term of enlistment ended, the regiment was discharged, and Lieut. Wallace returned to Ottawa, to resume his business. Here he formed a partnership with his late instructor, Capt. Dickey, which continued until the latter was elected Judge, in 1848. He at once entered upon a large practice, where he distinguished himself as an excellent lawyer, and won an enviable reputation throughout the State. In 1848, he formed a partnership with Judge John C. Champlin, which continued until 1851. In 1850, he was appointed Deputy Marshal to take the census of the county of La Salle, the duties of which office he executed promptly and accurately. On the 18th of February,

1851, he was married to Martha Ann Dickey, daughter of Judge Dickey. In 1853, he was elected State Attorney for the Ninth Judicial Circuit, which he held for a single term of four years, executing the duties of the office with distinguished abilities, and in a manner to add greatly to his reputation as a lawyer. When the rebellion broke out, Lieutenant Wallace did all in his power to aid the Government. In May of that year, he was chosen Colonel of the 11th Regiment of Illinois Volunteers, for the three months service, rendezvoused at Springfield. Leaving the latter place on the 5th of May, he went to Villa Ridge, twelve miles north of Cairo, where he remained until the 20th of June, when he took command of the post at Bird's Point. This command he held, with occasional brief intermissions, until about the 1st of January, 1862. In the latter month, his regiment marched to Fort Jefferson. On the 1st and 2d of February, he was placed in command of the First Brigade of the Second Division (Gen. McClernand's) of Gen. Grant's army, and about the 12th of the month marched to Fort Donelson, in the taking of which he bore a conspicuous part, his regiment and brigade suffering severely. After remaining a short time at Fort Donelson, he returned to Fort Henry, whence his brigade embarked for Savannah Tenn. He arrived at this point early in March, and here received the confirmation of his appointment as Brigadier General.

At the memorable battle of Shiloh, on the 6th of April, he was in command of the First Division of Major General Grant's army, Major General C. F. Smith (since deceased) being sick at that time. On that day (Sunday), while leading his division, he was shot through the head, and fell from his horse. He was borne some distance by his aids, Capt. Hotchkiss and Lieut. Dickey, when they, supposing him dead, and being hard pressed by the enemy, laid him down upon the field, and continued the retreat, which had commenced just before Gen. Wallace received his death-wound. The next day, when the Federal troops regained possession of the ground, he was found covered with a blanket, his head being supported by another blanket

4

rolled up for a pillow, and still alive. His watch and purse had been taken from him. He was immediately carried to Gen. Grant's headquarters, at Savannah, where he died on the following Thursday. His wife arrived at Pittsburg Landing on the morning of the battle, and ministered to his wants until his death. His body was borne to his former home at Ottawa, where he was buried with distinguished honors in the family burial ground, by the masonic fraternity, of which the General was an honored member. The only military present were his aids, Capt. Hotchkiss and Lieut. Dickey. A striking feature in the funeral cortege, was the flag of the 11th regiment, which bore the marks of the hotly contested fields of Donelson and Shiloh. In person, Gen. Wallace was very tall and erect. In manner, he was dignified and somewhat reserved, though cordial in his intercourse with his associates. He had, to a greater degree than usually falls to the lot of man, the respect, esteem and confidence of every one who knew him; and I know of no one to whom Shakspere's lines could be more appropriate:

"In war was never lion raged more fierce,
In peace was never gentle lamb more mild."

At a meeting of the members of the Bar of the State of Illinois, held in the Court House of the Supreme Court, at Ottawa, on the 23d day of April, A.D. 1862, for the purpose of testifying their respect for the memory of and regret at the untimely decease of their late friend and brother, General William H. L. Wallace, the following resolutions were unanimously adopted:

Resolved, That the recent death of our esteemed friend and brother, the late W. H. L. Wallace, from wounds received while gallantly leading a division at the battle of Pittsburg Landing, the Bar of Illinois, in common with the people of the whole State, deplore the loss of a soldier, who, as well in his life as by the manner of his death on the field, has sealed by his blood this new testimony to the ineradicable devotion which the people of Illinois are manifesting in heroic deeds and patriotic sacrifices to that form of free government on this continent which domestic traitors are so wickedly attempting to overthrow.

Resolved, That while, as citizens, the State may regret the loss of the experienced chief who could successfully inspire by his personal during and valor the troops committed to his charge, and by his example and bravery command success in that desperate charge or assault of battle; and while to the grateful history of his country is now committed that fame which to remote ages will hereafter rank his name with the other heroic defenders of the Republic; yet the Bar

of Illinois have a sadder tribute to now render his memory, by an expression of the profound grief which they feel at this parting and loss of a friend and brother.

Resolved, That they knew in the late W. H. L. Wallace one who, while possessing all the virtues which adorn a private life of exemplary excellence, in his professional character he was also a man without a blemish. Of a persevering industry, a very high order of legal attainments, and the very highest order of intellectual capacity—he seemed above all to shine in the very spirit of intellectual, moral and professional rectitude. This was "the daily beauty of his life," which never ceased to distinguish him in that career of professional triumph which had placed him already in the very front rank of eminent professional men, in all his intercourse with his brethren of this Bar and the State. As brethren, therefore, of the profession which he honored in his life, as well as by his glorious death, we may well pause, as we now do, in the midst of our professional and other avocations, to drop a tear upon the tomb, and inscribe this brief tablet by recalling a few of the many virtues of his life.

Resolved, That we tender our deepest sympathies to the widow and family of our departed brother; in their bereavement we are impressed with the conviction that all mere words are inadequate to express that deep sense of affliction which the loss of such a husband must have caused to the bereaved and stricken one. We humbly commend her to the guardianship and care of Him from whom alone, at such a time, can come the only solace for hearts so afflicted. He only can "temper the wind to the shorn lamb."

Resolved, That Hon. Norman H. Purple, the Chairman of this meeting, be appointed to present a copy of these resolutions to the Supreme Court of this State, at its present session, and request that they may be entered on record among the proceedings of said Court.

Resolved, That the Secretary of this meeting furnish a copy of the proceedings of the meeting, and they be presented to the family of deceased.

Judge Purple then said: As chairman of this meeting, I have been desired to present these resolutions to this Court, with the request that they may be entered upon the records thereof. In doing this, I cannot forbear to add my feeble personal testimony to the intellectual ability, unflinching integrity, exalted patriotism and sterling moral worth of our deceased friend. It has been my good fortune to know him long and well. We have often met, both here and in other courts of the State; as lawyers, we have often had contests, but collisions, never. His very countenance was to me a guaranty of honesty and truthfulness—an index to a heart that knew no guile. I trusted him ever, and neither professionally or otherwise did he ever deceive me.

I never inquired where he was born, or whence he came, nor knew aught of his parentage or ancestry. But I loved the man, because I knew that he had head, soul and intellect and honor; because he was in all respects a MAN; and when I was first assured of his untimely fate, selfish as it may appear, I do believe that I felt more deeply and keenly the misfortune that I had lost a friend, than that the country had lost a gallant soldier and a brave, meritorious and most accomplished chieftain. I felt that one of the bright lights of the profession to which I had devoted my life was at once extinguished—that a link in the chain that had bound me to its arduous duties, and enlivened its dull routine, had been severed and forever broken.

I believe that these feelings and sentiments of the worth, character and virtue of the deceased are common to all, and find an echo in the hearts of all who have enjoyed the pleasure and honor of his acquaintance and friendship; and that the grief which, in the resolutions just read, we declared that we feel, is as real and profound as the language of the resolutions import.

But why speak of our sorrows or regrets while there is one, at least, who knew him far better than any one of us, to whom his loss is irreparable—one whose deep anguish and unmitigated grief approaches nearly the boundaries of despair? Yet, even she should draw consolation from the reflection that he died bravely fighting in defence of his country, and his country's Constitution—that during his whole life his honor has remained untarnished—that victory, though dearly bought, finally crowned his dying struggle, that posterity will bless, revere and honor his name forever. Valor and bravery in him was not a virtue; it was a necessity—an essential part of his moral and physical constitution. When his country's call to arms was sounded, he was compelled to go; and where the fight raged thickest and fiercest, the very impulses of his nature forced him to be foremost in the conflict.

But he sleeps now the sleep that knows no waking, until the trump of God shall call him. In the maturity of his strong intellect, in the full vigor of his manhood, he has sacrificed his life upon the altar of his country—and now reposes quietly and silently in his last resting place, without a blot upon his fair fame or a stain upon his memory.

"So sleep the brave who sink to rest
With all their country's honors blest."

Whereupon, Chief Justice Caton responded:

The Court received the announcement of the death of Gen. Wallace with emotions for the expression of which we find no adequate words. In his death the Bar has lost one of its brightest ornaments, the Court one of its safest advis-

ers, and our country one of its ablest defenders. His whole professional life has been passed among us, and we have known him well. All your words of encomium are but simple justice, and we know they proceed from the deepest convictions of their truth. All his instincts were those of a gentleman; all his impulses were of a noble and lofty character—his sensibilities refined and generous. He was certainly a man of a very high order of talent, and he was a very excellent lawyer. By his industry he studied the law closely, and by his clear judgment he applied it properly. He did honor to his profession: it is meet that his professional brethren should honor his memory.

Scarcely a year ago he was with us, engaged in a lucrative practice—the ornament and the delight of a large circle of friends, and enjoying the quiet endearments of domestic life, loving and beloved by a family worthy of him, now made desolate. At the very first call of his country for defenders, he abandoned his practice, he withdrew from his associates and friends at home, and tore himself from the domestic circle, and pledged his energies and his life to the vindication of his country's flag, which had been torn down and dishonored by rebel hands at Sumter—to the defence of that Constitution and those laws, the maintainance of which is indispensable to material greatness and happiness. For these he fought, for these he died.

For myself, I may say he was my near neighbor and my dear friend. He honored me with his confidence, and disclosed to me fully the patriotic impulses which led him to abandon all to defend his native land. If he was an able lawyer, so was he an able commander. If we mourn him as a departed friend and brother, so does the country mourn him as one of her ablest Generals gone.

With the glad news of victory, comes the sad lament of his death. Our gladness was turned to mourning. So it ever is, and so must it ever be in this sublunary world. With all our joys are mingled strains of sorrow. Happiness unalloyed is reserved for that brighter and better world promised to those who act well their part on earth, into the full fruition of which those who knew him best doubt not he is accepted.

The resolutions which have been adopted by the Bar will be entered upon the records of the Court, as a perpetual memorial of our appreciation of the worth of the late General Wallace, and the Clerk will furnish a copy of them and a copy of this order to the widow and family of the deceased, and out of respect to his memory the Court will now adjourn.

GEN. SHIELDS.

Brigadier General JAMES SHIELDS was born December 12th, 1810, in the village of Atmore, near the historic town of Dungannon, county Tyrone, Ireland. He spent his early boyhood in his native place, and was sixteen years of age at the time of his coming to the United States. He completed his education at an academy in Bloomfield, New Jersey, and first manifested a partiality for the army by joining a volunteer force, and serving as Second Lieutenant in the Seminole war in Florida, before he had attained his majority. At the expiration of the term for which he was commissioned, he moved to Illinois, about 1832, settled in Kaskaskia, on the banks of the river bearing that name, and not far from the Mississippi, where he opened a school, and numbered among his pupils John Pope, now in command of the army of Virginia.   Having, during the period of his keeping a school, duly qualified himself for the legal profession, he was admitted to practice, and soon acquired a very respectable standing. A few years later, he was elected to the lower house of the State Legislature, and speedily became a leading man among the Democratic representatives. Fluent and precise in debate,—industrious, methodical and conscientious in the discharge of his onerous duties; inspired by a praiseworthy ambition to excel, and governed by a rare purity of purpose, he won the admiration and steadfast friendship of the most eminent men of his party; and even those who were opposed to him in politics, gave him many proofs of cordial personal regard. It would be a digression from the plan of this memoir to enter into more minute details of his career in the General Assembly of Illinois.

Gov. Carlin appointed him Auditor of the State in 1840, and his appointment was immediately confirmed by the Senate. He labored indefatigably to bring order out of chaos, and contributed materially to the improvement of the financial policy of Illinois, as well as to the restoration of the credit of the State, which had suffered terribly in consequence of recklessness in banking, in land speculation, and in canal and railroad enterprises. His residence was at this time in Springfield.

On the resignation by Judge Douglas of his position as Associate Justice of the Supreme Court of Illinois, in 1843, James Shields (who had recently removed to Belleville), by a joint vote of both houses of the Legislature, was chosen to fill the vacancy. He acquitted himself very creditably in his new sphere of duty. President Polk offered him the desirable appointment of Commissioner of the General Land Office, in 1845, which he accepted, and resigning his judgeship, he removed to Washington. He entered into the national service under promising auspices, and thoroughly trained for business. He made quite a stir among the drones in his department, by giving specific instructions to each of his subordinates, and insisting that every one of them should honestly earn his salary. His skill and energy were fully appreciated by the President, who, on the commencement of hostilities against Mexico, nominated him Brigadier General of volunteers, which nomination the Senate presently confirmed, and he was formally commissioned on the 1st of July, 1846.

Early in the autumn of 1846, Gen. Shields joined the central division of Brigadier General Wool, and accompanied it in its march, overland, to Monclava, in the province of Coahuila, Mexico, where it arrived late in October. He left the division at this point, and, according to orders, repaired to the camp of Major General Taylor, at Camargo, a few miles west of Rio Grande. On the 14th of November, Commodore David Conner, commanding the Gulf squadron of the United States navy—afterwards of the Mexican garrison—took peaceable possession of Tampico; and Gen. Taylor, then commanding the army of the United States in Mexico, presently appointed Gen. Shields Military Governor of that city.

About the close of the winter of 1846-7, Gen. Shields was ordered to join Major General Winfield Scott, before Vera Cruz, and in the second week of March "landed with the army, having a small part of one of his old regiments (three companies of the 2d Illinois foot), and the New York regiment of new volunteers," Col. Ward B. Burnett. His brigade was assigned to the division of his countryman, Major General Robert Patterson (second in command of the army), and actively participated in the siege and capture of Vera Cruz, the emporium of Mexican commerce, with the Castle of San Juan d' Ulloa, the enemy's principal fortress, with five thousand prisoners and as many stands of arms, four hundred pieces of ordnance, and a large quantity of ordnance stores. Gen. Scott made special mention of his services, with those of other officers of the army, in General Order, No. 80, dated at headquarters, March 30th, 1847—as Gen. Patterson had done in his report sixteen days previously.

In General Order 111, April 17, arranging the army for the attack on the enemy's entrenchments at the pass of Cerro Gordo, to Gen. Twiggs' division and Gen. Shields' brigade was assigned the duty of seizing possession of the national road to Jalapa, in the rear of the enemy, and preventing a retreat. Two brigades, led by Gen. Shields and Col. B. Riley, of the regulars, stormed the enemy's camp, on the 18th, from nearly opposite directions, the command of Gen. Shields attacking the extreme left of the foe, and achieving a glorious victory, but, unfortunately, at a terrible cost, in the number of brave men killed and wounded. Whilst leading his brigade, " over rugged ascents and through dense chapparal, under a severe and continuous flank fire," to turn the enemy's position, the intrepid Shields "fell severely, if not mortally, wounded," and was carried from the field. Col. Baker, who fell at Ball's Bluff, succeeded to the command, completed the work so nobly begun by his immediate chief, and on the 21st of April reported the operations of the brigade.

A large copper ball having passed through the body and lungs of Gen. Shields, the army surgeons declared his wound mortal, and his case hopeless. A Mexican surgeon, a prisoner, offered his services to the General, examined the wound, and assured the suffering hero that he would live, if he would permit the removal of the coagulated blood. A desperate case called for desperate remedial measures, and Shields gave his consent. The kind Mexican drew a fine silk handkerchief through the wound and the body of the patient, thus removing the extravasated blood. It has been stated that daylight could be distinctly seen through the hole. Care and quiet

were necessary to his recovery, which, though slow, was steady.

Gen. Twiggs, commanding the 2d division of regulars, reporting on the 19th of April, to Gen. Scott, said :

" Of the conduct of the volunteer force under the brave Gen. Shields, I cannot speak in too high terms. * * * * The gallant General, with a shout from his men, pushed boldly for the road on the enemy's left, who, seeing their position completely turned, as well as driven from the hill, abandoned themselves to flight. Gen. Shields was here severely wounded, the command of the brigade devolving upon Col. Baker, who conducted it with ability."

Major General Scott, General-in-Chief, in his official report, dated Plain del Rio, fifty miles from Vera Cruz, 19th of April, mentioned the injury of Gen. Shields thus :

" Brigadier General Shields, a commander of activity, zeal and talent, is, I fear, if not dead, mortally wounded. He is some five miles from me at the moment;" adding, in a postscript, " I make a second postcript to say there is some hope, I am happy to learn, that Gen. Shields may survive his wounds."

He repeats his commendation in a supplementary report, dated Jalapa, April 23, adding :

" I am happy in communicating strong hopes for the recovery of the gallant Gen. Shields, who is so much improved as to have been brought to this place."

When the news of the fall of Gen. Shields reached the United States, the country resounded with his praise, and the leading journals published obituary notices of him, in which his merits were enthusiastically spoken of.

For "gallant and meritorious conduct" in this battle, he was breveted Major General of Volunteers in August, 1848.

A few months pass away ; the twelve months volunteers return to their homes ; reinforcements arrive for the war ; the army approaches nearer and nearer to the city of Mexico ; new battles are to be fought, fresh victories to be gained ; Gen. Shields chafes at his own compulsory inactivity. Preparations for the final work of the campaign are being pushed forward vigorously ; officers and men are eager to meet the foe, in a decisive contest. Gen. Shields joined his command at San Augustin, on the main road to and only nine miles from the capital, early in August, 1847. The attack on Contreras is in progress, 19th of that month.   The General-in-Chief communicates special orders to Gen. Shields, who promptly obeys.

Marching his brigade over rough and broken ground, partially covered with a low forest, he reached Contreras time enough to find Gen. Cadwallader's forces in position, observing the formidable strength of reinforcements pouring out of the capital, into the entrenchments of the enemy.   What follows, Gen. Shields himself will describe.

"On the 19th instant, about three o'clock in the afternoon, pursuant to the orders of the General commanding this division, I marched from this place with the New York and South Carolina regiments of volunteers, towards the battle-field of Contreras.   On reporting to the commander-in-chief, who occupied, on my arrival, a position which overlooked the field, he described to me, in a few words, the position of the contending forces, pointed out the route of my command, and briefly instructed me as to the disposition which would render my force the most serviceable.

"Directing my march upon the village near Contreras, the troops had to pass over ground covered with rocks and crags, and filled with chasms, which rendered the route almost impassable.   A deep, rugged ravine, along the bed of which rolled a rapid stream, was passed after dark, with great difficulty and exertion; and to rest the wearied troops after crossing, I directed them to lie upon their arms until midnight. While occupying this position, two strong pickets thrown out by my order, discovered, fired upon, and drove back a body of Mexican infantry moving through the fields in a direction from their position towards the city.   I have since learned that an attempt had in like manner been made by the enemy to pass the position on the main road, occupied by the 1st regiment of artillery, and with a like want of success.   About midnight I again resumed the march, and joined Brigadier General Smith, in the village already referred to.

"Gen. Smith, previous to my arrival, had made the most judicious arrangements for turning and surprising the Mexican position, about daybreak, and with which I could not wish to interfere.   This cast upon my command the necessity of holding the position to be evacuated by Gen. Smith, and which was threatened by the enemy's artillery and infantry on the right, and a large force of his cavalry on the left.   About daybreak, the enemy opened a brisk fire of grape and round shot upon the church and village in which my brigade was posted, and also upon a part of our troops displayed to divert him on his right and front—evidently unaware of the movement in progress to turn his position by the left and rear.   This continued until Col. Riley's brigade opened its fire from the rear, which was

delivered with such terrible effect that the whole Mexican force was thrown into the utmost consternation.

"At this juncture, I ordered the two regiments of my command to throw themselves on the main road, by which the enemy must retire, to intercept and cut off his retreat; and, although officers and men had suffered during the march of the night, and from exposure without shelter or cover to the incessant rain until daybreak, this movement was executed in good order, and with rapidity. The Palmetto regiment, crossing a deep ravine, deployed on both sides of the road, and opened a most destructive fire upon the mingled masses of infantry and cavalry; and the New York regiment, brought into line lower down, and on the road side, delivered its fire with a like effect.   At this point many of the enemy were killed and wounded; some 865 captured, of which 35 were officers, among the latter was Gen. Nicolas Mendoza.

"In the meantime, the enemy's cavalry, about 3,000 strong, which had been threatening our position during the morning, moved down towards us in good order, as if to attack. I immediately recalled the infantry, to place them in position to meet the threatened movement; but soon the cavalry changed its direction, and retreated towards the capital.   I now received an order from Gen. Twiggs to advance by the main road towards Mexico; and having posted Capt. Marshall's company of South Carolina volunteers, and Capt. Taylor's New York volunteers in charge of the prisoners and wounded, I moved off with the remainder of my force, and joined the positions of the 2d and 3d divisions, already en route on the main road.   On this march we were joined by the General-in-Chief, who assumed command of the whole, and the march continued uninterrupted until we arrived before Churubusco.   Here the enemy was found strongly fortified and posted with his main force, probably 25,000.

"The engagement was commenced by the 2d division, under Twiggs, soon joined by the 1st, under Worth, and was becoming general, when I was detached by the Commander-in-Chief, with my two regiments and Pierce's brigade—the 9th, 12th and 15th—with the mountain howitzer battery, and ordered to gain a position, if possible, to attack the enemy's rear, and intercept his retreat.

"Leaving Coyoacan by a left-hand road, and advancing about a mile upon it, I moved thence with my command towards the right, through a heavy corn-field, and gained an open but swampy field, in which is situated the hacienda De los Portales.   On the edge of this field, beyond the hacienda, I discovered the road by which the enemy must retire from Churubusco, and found his reserve of about 4,000 infantry, already occupied it, just in rear of the town.   As my command arrived, I established the right upon a point recommended by Capt. Lee, engineer officer, in whose skill and judgment I had the utmost confidence, and commenced a movement to the left, to flank the enemy on his right, and throw my troops between him and the city; but finding his right supported by a heavy body of cavalry, some 3,000 strong, and seeing, too, that with his infantry he answered to my movements by a corresponding one towards his right flank, gaining ground faster than I could, owing to the heavy mud and swamp through which I had to operate, I withdrew the men to the cover of the hacienda, and determined to attack him upon his front. I selected the Palmetto regiment as the base of my line, and this gallant regiment moved forward firmly and rapidly under a fire of musketry as terrible, perhaps, as any which soldiers ever faced; the New York 12th and 15th, deployed gallantly on the right, and the 9th on the left, and the whole advanced, opening their fire as they came up, and moving steadily forward. The enemy began to waver, and when my order to charge was given, the men rushed upon and scattered his broken ranks. As we reached the road, the advance of Worth's command appeared, driving the enemy from his stronghold of Churubusco. I took command of the front, and continued in pursuit until passed by Harney with his cavalry, who followed the routed foe into the very gates of the city.

" In this terrible battle, in which a strongly fortified enemy fought behind his works under the walls of his capital, our loss is necessarily severe. This loss, I regret to say, has fallen most severely upon my command. In the two regiments of my own brigade, numbering about 600 in the fight, the loss is reported 240 in killed and wounded.

"In this last engagement, my command captured 380 prisoners, including six officers. Of this number, 42 had deserted from the American army during the war, and at their head was found the notorious O'Reilly, who had fought against out troops at Monteray and elsewhere."

Major General Quitman, in his report to the General-in-Chief, dated San Augustin, August 26th, enclosing the report of Gen. Shields, says he has nothing to add to it, " except the expression of my unqualified admiration of the distinguished conduct of that gallant officer, and my approbation of the good conduct and gallantry of the portion of my division which had the good fortune to be actively engaged under his command."

The General-in-Chief, in his official report, August 28, bears generous testimony to the great ability displayed by Gen. Shields, in these hazardous movements, and makes special reference to his noble conduct, in waiving his right to command as senior officer, in favor of Gen. Persifer F. Smith, his junior, as mentioned in the foregoing extract from the report of Gen. Shields.

Major General Worth, in his report of August 23, is equally eulogistic of the gallantry of Gen. Shields, during the perilous hours of concert and co-operation; and brevet Brigadier General Smith, of the 1st brigade, 2d division of regulars, writing on the same day, expresses his great admiration of his courage and skill.

The command of Gen. Shields again distinguished itself in the attack on Chapultapec, and the advance against the city of Mexico. Its chivalrous leader, in his report dated "Mexico, Sept. 15, 1847," described his progress thus:

" We arrived at Tacubaya on the 11th inst., under cover of the night. About daylight next morning, my brigade was posted, by the order of the General of division, in a position to support a heavy battery, being known as battery No. 1, under the command of Capt. Drum, 4th artillery. This battery was erected on the Tacubaya road, in front of the castle of Chapultapec. My command continued in the performance of this duty, which was both arduous and laborious, during the whole of the ensuing day and night. While here, we furnished large details to aid in the erection of battery No. 2, under the direction of Capt. Huger, and also to support the battery when erected.

" During all this time, the most of my command was exposed to a most annoying fire from the castle and heights of Chapultapec, which they bore with the most perfect coolness and composure. I may as well mention here, that, during the day of the 12th, the General commanding the division pushed a bold and vigorous reconnoisance, in person, to the right, towards the church and enclosures, as well as the great aqueduct leading to Mexico; and this reconnoisance disclosed the existence of one or two strong batteries in that vicinity, and a strong infantry force, which lined the walls and enclosures.

" About eight o'clock, on the morning of 13th, pursuant to the order of the General of division, preparations began to be made for a general assault on the castle and environs. The storming parties, consisting of an efficient force from Twiggs' brigade under command of Capt. Casey, 2d infantry, and a selected force of 120 men from the whole division, under command of Major Twiggs, marine corps, as well as forty pioneers, under the command of Capt. Reynolds, marine corps, were moved forward along the road to the right, with the intention of crossing the fields and carrying the defences surrounding the castle. The marines, under Lieut. Col. Watson, were also ordered forward to support those parties. This force had not yet reached the point where it was to cross the field to the left, when a terrible fire of grape and musketry opened upon them from the stone wall and base of the hill in front, and the woods, walls and enclosures to the right. It became evident, in an instant, that the main force of the enemy, having been driven from the hill and castle by our artillery, had thrown itself in our front and on our right, under cover of woods, stone walls, buildings and enclosures. This induced the General, who saw the whole with a glance, to direct a new movement across the fields to the left. I received orders, therefore, to turn the Palmettos and New Yorkers in that direction. The Pennsylvania regiment received orders from him to make a similar movement. The Palmettos, New Yorkers and Pennsylvanians arrived at the point of detour, and received orders to cross the fields in succession; and, though the route was intercepted by deep ditches filled with water, and the whole movement was performed under a severe fire of musketry in front, from the hill, and behind stone walls, and a tremendous fire of grape and musketry from the woods and enclosures on the right, yet these gallant regiments advanced with unshaken firmness and intrepidity. The Palmettos gained the wall without firing a shot, broke through it, and ascended the hill in a body, to the support of the storming parties from the other division. Several of the New York companies ascended the hill with such rapidity that they united with the storming parties of the other divisions; and the New York flag, and company B of that regiment, under the command of a gallant young officer, Lieut. Reid, were among the first to mount the ramparts of the castle, and there display the stars and stripes to the admiration of the army. Lieut. Brower, commanding company F, same regiment, had the good fortune to capture Gen. Bravo, the Mexican commander of Chapultepec. The other officers and soldiers of the whole command, behaved with equal gallantry and good conduct. Lieut. Col. Baxter, commanding the New Yorkers, fell mortally wounded in this gallant charge. He was an officer of the most determined courage and intrepidity, and behaved with great gallantry, both at Contreras and Churubusco, and his loss has been severely felt, both by his regiment and the army. Major Burnham, upon whom the command next devolved, led it during the rest of the day with great gallantry and good conduct.

"In the meantime, the battle raged with increased fury on our right. The main body of the enemy seemed bent on maintaining that position, and thus keeping open the communication with the city. This imposed upon the small force in that direction the necessity

of maintaining an unequal contest against tremendous odds in numbers, and a most formidable position. The place, however, was finally carried, with considerable loss. Here Major Twiggs fell at the head of his command; he was a brave and veteran officer, and his loss has been most severely felt by the whole command. The marines, under their gallant commander, Lieut. Col. Watson, exhibited the courage and discipline for which that corps is so justly celebrated.

"A portion of the command being now supplied with ammunition, the whole advanced along the Tacubaya road, from arch to arch of the aqueduct, towards the Garita of Belen. The whole of this movement was conducted under the immediate eye and direction of the General commanding the division. The rifles and Palmettos led the advance. The enemy made another determined stand at a position on the road, above a mile from Chapultepec, and behind a strong breastwork across the road, flanked upon his right by a field redan, and protected upon the left by an impassable marsh.

"This position, however, was soon rapidly carried by the rifles and Palmettos, aided by a well directed fire from Drum's battery. The advance was now pushed forward to the Garita. Here the enemy made a most determined stand; and as the ground to the right and left was marshy and impracticable, the movements forward, from arch to arch, became slow and hazardous, and had to be made under a terrible fire of round shot, grape, canister and musketry. The loss here was necessarily severe, but richly compensated for by the capture of the Garita—the entrance to the city. The Garita was captured between one and two o'clock, and from then till dark that position was maintained under the most terrible fire on the part of the enemy.

"Beyond this Garita, about three o'clock in the afternoon, Major Gladden, commanding the Palmettos—a brave, active and gallant officer—received a severe wound, and was carried off the field.

"About dark I was compelled to withdraw from the ground, in consequence of a wound received in my left arm, in the early part of the day, during the assault on Chapultepec. My whole body became paralyzed from the influence of the arm, and I was carried by the officers of my staff to the nearest house, to obtain medical assistance.

"Capt. F. N. Page, my Assistant Adjutant General, an officer of great gallantry and intrepidity, received a slight wound from a grape shot, in the side, while standing near me, awaiting my orders. My aid-de-camp, Lieut. Hammond, 3d artillery, whose services and gallantry have distinguished him in every field, escaped himself, but had his horse killed while advancing along the arches. My own horse was also shot near the same place. I have only to add, without specifying names and particulars, that my whole command behaved with the most distinguished intrepidity during the day, and have merited, I hope, the approbation of the General commanding the division."

Major General Quitman (who led the advance into the city of Mexico), in his report of the 29th of September, of the movements and operations of the portion of the army under his command, from the afternoon of the 11th to the raising of the American flag on the National Palace of Mexico, on the 14th, renews the expression of his exalted opinion of Gen. Shields, and his activity and daring, adding that:

"Brigadier General Shields had solicited from me the command of the storming parties on the morning of the 13th. Not feeling justified in permitting so great an exposure of an officer of his rank, with an inadequate command, and requiring his invaluable services, with his brigade, the application was declined. Until carried from the field on the night of the 13th, in consequence of the severe wound received in the morning, he was conspicuous for his gallantry, energy and skill."

Again, in the same report, referring to the storming of Chapultapec, and to the promptness and intrepidity of the battalion of marines and the New York and South Carolina regiments, belonging to the immediate command of Gen. Shields, as well as the 2d Pennsylvania regiment, led by Lieut. Col. John W. Geary, and for a while acting under his orders, Gen. Quitman states that " in directing the advance, Brigadier General Shields was severely wounded in the arm. No persuasions, however, could induce that officer to leave his command, or quit the field."

The General-in-Chief, in his official account of the brilliant operations of the American army, on the 12th, 13th and 14th of September, dated " National Palace of Mexico, Sept. 18, 1847," is equally complimentary to Gen. Shields and the gallant men of his command. He makes special and commendatory mention of " Shields badly wounded before Chapultapec and refusing to retire."

He returned to Belleville, Illinois, after the war. In January, 1849, he was elected by the Legislature of Illinois, U. S. Senator for six years, and took his seat at the extra session on March 4th, 1849. A question was raised as to his eligibility, his technical citizenship under his naturalization not reaching nine years

until October, 1849. During the discussion of this subject, he resigned, and the Legislature the next fall re-elected him. He served until March 3d, 1855, when he was succeeded by Judge Trumbull. He removed, in 1856, to Minnesota, and commenced lumbering on a farm in Faribault county. The first Legislature of that State elected him, in 1857, U. S. Senator. In classifying the terms of the new Senators, Gen. Shields won the short term, expiring March 3d, 1858. At the expiration of that time, he resumed his agricultural pursuits, but in the spring of 1860 moved to California, where he was residing when the war broke out, when he was appointed Brig. Gen. of Volunteers. He was attached to the army of the Shenandoah, and was present at the battle of Winchester, of which the General gives the following informal description in a private letter dated March 26th, 1862:

" I will give you a brief account of our late operations. My reconnoisance beyond Strasburg, on the 18th and 19th insts., discovered Jackson, reinforced, in a strong position, near New Market, within supporting distance of the main body of the rebels under Johnson. It was necessary to decoy him from that position. Therefore, I fell back rapidly to Winchester, on the 20th, as if in retreat, marching my whole command nearly thirty miles in one day. My force at night was placed in a secluded position, two miles from Winchester, on the Martinsburg road. On the 21st, the rebel cavalry, under Ashby, showed themselves to our pickets, within sight of Winchester. On the 22d, all of Gen. Banks' command, with the exception of my division, evacuated Winchester, en route for Centerville. This movement, and the masked position of my division, made an impression upon the inhabitants, some of whom were in secret communication with the enemy, that our army had left, and that nothing remained but a few regiments to garrison this place. Jackson was signalled to this effect. I saw their signals and divined their meaning. About five o'clock on the afternoon of the 22d, Ashby, believing the town was almost evacuated, attacked our pickets and drove them in. This success increased his delusion. It became necessary, however, to repulse them for the time being. I, therefore, ordered forward a brigade, and placed it in front, between Winchester and the enemy. I only let them see, however, two regiments of infantry, two batteries of artillery and a small force of cavalry, which he mistook as the whole force left to garrison and protect the place. In a little skirmish that evening, while placing the artillery in position, I was struck by a fragment of a shell, which broke my arm above the elbow, injuring my shoulder, and damaged me otherwise to such an extent that I have lain prostrate ever since. I commenced making preparations for any emergency that might occur that night or the next morning. Under cover of the night I ordered an entire brigade (Kimball's) to take up a strong position in advance. I pushed forward four batteries, having them placed in a strong position to support the infantry. I placed Sullivan's brigade on both flanks, to prevent surprise and to keep my flanks from being turned, and I held Tyler's brigade in reserve, to operate against any point that might be assailed in front. In this position I awaited and expected the enemy's attack the next morning. My advance brigade was two miles from the town, its pickets extending perhaps a mile farther along the turnpike to Strasburg. About eight o'clock in the morning I sent forward two experienced officers to reconnoitre the front, and report indications of the enemy. They returned in an hour, reporting no enemy in sight except Ashby's force of cavalry, infantry and artillery, which by this time had become familiar and contemptible to us. Gen. Banks, who was yet here in person, upon hearing this report, concluded that Jackson could not be in front, or be decoyed away so far from the main body of the rebel army. In this opinion I, too, began to concur, concluding that Jackson was too sagacious to be caught in such a trap. Gen. Banks, therefore, left for Washington. His staff of officers was directed to follow the same day, by way of Centerville. Knowing, however, the crafty enemy I had to deal with, I omitted no precaution. My whole force was concentrated and prepared to support Kimball's brigade, which was in advance. About half-past ten o'clock it became evident we had a considerable force before us; but the enemy still concealed himself so adroitly in the woods that it was impossible to estimate it. I ordered a portion of the artillery forward, to open fire and unmask them. By degrees they began to show themselves. They planted battery after battery in strong positions, on the centre and on both flanks. Our artillery responded, and this continued until about half-past three o'clock in the afternoon, when I directed a column of infantry to carry a battery on their left flank, and to assail that flank, which was done promptly and splendidly by Tyler's brigade, aided by some regiments from the other brigades. The fire of the infantry was so close and destructive that it made havoc in their ranks. The result was the capture of their guns on the left, and the forcing back of that wing on the centre, thus placing them in a position to be routed by a general attack, which was made about five o'clock, by all the infantry, and succeeded in driving them in flight from the field. Night fell upon us at this stage, leaving us in possession of the field

of battle, two guns and four caissons, three hundred prisoners, and about one thousand stand of small arms. Our killed in this engagement cannot exceed one hundred men, wounded two hundred and thirty-three. The enemy's killed and wounded exceed one thousand. The inhabitants of the adjacent villages carried them to their houses as they were removed from the field of battle. Houses between the battle-field and Strasburg, and even far beyond, have since been found filled with the dead and dying of the enemy. Graves have been discovered far removed from the road, where the inhabitants of the country buried them as they died. Gen. Banks, in his pursuit of the enemy beyond Strasburg afterwards, found houses on the road twenty-two miles from the battle-field, filled in this manner, and presenting the most ghastly spectacle. The havoc made in the ranks of the rebels has struck this whole region of country with terror. Such a blow has never fallen on them before, and it is more crushing because wholly unexpected. Jackson and his stone-wall brigade, and all the other brigades accompanying him, will never meet this division again in battle. During the night they managed to carry off their artillery in the darkness. We opened upon them by early daylight the next morning, and they commenced to retreat. Gen. Banks returned from Harper's Ferry between nine and ten o'clock a. m., and placed himself, at my request, at the head of the command, ten miles from the battle-field, pursuing the enemy. Reinforcements, which we had ordered back from Williams' division, and which I had ordered forward during the night, now came pouring in, and with all these we continued the pursuit, pressing them with vigor and with repeated and destructive attacks as far as Woodstock, where we halted from mere exhaustion. The enemy's sufferings have been terrible, and such as they have nowhere else endured since the commencement of this war; and yet such were their gallantry and high state of discipline, that at no time during the battle or pursuit did they give way to panic. They fled to Mount Jackson, and are by this time, no doubt, in communication with the main body of the rebel army. I hope to be able in a few days to ride in a buggy, and place myself at the head of my command; but I have neither sufficient force nor sufficient rank to do that service to the country that I hope and feel I am capable of. No man could be better treated than I am by Gen. Banks; and yet, if he and his command had been here on the 23d, you would have heard nothing of a fight, because our wily enemy would not have been entrapped. I want an efficient cavalry regiment—the 3d U. S. Cavalry, for instance—and additional infantry. I can do the country service if they give me a chance.   JAMES SHIELDS."

GEN. SCHOFIELD.

Brig. Gen. JOHN MCALLISTER SCHOFIELD, in command of the State of Missouri, was born Sept. 29th, 1831, in Chatauque county, N. Y. His father, Rev. J. V. Schofield, removed with his family, in 1843, to Illinois. His grandfather John McAllister was an officer in the war of 1812, and, also, his grandfather James Schofield. His father had not the means to give his boys a collegiate education, and when his eldest son was leaving home for an eastern college, the General, then a boy fifteen years old, thought he might have an education also, and resolved from that hour to get it. At the age of seventeen he had made good proficiency in study, and had taught a district school the winter of that year. In the following spring he was appointed a cadet in West Point, upon the recommendation of Hon. T. J. Turner, then representative in Congress from northern Illinois. The appointment was unthought of and unsought for by any one, and was given as an expression of regard for the General's father, and a knowledge of the boy's desires and capacity for study, especially mathematics. He took a high stand in his class as a mathematician, and was popular with his Professors and fellows in the Academy. He graduated in June, 1853; was brevetted Second Lieutenant in the 2d artillery, and stationed for two years at Fort Moultrie, S. C., and Fort Casser, Florida. He was then called to West Point as instructor in natural philosophy. He was popular as a teacher and a man. He spent much time in the observatory, in taking astronomical observations, both for his own love of science, and to aid scientific men. In 1857, he married the daughter of Prof. Wm. Bartlett, the well known author of works on natural philosophy to be used in his own department at West Point. The General remained at West Point for five years, and then obtained a leave of absence, to occupy the chair of natural philosophy in Washington University, St. Louis, Mo., which place he was filling when the rebellion broke out. By an order from Washington, he was detailed to muster into service troops from Missouri. He administered the oath to over 10,000 men, and was appointed Major in the 1st Missouri Infantry. His rank in the regular army at the

time was First Lieutenant, and May 14, 1861, he was appointed Captain, and Nov. 21, 1861, Brigadier General of Volunteers. He led one regiment to the capture of Camp Jackson, and was detailed to escort the prisoners to the arsenal, and administered to them the oath. When Gen. Lyon left for Boonville, he was left in command of the arsenal, and after the battle there, he joined Lyon, as Assistant Adjutant General and chief of staff. In that march to Springfield, and the terrible battle there fought, he was one of Gen. Lyon's chief advisers. They slept together under the same blanket for three hours, in sight of the camp fires of Wilson's Creek, where the hero and true patriot "slept his last sleep, and fought his last battle."

Gen. Schofield, by his skill and ability, won the confidence of all in that noble little army. He was with Gen. Lyon constantly until he fell in that fearful struggle for victory over a greatly superior force. Both before and after Gen. Lyon's death, he was in the thickest of the fight, had a horse shot from under him, his sword cracked with a bullet, and the beard under his chin cut by another. When the battle had raged with fierceness for three hours, Gen. Lyon was slightly wounded, and it was yet uncertain how the scales would turn. All things seemed against success. At this critical point he said to Gen. Schofield, "Major, I fear the day is lost." "No," he replied, "let us try it again." The Major then led the 1st Iowa regiment to the support of Totten's battery, and ordered them to stand by it, and right nobly did they obey the command. Gen. Lyon at the same time took the 2d Kansas regiment into action, and fell while gallantly leading them to the conflict. Gen. Schofield started to find Lyon, and met his servant and others bringing him off the field, dead. Such was the critical state of the battle that he did not report the fact to Major Sturges, upon whom the command then devolved, for half an hour. He then told him that Gen. Lyon was killed, and asked for orders. The battle then raged with increased intensity for three hours more, until that vastly superior force was repelled the fourth time from their chosen ground. Major Sturges, in making his report, acknowledged his indebtedness to the official report of Gen. Schofield, and in many instances copied it verbatim, and remarked that "he did not wish to particularize any, but he could not forbear mentioning the conduct of Major Schofield, for his coolness and bravery as he passed over the battlefield, giving orders and leading regiments into action, exposed to the fire of both armies. It gave confidence to the soldiers, and was the common theme of remark." One of the correspondents on the field remarked the same thing, and wrote, "A finer gentleman, a truer patriot and a braver soldier, never lived." The Chaplain of one of the regiments, the Missouri 1st, who was on the battle-field, and in the whole march, says, "To Gen. Schofield's untiring energy, perhaps more than any other officer in the gallant little army, is the country indebted for their safe retreat to Rolla, with their valuable train and stores."

Gen. Schofield organized a battery, in October, 1861, at the St. Louis Arsenal, joined Col. Carlin's force at Pilot Knob, marched to Fredericktown, where Col. Plummer's command from Cape Girardeau met them, attacked Jeff. Thompson, and gained the brilliant victory of Fredericktown, all in the short space of four days. Immediately after his appointment as Brigadier General of Volunteers, on the 27th of November, 1861, he was assigned to the command of the militia of Missouri, authorized by the War Department, to be raised for service during the war. This force was placed in active service as fast as their company organizations were completed, and long before they could be properly organized into regiments. Before the expiration of four months, he had organized, armed and equipped, and placed in the field, sixteen regiments, and this, too, after Missouri had furnished over 40,000 men to the United States volunteer forces, and 50,000 to the rebels. He took the field in person, about the 25th of December, 1861, to restore the peace of the State north of the Missouri river, where, by a general and concentrated uprising of the rebels, the entire line of the North Missouri Railroad was broken up. Nearly every bridge, several station houses, water tanks, and two or three trains of cars burned, and the whole country in a state of terror and alarm. In less than one month he had scattered and driven out the rebel bands, captured some fifty of the bridge burners, and restored peace and quiet. When Gen. Halleck took the field, immediately after the battle of Corinth, about four-fifths of the State, with some 25,000 troops of volunteers and militia, were under his command, and on the 1st of June, 1862, the district of Missouri, comprising the entire State, was placed under his command. His headquarters are in St. Louis, and his troops, some 30,000 in Missouri, now occupy every important post in the State, and are holding in check fully an equal number of rebels, now gathering in Arkansas, and threatening Missouri, together with several bands of guerrillas, numbering from 100 to 3,000 each.

Gen. Schofield was selected as one of the three officers of the Board appointed by the President to inspect the naval flotilla, at Cairo, before it was regularly placed in service, in January, 1862. He is industrious, and emphatically a great worker, devoting from twelve to fifteen hours each day to his office, in St. Louis, Mo.

COL. ELLSWORTH.

Life is not lost, from which is bought
Endless renown.   *Spenser.*

Although not in command of one of her regiments, at the time he fell—almost the first victim of the rebellion—Illinois claims the young hero, Ellsworth, as one of her most distinguished officers. It was on her soil he manifested his love for the profession of arms, and in her principal city that he first made his name familiar as a household word, by organizing and drilling to such marvellous perfection, the famous United States Zouave Cadets, who became known far and wide by their peculiar dress, and the novelty and celerity of their movements.

EPHRAIM ELMER ELLSWORTH was born at Malta, Saratoga County, New York, on the 11th of April, 1837. His early years were shadowed by the total wreck of his father's fortune, in the financial troubles which, about the period of his birth, swept over the land. His father never recovered; disaster followed disaster, and after learning the English rudiments at the village school, Elmer went out, unaided, into the wide world, to seek his fortunes. After various employments in Troy and New York, and ineffectual attempts to enter West Point, he determined to go to Illinois. Before he was twenty-one years of age, he was successfully engaged in business as a patent agent in Chicago. Energetic and attentive to his affairs, he was building up his fortune; but like many a true man, beheld the fruit of his toil swept away by the villainy of one whom he had trusted.

Having perfectly mastered Hardee's System of Tactics, become a perfect adept in gymnastics, and made himself an unequalled swordsman and marksman, he gathered around him a number of young men, who entered with spirit into his system, and on the 4th day of May, 1857, organized the United States Zouave Cadets, of Chicago, the first Zouave company ever seen in this country. Total abstinence from intoxicating liquors and tobacco was a strict law, the violation of which blotted the name of the offender from the roll. This corps he trained, as opportunity offered, for about a year, and at the same time gave attention to similar organizations in Lockport

and Springfield. At the United States Agricultural Fair, Ellsworth's Chicago Zouaves won the colors to be awarded to the company exhibiting greatest efficiency in drill.

The novelty and picturesqueness of the dress, combined with the exactness and celerity of their evolutions, soon made the Zouaves and their young leader known far and wide; and in July, 1860, they made a tour to the East, inviting any military companies to compete with them for the colors won at the Fair. Their exhibitions were visited by immense assemblies of people. In the city of New York, the Academy of Music was filled to overflowing, to witness their marvellous movements, at one moment.

In the last Presidential canvass, Ellsworth was a warm supporter of Lincoln, and aided the cause by his eloquent and stirring appeals in various parts of the State. During the session of the Legislature, he actively exerted himself to obtain the passage of a military bill which would put Illinois in a state of preparation; but in this he was defeated through the obtuseness of the "grave and reverend seigniors," who were blind to the coming storm, so clearly seen by him. At the request of the President elect, Ellsworth accompanied him to Washington, and received a Lieutenant's commission, as a preliminary to his entrance into the War Department.

When Sumter fell, Ellsworth felt that his time had come. He threw up his commission, and hastened to New York. A short interview with the Chief of the Fire Department settled all to his satisfaction. An appeal was made to the firemen, and in two days twelve hundred had enrolled their names. Ten companies were accepted, and at once proceeded to Fort Hamilton, to drill. For weeks the young soldier labored day and night at the herculean task of bringing his new regiment into discipline, but it was labor that he loved, and the jaded look which his countenance wore amid the chicanery and corruption of Washington, disappeared. New York became enthusiastic over Ellsworth's Fire Zouaves, over whom he had acquired perfect control. Three stands of colors were presented to them before their departure. On the 2d of

May, Col. Ellsworth, at the head of his regiment, entered Washington, amid an ovation equalling that which had attended his departure from New York.

On the 22d, orders were issued for the regiment to prepare to march to Alexandria. The day following, the young soldier wrote two letters—one to her who was to be his wife, the other to his parents, in these touching and prophetic words:

HEAD QUARTERS FIRST ZOUAVES, }
Washington, May 23, 1861. } ·

MY DEAR FATHER AND MOTHER:

The Regiment is ordered to move across the river to-night. We have no means of knowing what reception we are to meet with. I am inclined to the opinion that our entrance into Alexandria will be hotly contested, as I am just informed a large force was to have arrived there to-day. Should this happen, my dear parents, it may be my lot to be injured in some manner. Whatever may happen, cherish the consolation that I was engaged in the performance of a sacred duty; and to-night, thinking over the probabilities of the morrow and the occurrences of the past, I am perfectly willing to accept whatever my portion may be, confident that He who noteth even the fate of a sparrow, will have some purpose even in the fate of one like me.

My darling and ever loved parents, good-bye. God bless, protect and comfort you.

ELMER.

Before the early dawn, on the 24th, Ellsworth's regiment reached Alexandria. The "Pawnee," lying in the stream, had already proposed terms of submission to the town, which the rebels had accepted, agreeing to evacuate the place. Learning this, and satisfied that no resistance would be offered, Col. Ellsworth gave the necessary instructions to his officers to interrupt railway communication, and proceeded in person, at the head of a small detachment, to seize the telegraph office. On the way, he caught sight of a secession flag floating from the Marshall House, an inferior inn. Acting on the impulse of the moment, he entered with his party, and meeting a man, asked who placed the flag there. The person, who proved to be the proprietor, James T. Jackson, professed to know nothing about it, saying he was only a lodger. Ellsworth immediately cut down the flag, and was descending the stairs with it, when Jackson sprang forward and fired. Private T. Brownell, now Lieut. Brownell, U. S. A., who was in front of the Colonel, endeavored to strike up the weapon, but the rebel's grasp was too firm; a slug entered Ellsworth's side, between the fourth and fifth ribs, driving into his very heart a gold circlet, with the legend, "*Non nobis sed pro patria.*" Almost at the same instant, a ball from Brownell's rifle ended the murderer's career. The party made a litter of their muskets, and carried Ellsworth to the steamer, which immediately returned to the navy yard, Washington. From there, by order of the President, his remains were removed to the East Room of the White House. There the funeral ceremonies took place, on the 25th of May, and amid the tolling of bells, his remains, followed by the President and his Cabinet, and thousands of soldiers and spectators, were borne to the depot. The progress of his lifeless remains attested the young martyr's popularity, and the hopes the country had built upon his ability and energy. At New York, he lay in state, in the Governor's room, and an immense funeral procession threaded its way to the steamer that bore him to the home of his grief-stricken parents, where, amid the fury of a fierce rain storm, the hero was laid in the silent tomb. Thus passed away "poor Ellsworth! a fellow of genius and initiative," to quote the words of one who himself fell soon after, in the same glorious cause—the gallant Winthrop. Oh cursed spite of war, to silence such a genius—such a true man!

Col. Ellsworth's personal appearance is thus accurately described by one who knew him well and intimately: "His person was strikingly prepossessing. His form, though slight, was very compact and commanding; the head statuesquely poised, and covered with a luxuriance of curling black hair; a hazel eye, bright though serene—the eye of a gentleman as well as a soldier; a nose such as you see on Roman medals; a light mustache just shading the lips, that were continually curling into the sunniest smiles. His voice, deep and musical, instantly attracted attention; and his address, though not without soldierly brusqueness, was sincere and courteous."

One who visited the parents and the grave of the young martyr, a few weeks after his death, writes: " A wayfaring man for the night at the rural and quiet little village of Mechanicsville, the first object that attracted my attention early in the morning, was the hoisting of the 'Stars and Stripes' on the brow of an opposite and neighboring hill. There rests the youthful and brave Ellsworth. At the foot of the hill-side, near by, is the cottage of his father and mother, surrounded by some lovely flowers and green shrubbery, more striking in their fragrance and beauties, from the freshness of a recent shower. Accompanied by an intelligent lady, an intimate friend of the parents, we made in the afternoon a visit to the afflicted home. It was a visit of not merely idle curiosity, but of Christian sympathy to the mourners in their deep affliction and bereavement. We were cordially welcomed. On the wall hung his sword, belt, and military cap, with his likeness; and beneath, upon a side-table, his pocket Bible—a new volume, and bound in blue velvet. We are Bible readers ourselves, and upon opening the precious pages, its silken index pointed to the seventeenth chapter of St. John, with a pencil X at its top—most remarkable words: *'These words spake Jesus, and lifted up His eyes to heaven, and said, Father, the hour is come; glorify thy Son, that thy Son also may glorify Thee. . . . I have glorified Thee on the earth: I have finished the work which Thou gavest me to do. . . . And now I am no more in the world, and I came to Thee,'* etc., etc. Remarkable words are these we again add. 'I know not,' said the mother, weeping, 'where this Bible came from; but that may have been the *last* chapter of God's holy Word which Elmer over read in this world!' The fourteenth chapter was also marked: *'Let not your heart be troubled: ye believe in God, believe also in me. In my Father's house are many mansions,'* etc. Mysterious coincidence between these gracious divin promises and the sudden call of the youthful warrior to the Spirit Land! So it seemed to our minds. Both parents were present during our visit, and dwelt with weeping fondness upon the excellences of their departed son. Among his exalted virtues was pre-eminent the affection and devotion to his parents. To this they fondly referred more than to anything else. He was an illustrious example of this noble Christian trait, and one alas! alas! wanting in some children of our day. From the dwelling, we visited the new-made grave of Ellsworth, in the beautiful rural cemetery of Mechanics-ville, and near by, directly in the rear of his parents' garden. No spot could be better selected for the purpose. It lies on the top of a hill, affording a magnificent prospect of hills and valleys, winding streams, distant villages, forests and cultivated fields. Singular coincidence! Stillwater with *'Bemis Heights,'* toward the north, are in plain sight. What associations! A lofty pole and magnificent National flag already marks the grave of Col. Ellsworth. When it was elevated, at sunrise, a day or two ago, a single visitor, who was a stranger from North Carolina, made his appearance, and requested that he might hoist the 'Stars and Stripes' on this honored mount: his patriotic wish was granted, when he continued his journey toward his native State."

A noble regiment, to which each county gave its quota, every village and hamlet of his native State furnishing a man, and known as the "Ellsworth Avengers," was raised as his fittest, though not his only monument.

COL. CUMMING.

Col. GILBERT W. CUMMING, of the 51st Ill. Volunteers, was born in Delaware county, in the State of New York, and is now forty-five years of age. His parents came from the Highlands of Scotland, where his father's family suffered severely for their loyal adherence to the house of Stuart, in 1745. At an early age he was anxious to enter the legal profession, but owing to family loss of property, was apprenticed to a carriage maker in his native town, and devoted all the spare hours of his apprenticeship to study. At the age of sixteen he enlisted in an independent military company, and gave such evidence of a military taste and capacity, that he was soon appointed to office in his company, and by strict attention to his military duties and great perseverance in the acquirement of military knowledge, he rose to the command of a regiment, and afterwards received considerable military instruction from Major Le Brun, one of Napoleon's old officers. He was always a great student, and a good education acquired by his own personal efforts, has made him a thoroughly self-made man. The progress made in study while an apprentice, so far stimulated his early ideas of the legal profession, that, soon after becoming of age, he commenced the study of the law, and after being licensed to practice soon became one of the leading lawyers of his county. In 1845 the Anti-Rent troubles in the State of New York assumed the form of an armed resistance to the laws, and Sheriff Steele was basely murdered by an armed and disguised band of Anti-Renters, in Delaware county, while in the discharge of his official duties, which occasioned a rising of the Anti-Renters in Schoharie county, where Col. Cumming was then residing. He was thereupon ordered out at the head of a regiment to maintain the peace of the infected district, and by his skillful management of the forces under his command, and his judicious treatment of the Anti-Renters, soon restored the supremacy of the laws, and quelled that singular but dangerous rebellion in his county. In 1853, he removed with his family to Janesville, Wis., where for several years he had a large practice, and stood high in his profession. In 1858,

he removed to Chicago, where his family still reside. Here he continued the practice of his profession until September, 1861, when he devoted his time, with success, to raising a regiment for the war, and was appointed Colonel of the regiment, the 51st Illinois Volunteers, by Gov. Yates, on the 20th of September, 1861. In addition to this regiment, and to be attached to the same, Col. Cumming raised a battery of artillery and a company of cavalry. He was stationed at Camp Douglas until February, 1862, when he was ordered with his regiment to Cairo. Finding the extremely muddy and wet condition of his camp at Cairo was largely increasing his sick list, he obtained from Gen. Cullum—Gen. Halleck's chief of staff, then at Cairo—permission to remove his command to the Kentucky shore, opposite Cairo, which he named Camp Cullum. About this time, a scheming set of politicians in the Illinois Constitutional Convention, then in session at Springfield, inserted a provision in the new Constitution to turn Gov. Yates out of office before the expiration of his term, and in furtherance of this object sought to arouse old political prejudices against the Governor by addressing a resolution of the Convention to the Illinois officers in the field, inquiring whether their men were as well equipped as the soldiers from other States, and if not, whether the deficiency was owing to the fault of any of the Illinois State officers? and thus induce replies from which they might manufacture excuses for their intended slaughter of the Governor. One of the Convention circulars, containing this resolution, was sent to Col. Cumming, at Camp Cullum, who, indignant at such a base attempt to injure the highest officer in the State, whose patriotic labors were worthy of exalted praise, wrote to the Convention committee the following reply, which, speaks for itself:

HEADQUARTERS 51ST REG'T ILL. VOLS. }
Camp Cullum, Ky., Cairo Dist., March 3, '62. }
JAMES W. SINGLETON, ESQ.:

Dear Sir:—I am in receipt of your circular, containing a copy of the resolution of the Illinois Constitutional Convention, requesting information concerning the equipments furnished the Illinois troops, etc., and am greatly surprised to find the Convention arrogating to itself powers which do not belong to it.

Your Convention is only authorized to make a new Constitution for the State, and according to all well settled rules of law, can have no power or authority whatever beyond that specific object. Why, then, the inquiry contained in the resolution? To what part of a new Constitution does it point? and how or in what manner can any provision of the Constitution which the Convention is to make change or affect the equipments of the Illinois troops now in the field? The subject matter of the inquiry embraced in the resolution, clearly shows that the Convention is intermeddling with matters that are really none of its business, and that, too, with the evident intention of creating prejudice against the present State officers, and making political capital for members of the Convention. Such a course is unworthy of the high trust reposed in that important body, and the responsible duties it owes to the people, and ought impartially to perform. Illinois cannot be benefited by assumptions of power on the part of her constitutional delegates which can only stand as a record of shame and reproach in the history of the State. Such, I am constrained to say, are the peculiar characteristics of the communication addressed by you to me. The resolution is aimed at the present State officers. If the Convention will take the trouble to ascertain the facts, they will find that the State had neither money nor credit when this war commenced, and yet, without these necessary aids at hand, the Governor has raised, armed, equipped and sent into the field over 70,000 men. If, as has sometimes been said, "A man is a fact," then Illinois has this large number of them, which will refute and forever silence the implied slander contained in this extrajudicial resolution of the Convention. You say you are instructed to request me to make such suggestions as my observation and experience may dictate, etc. I have so far acted upon this request, and in addition would respectfully suggest, that if the Convention will attend to its legitimate duties and business, it may gain the respect it has now lost, and be of some benefit to the State. In conclusion, and by way of avoiding a misinterpretation of my remarks, permit me to assure you that this answer to your circular is not induced by political friendship for the Governor of this State. With him or his party I have no political affinities; I belong to another school; but during the war I have no politics but the Laws and Constitution of the United States. And yet I cannot, in justice to the Governor and the State he has honored by his unceasing labors for the common weal, withhold this truthful tribute to his patriotism and successful efforts under such trying difficulties. I also feel justified in saying, that Illinois will look with pride and satisfaction upon her soldiers, raised, armed and equipped by her State officers in defence of the Union.

I have the honor to be, very respectfully, your obedient servant.　　　　G. W. CUMMING,
Col. Comd'g 51st Regt. Ill. Vol.

This letter fell like a bombshell in the Convention, and was published with such manifest approval by the press throughout the State, that the constitutional wire-pullers were obliged to abandon their persecution of the Governor, and cover their retreat by passing resolutions highly complimentary to him and his war measures.

On the 4th of March, Col. Cumming was ordered with his regiment to Bertrand, in Missouri, where he was placed in command of several regiments, and soon after was ordered with his brigade to New Madrid, where he joined the army of the Mississippi, under Maj. General Pope, and was there assigned to the command of the 2d brigade in the division of Gen. Paine. On the 13th of March he was at the battle of New Madrid, at the head of his brigade, where he received the thanks of his superior officers for his coolness and the good conduct of himself, his officers and men, in that engagement. On the 7th of April, he was with his command at the taking of Island No. 10, and led his brigade in hot pursuit of the enemy from that place to Tiptonville, where, as part of Gen. Paine's division, he participated in the capture of over six thousand of the rebels, including two general officers, several Colonels and regimental officers, with all their arms, equipments and stores. Gen. Pope here placed Col. Cumming in charge of these prisoners, arms and stores, with directions to ship them, with suitable guards, to New Madrid. Having successfully accomplished this laborious task, he returned to New Madrid, where he received from Gen. Halleck the flattering order to have inscribed upon the colors of the regiments in his brigade, "New Madrid and Island No. 10." He next proceeded with his command to Fort Pillow, and was there engaged in the investment of that place, when he was ordered up the Tennessee to join Gen. Halleck before Corinth.

From the battle of New Madrid to the evacuation of Corinth, Col. Cumming's brigade was always in the advance, and in every fight and skirmish.

Col. Cumming is very popular with his officers and men, always having an eye to their care and comfort. He is a strict disciplinarian, is amply possessed of the qualities which make him a valuable officer, and has always received the approbation of his superiors.

COL. HARRIS.

THOMAS WOOLEN HARRIS, Colonel of the 54th Regiment Illinois Volunteers, was born in Newport, Ky., June 28th, 1822, and is the oldest of ten children. He is of the old Revolutionary stock, his grandfather, Thomas Harris, having served through the long years of our struggle for independence. He married Miss Nancy Woolen, of Virginia, removing from Maryland to the then wilderness of the dark and bloody ground, and settled at Crab Orchard. Trained to hardships, and accustomed to danger, he here made his home, and saw his children growing up around him, amid the perils and struggles of border life. Edward Harris, father of the Colonel, was born in Georgetown, to which place he removed and continued to reside for many years. The Colonel while a boy served an apprenticeship at the carpenter trade, which he pursued until he reached the age of twenty-three years, when he turned his attention to milling. In 1848, he went to Indiana, and soon afterwards engaged in the mill business at New Philadelphia, purchasing the ground and founding the town of Harristown, Washington county. He held an important office under President Fillmore's administration, was President of a Railroad, and in all county and State matters took an active interest. Owing to the failing health of his wife, unaccustomed to a northern climate, he visited the extreme southern States, and returning as far as Tremble county, Ky., engaged in merchandizing. Remaining but a short time, and attracted by the growing prosperity of Illinois, he removed to that State, and settled in Shelbyville, Shelby county, where he has since resided. Here he engaged extensively in mercantile business and land speculations, making valuable additions to the town. His residence, recently erected, is a model of architecture and convenience, and is one of the finest buildings in central Illinois.

Col. Harris commenced his political career as a Whig, and continued a staunch supporter of that organization until its decease. When the lamented Douglas, taking issue with a corrupt administration, came home to proclaim his Territorial policy to the people of Illinois, by which he sought to avert the impending conflict of arms, Col. Harris became one of his most ardent supporters, and labored unceasingly upon the stump and in private caucus for the success of the policy which he had avowed. Elected to the Legislature in the memorable campaign of 1860, receiving the nomination over the most distinguished members of the Democratic party in the counties of Shelby and Cumberland, a district noted for its eminent talent, and running against an opponent whose ability and personal qualities had made deservedly popular, he carried the district by over 1,200 majority, an increase over former Democratic majorities of nearly 100 per cent.

In the Legislature, his active interest in all that concerned the welfare of the State, and his superior business qualifications, soon made him a prominent actor in all important matters of legislation. He was on several important committees, among which were those of Finance and Education. Through his exertions mainly, the State became an interested party in the State Normal University, and this noble monument of the growing interest of the people in the cause of education placed upon a sure and solid foundation. To Col. Harris belongs the honor of having introduced the first bill for founding an Agricultural College, standing at first almost alone in its support. Afterwards he had the satisfaction of seeing this measure adopted by the State, and to the agricultural portions of the community secured the invaluable aid which such an institution must in time afford. The journal of the House will show that he never occupied the time of the House with long speeches, but on the stump and before the people gave free and full expression to his opinions upon public affairs. In the House he appeared as the representative of the people, legislating for the good of all, and not as the partizan seeking alone party ends. This is evidenced from the fact that, although politically the majority of the House was against him, he never introduced a bill that failed to pass. Few men can show such brilliant success as a legislator, or such a record of usefulness in one legislative session.

When events in their rapid succession showed

COL. HARRIS.

that Southern traitors were determined to rule or ruin the glorious government under whose fostering care they had been reared, educated and honored, Col. Harris rallied immediately beneath the flag of the Union, and recognizing the truth of the declaration of the patriot Douglas, that there could be but two parties in the country during the war,—patriots and traitors,—gave to the Government his hearty and unqualified support, encouraging enlistments, denouncing the authors of the rebellion, cheering with words of comfort and material aid those who for a time must be left without a protector, he gave his whole soul to the cause of his country. As soon as the complicated affairs of his extensive business could be arranged, and he obtained a release from his legislative duties, he drew the sword in the cause, and gathered around him the young men of the central portion of the State. He became identified with the scheme of organizing the "Kentucky Brigade," an order for which had been issued by the War Department, but through neglect seemed about to fail. Through his exertions, assisted by Col. McCarty, of Douglas county, the State was enabled to put four fine regiments in the field, at a time when recruiting was most difficult.

Commissioned Colonel of the first regiment filled, he immediately reported at Cairo, where he remained but a short time, from thence being ordered with his command to Columbus, Ky. Although suffering from a severe disease, caused by over-exertion,—being confined for days to his bed during the organization of his regiment,—he assumed command of this important post. His regiment was here assigned the laborious task of throwing up new works, opening magazines, and turning the old bastion, over which the enemy's guns had dealt their terrible showers of projectiles upon our forces, on the bloody field of Belmont, and threatened our iron-clad fleet, so as to command the river below. While these fortifications are evidences of the earnestness and determination with which the rebels are carrying on the war, they tell no loss of patience and patriotism of the brave men who labored so uncomplainingly through the long hot months of spring and summer at this tame and aggravating employment, while their brothers in arms were winning laurels upon the battle-fields of Tennessee and Arkansas.

Failing rapidly in strength, repeatedly warned of the danger he was in, in remaining at his post, it was only when confined to his bed that Col. Harris could be induced to accept a leave of absence from his command, and seek in a more congenial climate, where he could secure the advice of eminent medical talent, that health which was denied him on the banks of the Mississippi. After an absence of several weeks, he returned to his regiment, with his health partially restored, and at once took command and pushed forward the work on the bluffs.

The Tennessee river becoming dangerous for the transportation of military supplies, the government repaired and opened to travel the Mobile and Ohio Railroad, as far south as Corinth, the northern terminus being at Columbus. To Col. Harris was entrusted the task of repairing bridges, erecting block-houses, and guarding the road as far south as the Big Obion river, in Tennessee. Several fine block-houses have been erected, and although his camps rarely pass a night without an alarm, the travel upon this section of the road has been uninterrupted.

The Colonel makes his headquarters at Union City, Tenn., from whence he is continually sending out scouting expeditions to disperse and destroy the rebel bands who are continually ravaging the country between the railroad and the Hatchie river. Overtaking one of these parties, numbering full 400, in a recent expedition, at Merryweather's ferry, on the Obion, the Colonel, with 42 men from Co. C, 2d Illinois Cavalry, completely routed them, killing 38, and taking 13 prisoners, and between 40 and 50 horses, with a loss of two officers, Lieuts. Terry and Goodheart, and one private on our side. This skirmish completely cleared the country between the Mississippi and Obion rivers, which had long been infested by rebel bands, who have driven the Union citizens from their homes, and destroyed their property. The Colonel is now in the prime of life, and has regained his lost health. In the saddle almost continually for days at a time, Illinois has not in the field an officer more devoted to his country, or more energetic in maintaining the integrity of its flag.

Col. Harris is entirely a self-made man, and pursues with untiring energy whatever he undertakes. Always taking an active interest in all that concerns the welfare of society or the State, he has long made it a rule of his life to distribute one-third of his not annual earnings for the benefit of public improvements and private charities.

COL. OSBORN.

THOMAS O. OSBORN, Colonel of the 39th Regiment Illinois Volunteers, was born August 11th, 1832, in Jersey, Licking county, Ohio. After preparatory studies in the schools of his native town, he entered the Ohio University, where he graduated with honor in 1854. After leaving college, he commenced the study of law with Lewis Wallace (now Major General Wallace) at Crawfordsville, Ind. On being admitted to practice, he removed to Chicago in the fall of 1857.

At the very commencement of the present rebellion, when the first gun fired at Fort Sumpter sent a thrill through the hearts of the nation, he was among the foremost in the proffer of his services to Government; and, throwing aside business, he devoted his time and means to the organization of a regiment, which was soon accomplished and offered to the Secretary of War, but its acceptance was delayed until July, and was not mustered into the service of the U. S. until Aug. 5th, 1861.

The regiment remained in camp at Chicago until October 13th, when it was sent to Benton barracks, St. Louis, Mo. It was then sent to Williamsport, Md., to form a portion of Ward Lamon's brigade. It was here that a vacancy occurred in the colonelcy, and Col. Osborn, who was then filling the position of Lieut. Col., with honor to himself and the regiment, was promoted to fill it.

After his accession to this office, he evinced that commendable zeal in study and in the welfare of his men, together with that patriotism and valor which has not only made him the true and efficient officer that he has proved himself, but which has insured the respect, confidence and love of his whole command.

At the time Jackson made his first raid into Morgan county, Va., Colonel Osborn, with his command, was stationed at Alpine station, with a force not exceeding 800 effective men, with a section of battery, to guard the Baltimore and Ohio Railroad between Alpine and Great Cacapon. Jackson, at the time, had a force numerically estimated at 15,000, with 30 pieces of artillery. This whole force he succeeded in keeping at bay for the space of twenty-four hours, and then made good his retreat across the Potomac river, under fire of the enemy, with the loss of one man drowned and fourteen taken prisoners. His conduct while stationed along this line of road was such as to call forth from the late Gen. Lander the warmest praise and confidence, and he was at once entrusted with the charge of constructing and defending the road to Martinsburg.

At the battle of Winchester, April 23, 1862, his regiment occupied a position on the left wing, being ordered with two companies of the 8th Ohio to support a section of battery, and were for several hours exposed to a galling fire. After lying upon their arms during the night succeeding the battle, they took the lead at daybreak in the pursuit of the enemy, which was maintained until reaching Strasburg.

Col. Osborn has participated in every move that has been made in the Valley under Gen. Shields—crossing the Massanutten mountain, his command for a time was engaged in protecting the bridges over the Shenandoah river —then, with the division, they performed the march to Fredericksburg, and to take a forced march back again to the support of General Banks.

During the seven days' fight before Richmond, two brigades of Shields' division were ordered to join McClellan. Col. Osborn was then in command of one of these; they reached Harrison's Landing in time to perform efficient service during the retreat from Malvern Hill. He is now stationed with his regiment at Fortress Monroe, Virginia.

COL. OSBORN.

GEN. TURCHIN.

JOHN B. TURCHIN was born in the valley of the Don, near the Black Sea, Jan. 18th, 1822. At fourteen years of age he was put into the Military School at St. Petersburg, and went through the thorough course required by the great academy, and was made a Lieutenant in the Russian army, where he remained until he was promoted to a Captaincy, when, being selected as one of the *"Etat" Major* Staff, he was again sent to the School, where, during three years' study, he perfected himself in all branches of the military art—Cavalry, Infantry, Artillery and Engineering. He graduated with honor, and on the opening of the Crimean war with England and France, was made the First Assistant of the Chief of the Grand Duke—the present Emperor—a position corresponding in our service to the First Assistant Adjutant General to a Commander of Division—in which he did good service. The plan of defence of the coast of Finland was prepared by him, and cordially adopted by the highest military authority of the empire. After the war, having imbibed Democratic notions, and being thoroughly disgusted thereby with the Russian government and the tyranny of the army, he obtained a year's furlough for the purpose of visiting Germany. When there he determined to make his way to America, and accordingly came to this country in 1856. Soon after his arrival he was employed in the Engineer Department of the Illinois Central R. R. Co., where he won the esteem and admiration of all who had occasion to become acquainted with his extensive acquirements.

In July, 1861, he was appointed by Gov. Yates to the Colonelcy of the 19th Regiment, and at once took command and proceeded to Palmyra, Mo. Since that time Col. Turchin has been constantly with his regiment in Missouri and Kentucky, and recently in Alabama, where he took an active part in the capture of Huntsville, Tuscumbia and Decatur. Out of the long list of Brigadier Generals, whose nominations were not acted upon by the Senate two days before the close of the Session in July, 1862, exceptions were made of two names, which were confirmed. One of these was John B. Turchin, as skillful and

brave a soldier as Illinois has sent into the field—a General who believes in making war as war should be made. To this peculiarity and to the persecution which he endured from others who lacked his faith, his promotion is chiefly due.

Early in July, Gen. (then Col.) Turchin was court-martialed on the following charges, preferred against him by C. C. Gilbert, Capt. 1st Infantry, acting Inspector General:

Charge 1st.—Neglect of duty.
Charge 2d.—Conduct unbecoming an officer and gentleman.
Charge 3d.—Disobedience of orders.

The specifications in the first charge set forth minutely each act committed by the soldiery—pillaging houses, plundering stores, forcing trunks, iron safes and wardrobes, destroying thousands of dollars in notes of hand, burning goods, carrying off silver plate and jewelry, watches and money, and last of all, committing an indecent outrage on the persons of two servant girls. The second charge specifies that Col. Turchin was cognizant of these outrages, and failed to enforce his authority to prevent them, and also contracted debts and refused to liquidate them. The third and last charge embraces in its specification that the Colonel disobeyed a special order from headquarters in allowing the village to be plundered. To the charges and specifications Col. Turchin, with one exception, entered the plea of "not guilty."

The members of the court, which convened at Huntsville, Ala., were Brig. Gen. Garfield, Ohio, commanding the 20th brigade, president; Col. (now General) Ammen, 24th Ohio, and commanding the 10th brigade; Col. Beaty, 3d Ohio; Col. Jones, 42d Indiana; Col. Sedgwick, 2d Kentucky; Col. Pope, 15th Kentucky; Col. Mundy, 23d Kentucky. Capt. Swayne, U. S. Infantry, was attached to the court as Judge Advocate.

The witnesses brought to sustain the charges were parties suspected of disloyalty, and Col. Turchin, who bore himself with the most commendable dignity, in cross-examining them, merely asked the one question: "Are you a loyal man?" which question was disallowed by the Judge Advocate.

Col. Turchin addressed the court, detailing his operations while in command—all of which resulted successfully for the cause of the Union, and none of which were outside the strict line of military duty. He had brought to bear his military knowledge acquired in European campaigns, and, owing to the ignorance of our soldiers, had taken upon himself the duties of subordinates, that his plans might not fail.

"I was charged," said he, "with taking and keeping at my quarters a mulatto boy named Joe, belonging to Mr. Vasser, a resident of Athens. I proved by the witness, that, having used him in scouting expeditions, and for obtaining valuable information about the enemy, I gave him, in accordance with the orders of Gen. Mitchell, protection inside of our lines. Gen. Mitchell's policy with regard to negroes (sanctioned, probably, by higher authority), consisted in using them for military purposes, and giving them protection for valuable services. I consider this eminently proper. If we had war with England, and sent an expedition to attack that country, we would land our forces in Ireland, because we know that the people of Ireland hate their oppressors—the English—and would readily join us. For a similar reason Garibaldi, before he moved on Naples, invaded Sicily. We invade the southern States, where, with few exceptions, the white population is against us, and from them we can get no information concerning the enemy. In our hearts we know that our only friends here are negroes; but, imbued with prejudice, we are ashamed manfully to acknowledge it. As a matter of necessity, we use negroes for our purposes—they communicating with us readily about their masters, and about the movements of the enemy; and, after thus putting them in a position hostile to the mass of the white population of the South, we basely and meanly surrender them to their enemies.

"Our policy vacillates. One General gives them a temporary protection, promising them freedom; another, superseding the first, drives them out of the lines, leaving them to the mercy of their owners, who, looking upon them as their mortal enemies, hang them the first convenient opportunity. When I retreated from Tuscumbia, I heard, and I have conclusive reasons to believe it true, that there were four or five negroes hung on the following day, because they had given us some valuable information. Humanity, for permitting this great wrong, cries out against it."

The Colonel then enumerated the numerous advantages derived by the rebels from their slaves, and the many important uses which our army might make of them—among others, forming them into regiments, drilled, armed and equipped, to guard the country over which we have passed, and keep open communication with our rear.

He complained that the testimony of disloyal men should be placed on record to blast the fair fame of himself and his troops, and continued his address as follows:

"I have everywhere in Missouri, in Kentucky, in Tennessee, and in Alabama, been hated by secessionists, and I consider it my best recommendation as a loyal officer; but I defy any one to find a single Union man, who has been in connection with me, that will make a complaint against me.

"The more lenient we are with secessionists, the more insolent they become; and if we do not prosecute this war with vigor, using all the means that we can bring to bear against the enemy, including the emancipation of slaves, the ruin of this country is inevitable.

"The problem before us is grand. Universal freedom is at stake; and I feel humiliated when I think that this hitherto considered great and generous people may show the world their incapacity to master the present difficulties, and enjoy the blessings of self-government."

Then, turning to the members of the court, and speaking as if he were a teacher addressing his pupils, instead of an accused man pleading before his judges, he thus concluded:

"I have pointed out some defects in our army organization, and proposed some improvements therein, and if the members of this court will notice those points, and will present them to the higher authorities for consideration, I will feel happy in thinking that this court-martial may not have been held altogether in vain."

This conclusion, in its severe simplicity, I cannot but regard as beautiful. The last thought of the gallant soldier, instead of taking the form of a passionate peroration to move the judges in his favor, is directed to the good of the service, and the benefit of his adopted country. He was found guilty by the court, but its decision was annulled by his appointment as a Brigadier General after the court had been organized.

On his arrival in Chicago, on the evening of August 10th, he was received with a splendid ovation, at Bryan Hall, on which occasion he made the following brief and manly address:

Fellow Citizens of Chicago:—When I left this city with my regiment, I never expected to receive such a reception as this. *I have simp-*

ly done my duty; that's all I have done. (Enthusiastic applause). I did my duty as a soldier, and I trust as an American citizen also. (Applause). Although I am not versed in politics, I made my mind up that the cause of this rebellion was slavery, and I acted upon the principle that the cause should be removed. (Long continued applause). At the same time, I know also that the same men who were relying upon the power of slavery must not be handled with soft gloves, but a little roughly, and so I handled them a little roughly. (Applause). I don't know whether to call it a happy or an unhappy result that my superior officer did not approve of it, and thought differently. He thought that I must be court-martialed and dismissed from the service. (Groans and hisses for Don Carlos Buell, and cries "You shall go back, General.") My wife informs me that she has a commission, making me a Brigadier General, in her pocket, but I haven't got it, and haven't seen it. (Applause, and three cheers for Madame Turchin). As much as I rejoice to see this kind, and I may say great reception, it would be more pleasant to have my poor boys of the 19th with me—now strung along that railroad. (Cries, "Shame, shame.") They are punished for me, and as you sympathize with me, I want you to sympathize with them. There are five regiments at Huntsville: the 1st Wisconsin at Morris, another at Athens, another at Pulaski, and several at Columbia, all upon or contiguous to this line of railroad. It would seem as if there might be sent from each of these one or two companies to guard this road. They would not feel it. But, no! Our boys are posted in squads of fifteen or twenty for eighty miles. It is low minded; it is contemptible. I cannot but feel the greatest contempt for a man, who, at the head of a powerful army, will behave thus towards soldiers. I do not care for myself, but it is a shame to punish my men.

I have studied secession and secessionists in Missouri, Kentucky, Tennessee and Alabama, and I tell you it is of no use to fight against them unless we use every means in our power. They are too powerful to be fought otherwise. Who are these guerrillas? They are citizens who pretend to be peaceful, but who are plotting treason all the time. They are all the time looking out for a straggling Yankee. As soon as he finds one, he gets two neighbors; they take their shot guns, go out and catch him. They look out for pickets, and shoot them. You know how they murdered Gen. McCook. That is what I call a war of extermination. We must do the same; and until we use all men, slaves included, we cannot put them down. (Applause).

What I have done is not much; but what I could do, were I allowed, might amount to something. My friends, I must close. We have been talking about the Union a great while. Let us now talk and hurrah for conquest. (Applause).

The General closed amidst long continued cheering, which was twice and thrice renewed as the commission was exhibited to the audience, appointing Col. Turchin a Brigadier General, and setting aside the verdict of the court-martial.

The General was married in 1852, and his wife, also a native of Russia, accompanied him throughout all his campaigns in Missouri, Kentucky and Alabama, as she did during the war of the Crimea, with the utmost fortitude, enduring all the hardships incident to a soldier's life. To ride on horseback forty or fifty miles per day was to her a mere matter of amusement; and in the march of the 19th Illinois from Winchester to Bellefonte, she took command of the vanguard, and gave most vigorous and valuable directions for driving off and punishing the infamous bushwhackers who infested the road. These and similar things had so much excited the admiration of Gen. Turchin's men, that they would have followed his gallant wife into the field of battle with all the enthusiasm that fired the hearts of the French when gathered around the standard of the Maid of Orleans.

COL. CUSHMAN.

WILLIAM H. W. CUSHMAN was born at Free-town, Mass., May 13, 1813. He is a lineal descendant, of the eighth generation, of Robert Cushman, one of the Pilgrim Colonists who left England to escape the exactions of the Established Church, and to secure entire "freedom to worship God." His father, Hon. Hercules Cushman, was a lawyer, and a man of respectability, who graduated at Dartmouth College, from which he received the degree of A.M. He represented the town of Middleton in the Legislature of Massachusetts in the years 1811 and 1812, and Freetown in the years 1817 and 1819. In 1827 and 1828 he was a member of the Governor's Council of Massachusetts, for British county, and was a Colonel in the militia for six years, from 1822 to 1827 inclusive. His mother was the daughter of Gen. Abdiel Washburn, of Plymouth county, Mass. At the age of eleven he was sent to the American Literary, Scientific and Military Academy, at Norwich, Vt., then under the charge of Capt. Alden Partridge, the founder of that institution. He remained there some two years, made good progress in his studies, and received an honorable discharge.

In speaking of his early education, in a letter written a few years since to a friend, he remarks: "My father had a notion to make a man of me, and kept me at school all the time from ten to sixteen years of age, when my health failed, and from necessity I was obliged to disappoint him. If I had been kept at home till my mind was more mature, and had not been overburdened till disgusted with books, perhaps his plans would have been successful, though I have my doubts." His father undoubtedly designed to give him a collegiate education, and have him follow the legal profession.

Being of an active temperament, he commenced the mercantile business at Middleton, in the year 1831, at the age of eighteen, and did a very good and extensive business. In 1832, he was commissioned by Gov. Lincoln, of Massachusetts, Adjutant in the 4th Regiment, 5th Division, of the Massachusetts Militia, and received his discharge 21st February, 1834. He removed to Ottawa, La Salle coun-

ty, Ill., in October of the same year, and continued the business of merchandizing. He has now resided in Ottawa about twenty-eight years, and has become one of the "Old Settlers" of the wealthy and populous county of La Salle. During the whole time he has been extensively and profitably engaged in trade and as manufacturer and banker, and is now among the most wealthy men in Northern Illinois.

In 1842, the completion of the Illinois and Michigan Canal was considered of much importance in his section of the State, and as he had a peculiar faculty of arranging and successfully carrying out financial operations, he was elected to the House of Representatives of the State, for the term of two years, and in 1844 was again elected by his constituents to the same office. The result of his labors in the Legislature shows that the people were wise in their choice.

He was a candidate of the Democratic party in 1856 for the State Senate, but the district being largely Republican, he was defeated, though his vote exceeded the vote of his party, owing to his personal popularity. In the Presidential contest of 1860, he was one of the electors at large on the Democratic ticket, and was earnest and efficient in his advocacy of the claims of Mr. Douglas. He has filled several important county offices, particularly those of a financial character, and has always been faithful to his trusts.

It seems that his early military education has not been forgotten, but has been turned to good account. On the 24th day of June, 1847, he was commissioned by Gov. French, "Captain of the Ottawa Cavalry, 14th Odd Battalion," which office he held until September, 1861, when he was appointed by Gov. Yates to the command, as Colonel, of the 53d Regiment Illinois Volunteers.

The chief qualities of his mind, which have led to his remarkable success in life, are activity, integrity and good judgment. "*Omnia vincit labor*" is his maxim, and most faithfully has he adhered to it. The result in his case is very obvious, and may be easily stated. He has much wealth, many and ardent friends, and a most excellent reputation. The perfect

COL. CUSHMAN.

integrity and uprightness of his life have given him the entire confidence of the community in which he resides. During the period of his residence in Illinois, and with a widely extended business, he has seldom had any difficulty or controversies which he could not harmonize to the satisfaction of all. He avoids lawsuits as he would the plague, and seldom finds it necessary to resort to courts of justice to adjust his business matters with others. As a financial manager he has acquired a high reputation in the State of his adoption, and has by his talents and ability greatly aided in the business enterprises of the community. One great source of his pecuniary prosperity may be found in the fact that he has never entered into speculations, but has attended strictly to a regular, legitimate business. While he has thus been blessed in his "granary and his store," he has not forgotten those less fortunate than himself. He has always been ready to assist those who are willing to help themselves, and none who deserve success have applied to him for aid in vain. He is a liberal and cheerful giver, and benevolent and christian enterprises have always found in him a friend.

In his political principles, he is (as most of his family relations are) an "old-fashioned Jefferson Democrat," and yet he is tolerant and liberal in his feelings and conduct towards those who differ with him in political questions.

Aside from the distinguished features of his character alluded to, his love of country is an abiding principle which animates and controls his public conduct. Differing as he does in political sentiments with the present Administration, he was prepared from the moment the signal gun of the rebellion was fired, to devote himself to the service of his country, and yielding to its call, he took command of his regiment, and with it is now in the field. With him party considerations were forgotten when he saw his country in danger of being overthrown by its enemies.

As soon as his regiment was organized, he was ordered to Camp Douglas, where he was stationed until April, 1862, and then directed to repair to the field of active operations in Tennessee. Arriving there late, he did not participate in the battle of Shiloh, but since then he and his command have been continually on duty—sharing the hardships and perils of the campaign, under Generals Halleck and Grant, in the heart of the enemy's country.

From the character of the man, as developed in a long and successful life, it cannot be doubted that he will justify the confidence reposed in him by the country, and when an opportunity is presented, will distinguish himself as an able and courageous military leader. The only drawback to such expectations is found in the fact that for some years his health has been impaired, and may not be found equal to the exposures of camp life and the labors of his position. In person, Col. Cushman is thin and spare, of medium height, very erect, with deep set black eyes, and regular features. To a stranger, he wears an air of reserve, but to his friends he is genial and even playful in his temper. His friendships are of an enduring character, and when once formed, it is no ordinary event that will disturb them. He has been married three times. His present wife is the daughter of Hon. Cæsar Rodney, of the State of Delaware.

The limits of this sketch permit but a brief glance at the leading characteristics of Col. Cushman. Were a more detailed narrative allowable, it might be shown that he possesses in a remarkable degree those traits which distinguish the New England Puritan race to which he belongs, and which have made their impress upon the institutions of the country.

COL. POST.

Col. P. SIDNEY POST, of the 59th Regiment Illinois Volunteers, was born in the village of Florida, Orange county, N. Y., in 1833. He graduated at Union College, Schenectady, N. Y., in 1855, and immediately entered the law school at Poughkeepsie. While at the law school, his father, Gen. Peter Schuyler Post (a soldier of 1812) removed with his family to Galesburg, Ill., to which place Col. Post followed when admitted to the bar.

In the spring of 1857, he took up his residence in Wyandotte, Kansas, and commenced the practice of law, with marked success. Feeling the power which a newspaper exerts in a new and rapidly-advancing country, he purchased a printing office, and established the Wyandotte *Argus*, of which he finally assumed editorial control. He continued his double profession of lawyer and editor, and for a time holding the position of Probate Judge, until summoned to Illinois by the dangerous and fatal illness of his father, in the spring of 1861.

When the storm of war at last broke upon the country, he entered the service of the United States as 2d Lieutenant of a company raised in Knox county. The Government refused at that time to receive any more troops from Illinois, and this company was mustered into the 9th Regiment Missouri Volunteers, and afterwards changed, by order of the War Department, to the 59th Regiment Illinois Volunteers, the soldiers all being citizens of this State.

When the regiment was organized, J. C. Kelton, Assistant Adjutant General of the Department of the Mississippi, was appointed Colonel, and Col. Post, Adjutant. In January, 1862, the Majorship became vacant, and the Adjutant was made Major, and immediately took command of the regiment, on the midwinter march across Missouri, to join Gen. Curtis at Lebanon. He was with the army of the Southwest during the series of exciting and rapid marches which culminated in fighting the bloody battle of Pea Ridge. During the hottest of the engagement, Maj. Post was shot through the shoulder, but persistently refused to leave the field until utterly helpless from loss of blood. When the news of the battle of Pea Ridge reached Col. Kelton, who had been detached on Gen. Halleck's staff, he refused longer to retain his position, and resigned in favor of Col. Post, who was recommended by the officers of the regiment.

During eight months' active service in the field, Col. Post had not been off duty a single day, until disabled by wounds received in battle, and had won the Colonelcy with the concurrence of the officers of the regiment, though one of the youngest among them.

As soon as recovered sufficiently to be able to ride, he rejoined his regiment, then on its way to the expected scene of conflict, Corinth, Miss., and was assigned to the command of a brigade, which he marched into the entrenchments in front of that place, four days before its evacuation.

As an officer, Col. Post is of a dashing and energetic character. He is one of the youngest Colonels in the service, but owes his position solely to his merit as a brave and skillful officer, tried in the active duties of the field, and his officers and men alike have the utmost confidence in, and are thoroughly devoted to him. There is, perhaps, no other instance in this or any other war, of a man rising from the position of an officer of the lowest grade, to the command of a brigade, in the short space of ten months. Col. Post undoubtedly owes his rapid promotion as much to his personal qualities as a man of ability and honor, as to his well-known skill as a tactician and his gallantry in the field.

COL. HALL.

Col. CYRUS HALL was born in Fayette county, Illinois, August 29, 1822. His parents emigrated from Christian county, Kentucky, in 1819. His father dying in December, 1836, at the age of only fourteen he was left to manage his mother's business affairs, and did so successfully several years. In May, 1846, at the breaking out of the Mexican war, he volunteered in a company raised by Capt. Ferris Forman, at Vandalia, Ill. The regiment rendezvoused at Alton, Ill., and elected Capt. Ferris Forman, Colonel. It was designated as the 3d Regiment Illinois Volunteers. Mr. Hall was urged to accept the Captaincy of the company, but being inexperienced in military matters, declined doing so. He was chosen Orderly Sergeant, and served as such three months, when he was elected First Lieutenant, to fill the vacancy occasioned by the resignation of James T. B. Stappe, in his company, A. In this capacity he served through the campaign, or up to Jalappa, where the term of service for which the regiment enlisted being so near ending, Gen. Scott ordered the 3d back to New Orleans, to be mustered out of the United States service. Lieut. Hall was in two engagements—at the memorable battle of Cerro Gordo and the taking of Vera Cruz. He shared in the gallant charge led by the lamented Col. Baker, of the 4th Illinois Infantry. In a communication to the author, Lieut. Hall thus describes the capture of Vera Cruz:

"But the most magnificent sight that I ever beheld, was the bombardment of Vera Cruz by the American forces. From the time our army first landed until the surrender of the city, heavy details were constantly at work placing 64-pounders in position in the sand hills upon our line of investment. We would cut a niche in the sand hills, place three of those huge guns in position during the night, and at early dawn the brush would be cleared away; and the battery, being well manned from the men-of-war, would open out in magnificent style. But the most sublime spectacle was to watch the flight of the huge shells, thrown after night, from our batteries, and from the men-of-war outside the harbor, at the devoted city. Like fiery comets sent on errands of destruction, they coursed their angry way, shrieking and hissing through the air; and woe to the domicile, church or palace where their fiery course ended!"

Lieut. Hall was married in 1848, and settled upon the farm purchased by him before the war occurred, where he remained for seven years, engaged in farming and dealing in stock. His health then failing, he removed to Shelbyville, Ill., where he opened and conducted a hotel until the downfall of Fort Sumter, when he proceeded to raise a company of volunteers for the war. April 22d, he reported a full company, and was ordered to rendezvous at Jacksonville, on May 11th, by Gov. Yates. The regiment was organized under the Ten Regiment Bill, Hon. John M. Palmer elected Colonel, and was designated as the 14th Regiment Illinois Volunteers.

When the opportunity was presented to the 14th Regiment to enlist for three years, at the appointed hour, Capt. Hall, with one hundred and one men, marched up to Col. Palmer's headquarters, ready to take upon themselves the usual obligation, which elicited the following remark from Col. Palmer: "Capt. Hall, old Shelby has reason to be proud of your company!"

The regiment was ordered into Missouri, July 5th, and was detailed for service at several points on the Hannibal and St. Jo. and the North Missouri Railroads. August 13, they removed to Jefferson Barracks, and the next day were ordered to Rolla, on the southwest branch of the Pacific Railroad, to support Gen. Sigel, who was falling back upon that place, after the memorable battle at Wilson's Creek.

Capt. Hall served with his company (B) until Sept. 1st. Returning to his family at Shelbyville, he received the appointment of First Major in the 7th Regiment Illinois Cavalry, Col. Wm. Pitt Kellogg. Taking great interest in the reputation of the regiment, he applied himself very closely to the tactics, until Feb. 1st, when he was appointed Colonel of the 14th Regiment Illinois Volunteers—Col. Palmer having been promoted to a Brigadier Generalship. Col. Hall assumed command on board the steamer Continental, on the way to Fort Donelson, reaching that place fifteen hours after the surrender. Previous to his appointment, he was *chosen* Colonel by the officers and men of the regiment. At Fort

Donelson he was assigned to the 2d Brigade, Gen. Veatch, of Gen. Hurlbut's (4th) Division, where he still remains. At the battle of Shiloh, Col. Hall marched out his regiment, containing considerable less than six hundred men, of whom *two* hundred were killed and wounded—mostly on the first day of the battle, Sunday, April 6th. Of the closing scene of Monday's operations, Gen. Veatch, in his official report, says:

"Col. Hall, of the 14th Illinois, with his regiment, led that gallant charge, on Monday evening, which drove the enemy beyond our lines, and closed the struggle on that memorable day. In the heat of battle, he exhibited the skill and firmness of a veteran."

Col. Hall has furnished the author with the following brief account of the part taken by the 14th in the battle of Shiloh:

"Long will the 14th Regiment Illinois Volunteers remember the position so long and ably held by them upon the Corinth road! Here the solid columns of the rebel centre were thrust upon our lines with great fury, aided by a large artillery force. Notwithstanding the overwhelming force of the enemy, our position was held until our right and left was completely turned by the heavy columns of the rebels, and we were forced to fall back to prevent being entirely cut off. Here our gallant old flag received a large share of its forty-one bullet holes, and Color-Sergeant Fletcher Ebey was killed while nobly carrying the same. One other noble fellow—Wm. W. Standage, private of Co. I—was seriously injured about four o'clock that eventful day, while bearing the colors—having seized them when Ebey fell. Four o'clock found us much oppressed in spirits, and hard pressed by a superior force, but we had a line composed of the 4th (Gen. Hurlbut's) Division, which was never broken by the enemy. These were the men who, if necessary, would 'die in the last ditch.' Long, loud and ably did the heavy siege guns upon our left, aided by the gunboats and a few batteries, deal death and terror to the rebels, and soon after dark the enemy drew off, fell back, and bivouacked for the night—much to our joy and consolation.

"On Monday we were held in reserve until afternoon, not far from two o'clock, when we were ordered forward; came up lively through an old field, then across a skirt of woods to another field, where we came from column into line; were then ordered to cross the field and charge the enemy, which was in sight in the open woods beyond, composed of cavalry and infantry. The charge was made across the field on double-quick, the men yelling at the top of their voices. As soon as we were sufficiently near, the men were ordered to fire and advance. The enemy gave us a hearty welcome from a heavy battery upon the right, and from their small arms upon our left and front. Never did men behave more like veterans. After the rebels were entirely routed, we were ordered to halt and cease following them, which order was very reluctantly obeyed. We were placed, by the above gallant charge, in the possession of the last of the camps captured the day before. A singular coincidence occurred: The same field witnessed our review by Generals Grant and Hurlbut, our first disastrous stand in the morning, our subsequent retreat, and our final glorious charge and triumph on the second day, April 7th."

Col. Hall participated in the perilous approach to Corinth, in the two marches to Holly Springs from La Grange, and from La Grange to Memphis, where he still stands at the head of the old "Pious Fourteenth." He hesitates, however, to vouch for the *soubriquet* "Pious," since the long series of marches and hardships which his "boys" have undergone. But if severe fighting and cleaning out of rebels is "*practical* piety," he thinks his men possess that to an eminent degree.

COL. KELLOGG.

GEN. WHITE.

Brigadier General JULIUS WHITE, son of Lemuel and Emily White, was born at Cazenovia, Madison county, N. Y., Sept. 29th, 1816. He removed to Illinois in 1836, and has resided in Illinois, Missouri and Wisconsin since that time. He was a member of the Wisconsin Legislature in 1849, and was engaged in commercial pursuits and as an insurance agent up to the time the war broke out. Mr. White was appointed Collector of Customs at Chicago in the spring of 1861. He raised a regiment of infantry (the 37th Illinois, formerly known as the Fremont Rifle Regiment), and resigned the Collectorship upon being appointed to the command of the regiment, in Sept., 1861. He commanded the regiment during Fremont's expedition to Southwestern Missouri, in the fall of 1861, and was placed in command of a brigade, and marched with General Curtis into Arkansas in the ensuing winter. He was present at the battle of Pea Ridge, fought on the 6th, 7th and 8th days of March, 1862, and was promoted to the rank of Brigadier General for gallant conduct in that severely contested battle, to rank from June 9th, 1862. In accordance with orders, he proceeded to Washington early in July, after a brief visit to his family in Chicago, and joined his brigade, which forms a part of the army of Virginia.

Of the engagement at Martinsburg, in which the rebels were repulsed with considerable loss, Gen. White made the following report to Maj. Gen. Wool, dated Martinsburg, Va., Sept. 7, 1862:

"I have the honor to report that the enemy, consisting of 400 cavalry, who attacked my outposts, have been defeated, with the loss of about fifty prisoners, horses and arms, now in our possession. Our loss was two killed and ten wounded, including Capt. Grosvenor and Lieut. Logan, of the 12th Illinois cavalry. The loss of the enemy greatly exceeds our own, but is not accurately known."

On the 15th September, at the capture of Harper's Ferry, Va., by the enemy, commanded by Jackson, Gen. White, who had just joined our forces there with his command, was taken prisoner, and acting Brigadier Gen. Miles was killed.

COL. KELLOGG.

WM. PITT KELLOGG, Colonel 7th Regiment Illinois Cavalry, was born in Montpelier, Vermont, Dec. 8th, 1831, and removed to Illinois in 1848. He attended, for two years, the Norwich Military University in Vermont, under Gen. Truman B. Ransom, father of Col. Ransom of the 11th Regiment Illinois Volunteers. After which, he read law with Hon. E. G. Johnson of Peoria, and commenced practice in Fulton county, Illinois, in 1855. The year following, Mr. Kellogg was a candidate for the State Legislature, but by a coalition between the Democrats and Americans, he was defeated by a small majority, although he ran some two hundred votes ahead of his ticket. In 1860 he was chosen Republican Elector, and was appointed by Mr. Lincoln, in March, 1861, Chief Justice of Nebraska. In Sept. of the same year, Gov. Yates offered him a commission as Col. of the 7th Regt. Illinois Cavalry, when Mr. Kellogg obtained leave of absence from the Territory, and entered the service. He was present at the taking of New Madrid, where his regiment captured four guns from the enemy. Col. Kellogg accompanied Gen. Pope's army up the Tennessee river, and took part in the capture of Corinth. In July, 1862, the Col. left his regiment temporarily in order to hold court at Omaha, N. T., at the usual time, but will soon again join the 7th, now stationed at Tuscumbia, Ala.

COL. DICKEY.

THEOPHILUS LYLE DICKEY is a son of the Rev. John Dickey, of Kentucky, a clergyman of the Presbyterian Church, and one of the pioneers of the church militant in the regions along the Ohio river, in the early settlement of the country.

He was born in Paris, Kentucky, November 12th, 1812. Being of an ingenuous nature, and at the same time discriminating mind, as well as trained by a man of the eminent apostolical and puritanic character of his distinguished father, he early imbibed towards the institution of domestic slavery sentiments of the deepest abhorrence. These were based mainly upon his personal observations of the treatment slaves received, and the influence of the system upon the character of the whole people.

An incident related by him, as occurring in his presence, while yet a youth, passing over the country in Kentucky, in company with his most excellent father, made a deep impression upon his mind. A copple of slaves—men, women and children—were passing, all fastened to a rope, on their way to a southern market, some singing, some crying, all influenced by the sweet strains of a band of music, under the leadership and presidency of a driver, with his whip-lashes and insignia of authority. Whereupon, the Rev. John Dickey, his father, having first straightened up his tall and majestic form, and boiling over with fervent indignation at the sight, awaited the coming of the leader. Immediately upon him this successor of the Apostles poured forth an irresistible strain of invective, such as the sight inspired, characterizing the business as it deserved, and warning the actors of the vengeance of God they were laying in store for themselves against the time to come.

Still, Judge Dickey, by the death of a maternal relative, himself, about the period of his arriving at lawful age, became a slaveholder by inheritance, owning about a dozen of the descendants of Africa. About the same time, he was married, and on looking to the serious affairs of life, his first act was to liberate all his slaves, and he formed the purpose of removing to a free State, resolved that the sacrifice of the character and destinies of his family, which he considered a necessary consequence of settlement in a slave State, and reliance for living on unrequited labor, too great to be endured, too costly to be purchased.

Thus, he struck for freedom, in 1835, and removed to Illinois, and settled in Macomb, McDonough county, where he studied law with Cyrus Walker, and the year following.was admitted to the bar. In 1837, Mr. Dickey removed to Rushville, Ill., where he remained until 1839, when he again removed and settled in Ottawa, his present residence. In 1846, he enlisted, and was elected Captain of a company in Col. Hardin's regiment, but soon after reaching Mexico, on account of ill health, was compelled to resign. In June, 1848, he was elected Judge of the Circuit Court, Ninth District, which position he resigned in 1852. After this date, he practised law in Chicago, the firm being Dickey, Mather & Taft. In the summer of 1861, he received authority from the Governor of Illinois to raise a regiment, and in October he proceeded to Springfield with his regiment, the 4th Illinois Cavalry. At Fort Donelson, Col. Dickey rendered most efficient service, in preventing the escape of a rebel column, and also distinguished himself at the battle of Shiloh. He is now Chief of Cavalry on Maj. Gen. Grant's Staff.

COL. BRACKETT.

ALBERT G. BRACKETT, Colonel of the 9th Regiment Illinois Cavalry, was born in Cherry Valley, Otsego county, New York, on the 14th day of February, 1829. In the autumn of 1846, he removed to Indiana, and the next spring he volunteered as a soldier in the Mexican war. He was chosen 2d Lieutenant of an Indiana regiment, and shortly after, 1st Lieutenant, in which capacity he continued until the close of the war, displaying, on different occasions, the greatest bravery. He was in the battle of Huamantla, at the siege of Puebla, and at the bombardment of Atlixco. His regiment was attached to Gen. Lane's command, and served through the campaign with great credit. At the close of the war, Lieut. Brackett prepared a volume entitled "A History of Lane's Brigade in Mexico," embodying his own personal observations.

On the 3d of March, 1855, he was appointed Captain in the 2d Regiment of U. S. Cavalry, and after having recruited a company of regulars at Rock Island, Illinois, was ordered to Texas, where he continued to serve against the Camanche and Apache Indians until the breaking out of the rebellion. During his stay in that region and on the frontier, he saw much active service. He had command of several important posts, and had frequent fights with the Camanches, whom he eventually conquered and brought to terms. Not only had Capt. Brackett to guard the country against Indian depredations, but he had frequently to repel the incursions of Cortenas and other Mexican bandits, who were accustomed to scour the country far and near, carrying off all that they could obtain, and hesitating not to commit murder if necessary to their success. The records of the department show amply his success on the frontier, in defending the country from the Indians and the Mexicans, and he had the honor of receiving the particular commendation and thanks of Gen. Scott for his conduct. He made his escape from Texas after the traitor, General Twiggs, had surrendered his whole command to the rebels, and after a great deal of difficulty, made his way to Florida, thence to Cuba, and from there to New York.

His company having been refitted at Carlisle Barracks, Pennsylvania, marched to Washington, and crossed the Potomac into Virginia with the first troops. At the battle of Blackburn's Ford, which took place on the Friday preceding the battle of Bull Run, Brackett's company of cavalry took an important part. They were exposed to the hottest of the enemy's fire, and not only served as cavalry, but assisted the artillery forces in bringing up their guns, and indeed were everywhere and anywhere that their services were needed. Capt. Brackett, during the fight, seeing one of the New York regiments leaving the field in disorder for want of officers competent to direct them, placed himself at their head, rallied them by word and example, and succeeded in taking them back to face the enemy.

At the battle of Bull Run, July 21, 1861, his cavalry was General McDowell's escort through the whole day, and were constantly exposed to the enemy's fire. In the disastrous flight, they covered the retreat, and by vigorous and intelligible action, did much to restore order and confidence in the host of men abandoned by their own appointed officers. No officer of his rank did more to retrieve the fortunes of the day than Capt. Brackett. His conduct received the approbation of his commanding officer.

In the fall and winter of 1861-2, he raised a splendid cavalry regiment (9th Regiment Illinois Cavalry) in the vicinity of Chicago, and in February, 1862, marched to Missouri, and thence to Arkansas, forming part of Steele's brigade of Gen. Curtis' army. On the 12th of June, 1862, he met and defeated a large rebel force at the Waddell Farm, Jackson county, Arkansas, and saved a valuable train belonging to the Government. Again, on the 27th of June, he attacked a superior force of the enemy at Stewart's Plantation, Jackson co., Ark., and fought them until dark, when the enemy retired, and next day sent in a flag of truce to obtain permission to bury their dead. The Illinois troops went into the engagement with "nerves of steel and hearts of oak," and displayed the greatest gallantry. In this action Col. Brackett was severely wounded, and is still (Sept. 16th) suffering from its effects. He is now stationed with his regiment at Helena, Arkansas. Col. Brackett has lately been promoted Major of Cavalry in the regular service, which certainly possesses no braver or more gallant officer, or one to whom the lines of the poet could be more properly applied:

"In war, was never lion raged more fierce;
In peace, was never gentle lamb more mild."

COL. STARRING.

FREDERICK A. STARRING, Colonel of the 72d Illinois Volunteers (1st Chicago Board of Trade Regiment), was born in Buffalo, N. Y., May 24, 1834. From his earliest childhood he evinced a strong love for the profession of arms. He received a military education, and fitted himself for the profession of civil engineering, after having spent three years of his boyhood as a sailor before the mast. In 1852, he went to Chicago, and was employed by the Illinois Central R. R. Co. in different departments until 1856.

In 1857, he proceeded to the south, and was absent most of the time until the breaking out of the rebellion, at which date he was Secretary of a railroad in Arkansas. Liberal offers were made to him to enter the southern army; but, leaving everything, he came from there early in May, 1861, in disguise, hunted and branded as a renegade and traitor to the south, sacrificing everything he possessed, with a price on his head—("a liberal reward for his scalp.") After many difficulties, he reached Louisville, and returned again to Ill., and tendered, June 1st, 1861, to the President a regiment, the skeleton organization of which was formed and framed by the lamented Col. E. E. Ellsworth, between whom and Col. Starring the warmest intimate personal friendship and confidence existed.

The regiment was not then received by the Government, and the companies went into different organizations already accepted. Col. Starring went to the Potomac, and remained until after the disastrous battle at Bull Run. He returned to Illinois, and was commissioned Major of the 46th Illinois Regt., and served in that regiment from Sept., 1861, to January, 1862, and was then transferred to the 2d Ill. Light Artillery, when that regiment was formed, as Major of the regiment. Col. S. was at Island No. 10, during the long bombardment; was stationed at Columbus, Ky., and was Chief of the Artillery, district of the Mississippi, at the time of his promotion to the command of the 1st Chicago Board of Trade Regiment, in August, 1862. This regiment, one of the best that Illinois has sent into the field, left Chicago en route for Kentucky, August 30th, and is now (Sept. 18th) stationed at Paducah, the post at that place being in command of Col. Starring. For versatile and technical knowledge of military tactics, the Col. of the 72d, although so young a soldier, has probably no superior among our volunteer officers.

GEN. HUNTER.

GEN. HUNTER.

Major General DAVID HUNTER was born in Washington, District of Columbia, July 26, 1802. His father, who was a Chaplain in the army, was a native of Virginia, of the family of Hunters of Winchester. He graduated at West Point in 1822, the twenty-fifth in rank in a class numbering forty, and was appointed 2d Lieutenant in the Infantry, his commission dating from July 1, 1822. He took command of Fort Dearborn, Chicago, Illinois, December 14, 1830, which he retained until May 20, 1831. During this period he was married to Miss Maria I. Kinzie, daughter of John Kinzie, the first permanent inhabitant of the city of Chicago, who settled there in 1804, the year following the erection of Fort Dearborn. Having risen to a 1st Lieutenancy, he was, in 1832, made a Captain of Dragoons, and twice crossed the Plains to the Rocky Mountains, on one of which long, perilous and fatiguing journeys he was accompanied by Mrs. Hunter, who has been the almost constant companion of her husband in all of his campaign life. In 1836, he resigned and entered into the forwarding business at Chicago, forming a copartnership with his brother-in-law, John H. Kinzie. In 1842, he rejoined the army as a Paymaster, in which position, with the rank of Major, the present administration found him. He accompanied the President from Springfield, en route for Washington, as far as Buffalo, N. Y., where, owing to the extraordinary pressure of the crowd, he suffered a dislocation of the collar-bone. May 14, 1861, he was appointed Col. of the 6th Regiment U. S. Cavalry, and at the disastrous battle of Bull Run, July 21st, 1861, commanded the main column of McDowell's army, and was severely wounded in the neck. August 13, 1861, he was made Major General of Volunteers, and superseded Maj. Gen. Fremont in the Department of Missouri, Nov. 2d, 1861. In assuming command, Gen. Hunter repudiated Fremont's agreement with Price in Missouri, and in his report to headquarters, assigned as his reasons that it would render the enforcement of martial law impossible, give absolute liberty to the propagandists of treason, and practically annul the confiscation act. Gen. Hunter afterwards had command

6

of the Department of Kansas, with his headquarters at Fort Leavenworth. While in command of this Department, he received the following complimentary dispatch from Gen. Halleck, dated St. Louis, February 19, 1862: "To you, more than any other man out of this Department, are we indebted for our success at Fort Donelson. In my strait for troops to reinforce Gen. Grant, I applied to you. You responded nobly, placing your forces at my disposal. This enabled me to win the victory. Accept my most heartfelt thanks."

In March, 1862, he was ordered to South Carolina, assuming command of the Department of the South, consisting of the States of South Carolina, Georgia and Florida, and establishing his headquarters at Hilton Head, Port Royal, S. C. On the 11th of the month following, Fort Pulaski surrendered to the forces under his command. May 9, 1862, Gen. Hunter issued a proclamation, declaring the slaves of all the rebels in his Department free, which was annulled by the President on the 19th of the same month. June 16th, a portion of the troops under Gen. Hunter's command met with a severe repulse at the battle of James Island, near Charleston, Brig. Gen. Benham having, in direct violation of Gen. Hunter's orders, made an attack upon the enemy. Having organized negro regiments in his Department, which was also done by another Federal officer, the following order was issued by the rebel authorities:

WAR DEPARTMENT,
ADJUTANT AND INSPECTOR GENERAL'S OFFICE,
RICHMOND, Aug. 21, 1862.
General Orders, No. 60.]

1. *Whereas*, Major General Hunter, recently in command of the enemy's forces on the coast of South Carolina, and Brigadier General Phelps, a military commander of the enemy in the State of Louisiana, have organized negro slaves for military service against their masters, citizens of this Confederacy:

And whereas, The Government of the United States has refused to answer an inquiry whether said conduct of its officers meets its sanction, and has thus left to this government no other means of repressing said crimes and outrages than by the adoption of such measures of retaliation as shall serve to prevent their repetition;

Ordered, That Major General Hunter and Brigadier General Phelps be no longer held and treated as public enemies of the Confederate States, but as outlaws; and that in the event of the capture of either of them, or that of any other commissioned officer employed in drilling, organizing, or instructing slaves, with a view to their armed service in this war, he shall not be regarded as a prisoner of war, but held in close confinement for execution as a felon, at such time and place as the President may order.

By order,   S. COOPER,
          Adjutant and Inspector General.

He remained in that Department until early in September, when, by order of the Commander-in-Chief, he proceeded to Washington, giving up the command of the Department of South Carolina to Gen. O. M. Mitchell. While there, he wrote the following letter to the Rev. Stephen H. Tyng, D.D., President of the National Freedman's Association of New York, dated Hilton Head, S. C., July 17, 1862. As Gen. Hunter is by education and choice a soldier, what he says in regard to the subject of slavery at this time has a weight and authority to which the opinions of few men are entitled.

SIR: I have the honor to acknowledge the receipt of your communication, dated June 2, 1862, expressing to me the approval of my course in regard to the freed slaves of this Department by the important and benevolent association of which you are President.

Satisfied of having attempted, in the absence of instructions, to do my duty in the matter according to the best lights of my judgment and a long experience, every assurance of sympathy from men whose characters I esteem is gratifying, and enables me to wait with more patience for those inevitable days which are to give a policy on the slavery question to our Government.

It is my only fear that the lesson may not be understood and acted upon until read in characters of blood at the fireside of every Northern family. To attain wisdom we must suffer; but that wisdom on the slavery question must finally be obtained, is my sustaining faith.

Our people are not dull of comprehension in regard to matters about which free play is given to their common sense. When a fire is spreading through a block of houses, they do not hesitate to batter down an intermediate house to save the remainder of the block. When the plague occupies an infected district, the district is quarantined, and every resource of science and industry put forth to rid the locality of its presence. The soldiers of health are by no means ordered to mount guard over each smitten house and see that the vested interests of pestilence are protected. "Break open doors, if they be not opened," is the

order on these occasions. "Let in fresh air and sunlight; let purity replace corruption."

But in presence of one great evil, which has so long brooded over our country, the intelligence of a large portion of our people would seem paralyzed and helpless. Their moral nerves lie torpid under its benumbing shadow. Its breath has been the pestilence of the political atmosphere in which our statesmen have been nurtured; and never, I fear, until its beak is dripping with the best blood of the country, and its talons tangled in her vitals, will the free masses of the loyal States be fully aroused to the necessity of abating the abomination at whatever cost and by whatever agencies.

This is written, not politically, but according to my profession in the military sense. Looking forward, there looms up a possibility (only too possible) of a peace which shall be nothing but an armistice, with every advantage secured to the Rebellion. Nothing can give us permanent peace but a successful prosecution of the war, with every weapon and energy at our command, to its logical and legitimate conclusion. The fomenting cause of the Rebellion must be abated; the axe must be laid to the root of the upas tree which has rained down such bitter fruit upon our country, before anything like a permanent peace can be justly hoped.

Already I see signs in many influential quarters, heretofore opposed to my views in favor of arming the blacks, of a change of sentiment. Our recent disasters before Richmond have served to illuminate many minds.

To speak of using the negroes merely for throwing up entrenchments, is a step in the right direction, though far short of what must be the end. It has the advantage, however, of making the further and final steps necessary; for men working in face of the enemy must have arms with which to protect themselves if suddenly attacked.

On the whole, there is much reason to be satisfied with the progress made by public sentiment, considering how deeply-rooted were the prejudices to be overcome, the general failure of the nation to realize at first the proportions of the war, and the impunity still extended to those Northern traitors who are the plunderers of the Government by means of fraudulent army and navy contracts, on the one hand, while using every energy of tongue and pen to excite discontent with our Government and sympathy with the more candid and courageous traitors of the South who are in arms against us.

In conclusion, it may not be inappropriate to say that in transmitting the approval of the National Freedman's Relief Association of my course, you were—doubtless, unconsciously—indorsing views which your own earnest eloquence had no slight share in maturing. Though without the pleasure of your personal acquaintance, I was, during a

GEN. McCLERNAND.

year, a member of your congregation, and take this opportunity of gratefully acknowledging my indebtedness to your teachings.

Your letter would have been earlier answered, had not pressing duties too fully occupied my time.

Believe me, Sir, very truly, your obliged and obedient servant, D. HUNTER.

P. S —None of the carefully fostered delusions by which slavery has sustained itself at the North, is more absurd than the bugbear of "a general migration of negroes to the North," as a necessary sequence of emancipation. So far is this from being the fact, that although it is well known that I give passes North to all negroes asking them, not more than a dozen have applied to me for such passes since my arrival here, their local attachments being apparently much stronger than with the white race. My experience leads me to believe that the exact reverse of the received opinion on this subject would form the rule, and that nearly if not quite all the negroes of the North would migrate South whenever they shall be at liberty to do so without fear of the auction-block.

Sincerely, D. H.

By Special Orders No. 286, a commission, over which Maj. Gen. Hunter presides, assembled at Washington, Sept. 25th, 1862, for the trial of such cases as might be brought before it. The investigation into the conduct of the officers against whom Gen. Pope brought charges, the surrender of Harper's Ferry, and other matters connected with the late battles in Maryland, are expected to come before the court.

GEN. McCLERNAND.

Major General JOHN ALEXANDER McCLERNAND was born in Breckinridge county, Ky., May 30th, 1812. Upon the death of his father, in 1816, his mother removed to Shawneetown, Illinois, where he acquired his education in the village school. When not attending school, he worked on a farm. In 1827, he commenced the study of the law, and was admitted to the bar in 1830. The same year he volunteered in the war against the Sac and Fox Indians, serving in the ranks as a private until the war was closed by the battle of Bad Axe. Ill health rendered it necessary, after his return home, that he should defer professional practice until his health should be restored by more active life. Accordingly, for two years, during 1833-4, he traded upon the Ohio and Mississippi rivers. With the pecuniary means thus acquired, he was better enabled to engage successfully in his profession.

In 1835, he established the first Democratic press that ever existed in Shawneetown. The paper published, of which he was the editor, was called the *Democrat*. In the same year he opened an office in Shawneetown, and commenced the practice of law in the several courts of the judicial circuit. He continued to practice his profession with success until his election to Congress, in 1843. In the meantime, he formed a partnership with Albert G. Caldwell, a gentleman who had finished his studies in Mr. McClernand's office.

His political principles are inflexibly those of a Democrat. "Born one of the people," he says, "he continues one of the people." The late General Ewing, formerly Senator in Congress from Illinois, when referring to him upon an exciting political question, said, "McClernand we can count upon; he is always for the Democracy and his friends."

In 1836, he was elected to the State Legislature from the county of Gallatin. He was then twenty-four years of age. Politics ran high. Gen. Jackson's administration was violently opposed. The Whigs expected to overthrow it, and with it, the ascendancy of the Democratic party. In this crisis, Governor Duncan, who had been repeatedly elected to Congress as a Democrat and political friend of Gen. Jackson, made a violent attack upon him, in his message to the Legislature of 1836. He denounced him or the abuse of executive patronage; for wasteful and increased expenditures; for vetoing the bill to recharter the United States Bank; for the removal of the deposits, and for other alleged delinquencies.

The friends of the Governor, at home and abroad, predicted that he would be able to revolutionize the politics of the State. The contest became fierce, and the excitement intense.

In this state of things, a legislative committee was raised to investigate the charges preferred by the Governor against the President. Mr. McClernand, in behalf of the committee, prepared and presented a report, which thoroughly discussed all the mooted political topics of the day, and defended and vindicated the administration of the President. It is known that the State was finally saved to the Democratic party.

During the same session of 1836-7, a system of internal improvements was adopted. Mr. McClernand had been elected, and, after his election, had been formally instructed by his constituents to support such a system. No alternative, therefore, was allowed him, but to violate instructions, or vote for the system if he retained his seat. Accordingly, he voted for the system, and advocated, in a speech, the general policy of public improvements by the States. He has subsequently stated, in the councils of the State, that he regretted the *necessity* for the part he took upon this question more than anything which had occurred in connection with his political career. Referring to this subject at a subsequent period, he thus expresses himself:

"If we look to the circumstances of the time, we shall find a satisfactory solution of the matter. Railroads and canals were the *mania* of the time. Banks had multiplied; paper money had become never so plenty; speculation had inflamed the public mind, and become rife throughout Europe and America. Causes of imperious and world-wide operation were driving nations and individuals, heedless and infatuated, upon the treacherous rocks of speculation. The extravagance committed by Illinois, was committed, in greater or less degree, by almost every State in the Union, and by thousands of individuals. Her failure, therefore, was not an exception, but a misfortune in which individuals and nations equally shared. The convulsion and the calamity were general; their causes originated in the great and mysterious law which appoints to human affairs the periodical fluctuations which are typified in the diurnal fluctuations of the sea."

During the same session of 1836-7, a controversy arose respecting the Illinois and Michigan Canal, which had well-nigh defeated that great and popular work. Mr. McClernand was an efficient and bold advocate of what is known as the "deep-cut plan," which, with some amendments, was finally adopted. After the controversy had been adjusted, the offices of commissioner and treasurer of the canal were tendered to him, and he was elected unanimously, we believe, by the Legislature.

In 1837, he entered upon the duties of this twofold office. In the spring of 1839, the State found herself without adequate means to carry on the work, and Mr. McClernand, deeming it useless to continue his connection with it, resigned the office. His faithful administration of his responsible trust upon the canal was responded to by complimentary resolutions adopted at public meetings.

In 1840, Mr. McClernand was elected a second time to the Legislature from the county of Gallatin. A large majority of Democrats were returned to both branches. The most exciting question of the session was the passage of the new Judiciary Bill. The Supreme Court had given great offence to the people of the State, not only on account of its decision on the *quo warranto*, but especially with reference to the right of aliens to vote under the Constitution of the State. The Legislature went to work to reform the judiciary, and this was done. In the debate upon the bill having this last-mentioned object in view, Mr. McClernand, on the authority of a highly respectable gentleman, made a statement imputing improper conduct to the Supreme Court in regard to a cause involving the exercise of the elective franchise, to which Theophilus W. Smith, of the Judges of the Supreme Court, took exception. The consequence was a challenge from Judge Smith, which was promptly accepted by Mr. McClernand, who immediately repaired to the place of meeting. But the Judge failed to do so, and the hostile meeting never took place.

In December, 1840, Mr. McClernand, Adam W. Snyder, then former representative in Congress, and afterward Democratic nominee for Governor, whose election was only prevented by his death, James H. Ralston, Isaac P. Walker and John W. Eldridge, were nominated by a State Convention for electors to support Martin Van Buren and Richard M. Johnson, Democratic candidates for President and Vice-President. The Whig ticket for electors,

Harrison and John Iarshall, Edwin B. ow President of the ter and Buckner S. s no ordinary one. ggle, protracted for State which might, decide the election. of about four thou- ind Johnson in that iajority in the whole . hundred.

id was a third time and the year follow- 'the Legislature, was) the twenty-eighth s seat, he married Sa-), of Jacksonville, Ill. s, he soon won the friends. His first he bill to remit the :kson by Judge Hall, i which he had cher- for that illustrious session of the same ard, as a member of .ands, a comprehen- t, accompanied by a ii diu the completion in Canal. In 1814, ;e of the usual time, ire, another election igress came on, and ected without oppo- . third time elected, isition in 1848 and i 1852 he was not is, but headed the :et. In 1854, Mr. Jacksonville, and in cticing law at both of the Committee on :ratic State Conven- ially repudiated Le- :d Senator Douglas. l for Congress in the iirved until the break- he resigned his seat, with Col. (now Brig. ind Col. P. B. Fouke, s, raised the McCler- iident appointed him .y 17, 1861, and he

immediately proceeded to Cairo, where he se- cured, during his administration of military affairs there, the respect and good-will of all under his command. He accompanied Gen. Grant to Belmont with his brigade, and in the engagement he displayed great military ca- pacity. The day after the battle, Gen. Mc- Clernand issued the following General Order (No. 15) to his gallant troops:

BRIGADE HEADQUARTERS, CAMP CAIRO, November 8, 1861.

The General commanding the First Brigade of Illinois Volunteers takes pleasure in meeting to-day those who conferred honor upon his command by their gallantry and good conduct on yesterday. Few of you had before seen a battle. You were but imperfectly disciplined, and supplied with inferior arms. Yet you marched upon a concealed enemy, of superior numbers, on ground of their own choosing.

You drove them steadily before you for two miles of continued fighting, and forced them to seek shelter in their entrenchments at Belmont, beneath the heavy batteries at Columbus. You drove them from their position, and destroyed their camp—bringing with you, on retiring, two hundred prisoners, two field-pieces, and a large amount of other property.

Reinforced from Columbus, they formed in large numbers in your rear, to cut you off, while the heavy guns were playing upon your ranks. Fighting the same ground over again, you drove them a second time. A portion of the com- mand, becoming separated from the rest, made a successful and well ordered movement by another route, and returned to the river. After a day of fatiguing marches, fighting as you marched, having been nearly six hours actually engaged, you re-embarked and returned to your camps.

On looking along your ranks to-day, the com- manding General has cause to mourn the ab- sence of many of his gallant men—the victims of inexorable war. Some laid down their lives on the battle-field, offering their blood freely, and giving their last and most glorious mo- ments to their country. Others bear honorable wounds, and suffer more than those who died, yet it is hoped they will resume their duties and win new honors.

While mourning the dead and offering sym- pathy to the suffering, the General commanding gratefully acknowledges his gratitude, and of- fers the thanks of a grateful country and State to the officers and soldiers of Illinois under his command, for their gallantry and good conduct.

When again called upon, he hopes to find you equally prompt, and better prepared for battle and for victory. By order of

JOHN A. McCLERNAND, Brigadier General Commanding.

Gen. McClernand was present at the capture of Fort Henry and also at Fort Donelson, where, with his noble division, composed exclusively of Illinois troops, he acted a prominent part in its capture. A Massachusetts writer penned the following lines on hearing of the glorious victory:

McClernand's division, composed of Oglesby's, Wallace's and McArthur's brigades, suffered terribly. They were composed of the Eighth, Ninth, Eleventh, Eighteenth, Twentieth, Twenty-ninth, Thirtieth, Thirty-first, Forty-fifth, Forty-eighth and Forty-ninth Illinois regiments.
The Eighth, Eighteenth, Twentieth and Twenty-first Illinois regiments occupied a position above the Fort. The four Illinois regiments held their ground full three hours. Nearly one-third had been killed and wounded. Yet the balance stood firm.

> O gales that dash th' Atlantic's swell
> Along our rocky shores!
> Whose thunders diapason well
> New England's glad hurrahs—
>
> Bear to the prairies of the West
> The echoes of our joy,
> The prayer that springs in every breast:
> "God bless thee—Illinois!"
>
> Oh! awful hours, when grape and shell
> Tore through th' unflinching line;

> "Stand firm, remove the men who fell,
> Close up and wait the sign."
>
> It came at last, "Now lads, the steel!"
> The rushing hosts deploy:
> "Charge, boys!"—the broken traitors reel—
> Huzza for Illinois!
>
> In vain thy rampart, Donelson,
> The living torrent bars;
> It leaps the wall, the fort is won,
> Up go the Stripes and Stars.
>
> Thy proudest mother's eyelids fill,
> As dares her gallant boy,
> And Plymouth Rock and Bunker Hill
> Yearn to thee—Illinois.

For gallantry displayed at the taking of Ft. Donelson, he was made a Major General, March 21, 1862. On the hotly-contested field of Shiloh, Gen. McClernand was present, and rendered valuable service in both day's battles. He was constantly in the field with his division from that date until September, when he was ordered to Springfield to assist Gov. Yates in organizing the new volunteer regiments raised under the President's calls for 600,000 men.

GEN. POPE.

Major General JOHN POPE was born in Kaskaskia, Illinois, March 12th, 1823. His father was the well known Judge Nathaniel Pope, of Virginia, who removed to Kentucky some time before the birth of his son, and afterwards settled in Illinois. He was a delegate to Congress from Illinois before its organization as a State, in 1828, and was afterwards appointed District Judge. His son was appointed a cadet in the West Point Military Academy, from Illinois, in 1838, having received a thoroughly good preliminary education, and acquitted himself so well at the Academy as to form one of the distinguished graduating class in 1842, and was commissioned a brevet Second Lieutenant in the corps of Topographical Engineers on the 1st of July of the same year. In the Mexican war, Lieut. Pope was attached to the army under Gen. Taylor. At the battle of Monterey he won his First Lieutenancy, the new commission bearing date Sept. 23, 1846; and for gallantry at Buena Vista was brevetted a Captain, his commission bearing date February 23, 1847.

In 1849, he conducted the Minnesota Exploring Expedition; having accomplished which, he was entrusted with the conduct of an expedition sent out by the Government to test the feasibility of boring artesian wells in the celebrated Staked Plain, stretching between Texas and New Mexico, for some hundreds of miles in length, and about seventy-five in width, and partially in the territory of each. The region takes its Spanish name from the fact that owing to its aridity and barrenness, the Indians were compelled to stake out tracks to enable them to cross it with rapidity and certainty. Not a drop of water is found throughout its extent, and yet, as it lies directly on the best overland mail routes between the eastern and western slopes of the Union, it was of the greatest importance that it should be made traversable. With a view to do this, the artesian well enterprise

GEN. POPE.

was undertaken by Capt. Pope, whose efforts and adventures on the desert form an interesting page in the annals of western exploration. In 1853 he was assigned to the command of one of the expeditions to survey the route of the Pacific Railroad. From 1854 until 1859, he was engaged in exploring the Rocky Mountains, during which period (July 1st, 1856) he took the actual rank of Captain in the Topographical Engineering corps, having previously been Captain by brevet. During the political campaign of 1860, he sympathized with the Republicans, and in an address on the subject of fortifications, read before the Literary Society of Cincinnati, he satirized the policy of President Buchanan in unsparing terms. He was court-martialed by Buchanan shortly afterwards, but upon the recommendation of Mr. Holt, Postmaster General, the matter was dropped. He was still a Captain in the Engineer corps when the rebellion of 1861 broke out, and was one of the officers detailed by the War Department to escort President Lincoln to Washington.

When the President called for four hundred thousand volunteers, Capt. Pope was named as a Brigadier General, receiving his commission May 17, 1861, and appointed to a command in Missouri. He stands ninth on the list of Brigadiers, those who precede him being Heintzelman, Keyes, Andrew Porter, Franklin, W. T. Sherman, Stone, Buell, and T. W. Sherman. Gen. Pope's operations in Northern Missouri, protecting railway communication and driving out guerilla parties, were attended with great success. The most important engagement with which he was then connected, was that which occurred at Blackwater, where, by the co-operation of Gen. J. C. Davis, a large number of rebel prisoners were taken, and their army routed. Gen. Halleck entrusted him with the command of the army of the Mississippi, destined to co-operate with Flag Officer Foote's flotilla. At the head of a well appointed army, General Pope left Commerce, Mo., marched on New Madrid, captured that place, and acted in concert with Com. Foote in driving the rebels from Island No. 10 into a well conceived trap, where about five thousand of them were taken prisoners by Gen. Pope's army.

When General Halleck assumed command of the army on the Upper Tennessee, in April, 1862, he arrested General Pope's course down the Mississippi, when he was about to commence the attack on Fort Pillow. With his army he proceeded, in obedience to orders, to Pittsburgh Landing, and was assigned a position on the extreme left of Halleck's army. Here he had command of one of the three grand divisions into which the Union force was divided, and by a brilliant piece of strategy succeeded in capturing a large number of rebel prisoners at Corinth. After the evacuation of Corinth, Gen. Pope pursued the enemy, under command of Gen. Beauregard, down the Mobile railroad, capturing many prisoners and munitions of war. He was engaged in this duty when summoned by the War Department to Washington, and assigned to the command of the troops in the Shenandoah Valley, consisting of three divisions, Fremont's, Banks' and McDowell's, June 26, 1862. On assuming command, General Pope issued the following address:

WASHINGTON, Monday, July 14, 1862.

To the Officers and Soldiers of the Army of Virginia:

By special assignment of the President of the United States, I have assumed command of this army.

I have spent two weeks in learning your whereabouts, your condition, and your wants; in preparing for your active operations, and in placing you in positions from which you can act promptly and to the purpose.

I have come to you from the West, where we have always seen the backs of our enemies—from an army whose business it has been to seek the adversary, and to beat him when found—whose policy has been *attack,* and not *defense.*

In but one instance has the enemy been able to place our Western armies in a defensive attitude.

I presume I have been called here to pursue the same system, and to lead you against the enemy. It is my purpose to do so, and that speedily.

I am sure you long for an opportunity to win the distinction you are capable of achieving; that opportunity I shall endeavor to give you.

Meantime, I desire you to dismiss from your minds certain phrases which I am sorry to find much in vogue among you.

I hear constantly of taking strong positions and holding them—of lines of retreat—and of bases of supplies. Let us discard such ideas.

The strongest position the soldier should desire to occupy, is one from which he can most easily advance against the enemy.

Let us study the probable lines of retreat of our opponents, and leave our own to take care of themselves.

Let us look before us, and not behind.

Success and glory are in the advance.

Disaster and shame lurk in the rear.

Let us act on this understanding, and it is safe to predict that your banners shall be inscribed with many a glorious deed, and that your names will be dear to your countrymen forever.

JOHN POPE,
Major Gen. Commanding.

On the 29th of July, Gen. Pope placed himself at the head of the army, by whom he was received with the utmost enthusiasm, and established his headquarters at Warrenton. Of the battle of Cedar Mountain, August 9th, the first engagement which occurred with the enemy after Gen. Pope assumed command of the army of Virginia, we have the following official account from the General commanding:

HEADQUARTERS ARMY OF VIRGINIA, } Cedar Mountain, Aug. 13, 1862, 5 p. m. }
To Maj. Gen. Halleck, General-in-Chief:

On Thursday morning, the enemy crossed the Rapidan at Barnett's Ford, in heavy force, and advanced strong on the road to Culpepper and Madison Court House. I had established my whole force on the turnpike between Culpepper and Sperryville, ready to concentrate at either place as soon as the enemy's plans were developed.

Early on Friday it became apparent that the move on Madison Court House was merely a feint to detain the army corps of Gen. Sigel at Sperryville, and that the main attack of the enemy would be at Culpepper, to which place I had thrown forward part of Banks' and McDowell's corps. Brig. Gen. Bayard, with part of the rear of McDowell's corps, who was in the advance near the Rapidan, fell slowly back, delaying and embarrassing the enemy's advance as far as possible, and capturing some of his men.

The forces of Banks and Sigel, and one of the divisions of McDowell's corps, were rapidly concentrated at Culpepper during Friday, and Friday night Banks' corps being pushed forward five miles south of Culpepper, with Rickett's division of McDowell's corps three miles in his rear.

The corps of Gen. Sigel, which had marched all night, was halted in Culpepper, to rest for a few hours.

On Saturday the enemy advanced rapidly to Cedar Mountain, the sides of which they occupied in heavy force.

Gen. Banks was instructed to take up his position on the ground occupied by Crawford's Brigade, of his command, which had been thrown out the day previous to observe the enemy's movements. He was directed not to advance beyond that point, and, if attacked by the enemy, to defend his position, and send back timely notice.

It was my desire to have time to give the corps of Gen. Sigel all the rest possible after their forced march, and to bring forward all the forces at my disposal.

The artillery of the enemy was opened early in the afternoon, but he made no advance until nearly 5 o'clock, at which time a few skirmishers were thrown forward on each side, under cover of the heavy wood in which his force was concealed.

The enemy pushed forward a strong force in the rear of his skirmishers, and Gen. Banks advanced to the attack.

The engagement did not fairly open until after six o'clock, and for an hour and a half was furious and unceasing.

Throughout the cannonading, which at first was desultory and directed mainly against the cavalry, I had continued to receive reports from Gen. Banks that no attack was apprehended, and that no considerable infantry force of the enemy had come forward.

Yet, toward evening, the increase in the artillery firing having satisfied me an engagement might be at hand, though the lateness of the hour rendered it unlikely, I ordered Gen. McDowell to advance Ricketts' division to support Gen. Banks, and directed Gen. Sigel to bring his men upon the ground as soon as possible.

I arrived personally on the field at seven P. M., and found the action raging furiously. The infantry fire was incessant and severe.

I found Gen. Banks holding the position he took up early in the morning. His losses were heavy.

Ricketts' division was immediately pushed forward, and occupied the right of Gen. Banks, the brigades of Crawford and Gordon being directed to change their position from the right and mass themselves in the centre.

Before this change could be effected it was quite dark, though the artillery fire continued at short range without intermission.

The artillery fire at night by the 2d and 5th Maine batteries in Ricketts' division of Gen. McDowell's corps, was most destructive, as was readily observable the next morning in the dead men and horses, and broken gun-carriages of the enemy's batteries which had been advanced against it.

Our troops rested on their arms during the night in line of battle, the heavy shelling being kept up on both sides until midnight.

At daylight the next morning the enemy fell back two miles from our front, and still higher up the mountain.

Our pickets at once advanced and occupied the ground.

The fatigue of the troops from long marches and excessive heat made it impossible for either side to resume the action on Sunday. The men were, therefore, allowed to rest and recruit the whole day, our only active operation being of cavalry on the enemy's flank and rear.

Monday was spent in burying the dead and in getting off the wounded.

The slaughter was severe on both sides, most of the fighting being hand to hand.

The dead bodies of both armies were found mingled together in masses over the whole ground of the conflict.

The burying of the dead was not completed until dark on Monday, the heat being so terrible that severe work was not possible.

On Monday night the enemy fled from the field, leaving many of his dead unburied and his wounded on the ground and along the road to Orange Court House, as will be seen from Gen. Buford's dispatch.

A cavalry and artillery force under Gen. Buford was immediately thrown forward in pursuit, and followed the enemy to the Rapidan, over which he passed with his rear guard by ten o'clock in the morning.

The behavior of Gen. Banks' corps during the action was very fine. No greater daring and gallantry could be exhibited by any troops. I cannot speak too highly of the coolness and intrepidity of Gen. Banks himself during the whole of the engagement. He was in the front, and exposed as much as any man in his command. His example was of the greatest benefit to his troops, and he merits and should receive the commendation of his Government.

Generals Williams, Augur, Gordon, Crawford, Prince, Green and Geary, behaved with conspicuous gallantry.

Augur and Geary were severely wounded, and Prince, by losing his way in the dark, while passing from one flank to another, fell into the hands of the enemy.

I desire publicly to express my appreciation of the prompt and skillful manner in which Generals McDowell and Sigel brought forward their respective commands, and established them on the field, and of their cheerful and hearty co-operation with me from beginning to end.

Brig. Gen. Roberts, chief of cavalry of this army, was with the advance of our forces on Friday and Saturday, and was conspicuous for his gallantry and for the valuable aid rendered to Gens. Banks and Crawford.

Our loss was about 1500 killed, wounded and missing, of whom 290 were taken prisoners. As might be expected, from the character of the engagement, a very large proportion of these were killed.

The enemy's loss in killed, wounded and prisoners, we are now satisfied, is much in excess of our own.

A full list of casualties will be transmitted as soon as possible, together with a detailed report, in which I shall endeavor to do justice to all.

On Sept. 3d, Gen. Pope made an official report, of which the following is an abstract, detailing his operations, extending over a period of seventeen days, prior to his being relieved at his own request of the command of the army of Virginia:

I have the honor to submit the following brief sketch of the operations of the army, since the 9th of August:

I moved from Sperryville, Little Washington and Warrenton, with the corps of Banks and Sigel, and one division of McDowell's corps, numbering in all 30,000 men, to meet the enemy, who had crossed the Rapidan, and was advancing upon Culpepper. The movement towards Gordonsville had completely succeeded in drawing off a large force from Richmond, and in relieving the army of the Potomac from much of the dangers which threatened its withdrawal from the peninsula.

The action of August 6th, at Cedar Mountain, with the forces under Jackson, which compelled his retreat across the Rapidan, made necessary still further reinforcements of the enemy from Richmond, and by this time, it being apparent that the army of the Potomac was evacuating the peninsula, the whole force of the enemy around Richmond was pushed forward with great rapidity to crush the army of Virginia before the forces evacuating the peninsula could be united with it.

I remained at Cedar Mountain, and still threatened to cross the Rapidan, until the 17th of August, at which time Gen. Robert Lee had assembled in our front, and within eight miles, nearly the whole of the rebel army. As soon as I ascertained this fact, and knew that the army of the Potomac was no longer in danger, I drew back my whole force across the Rappahannock, on the night of the 17th and day of the 18th, without loss of any kind, and one day in advance of Gen. Lee's proposed movements against me.

The enemy immediately appeared in my front at Rappahannock Station, to pass the river at that bridge and the numerous fords above and below, but without success. The line of the Upper Rappahannock, which I had been ordered to hold, that the enemy might be delayed long enough in his advance upon Washington, to enable the forces from the peninsula to land and effect a junction with me, was very weak, as it crossed at almost any point above the railroad bridge, by good fords. By constant vigilance and activity, and much severe fighting for three days, the enemy were gradually forced around from the railroad crossing to Waterloo bridge, west of Warrenton.

Meantime my force had been much reduced by loss in battle, and by fatigue and exposure, so that although I had been joined by a detachment under General Reno, and the other division of McDowell's corps, my force barely numbered 40,000 men. On the 22d a heavy rain fell, which rendered the fords of the river impassable for twenty-four hours. As soon as I discovered this, I concentrated my forces and marched rapidly upon Sulphur Springs and Waterloo bridge, to drive back the forces of the enemy which had succeeded in crossing at these points. This was successfully accomplished, and the bridges destroyed. I passed one day, or rather part of one, at Warrenton and beyond.

The enemy still continued to move slowly around, along the river, masking every ford with artillery and heavy forces of infantry, so that it was impossible for me to attack him, even with the greatly inferior forces under my command, without passing the river over fords strongly guarded, in the face of very superior numbers. The movement of Jackson through White Plains and in the direction of Thoroughfare Gap, while the main body of the enemy confronted me at Sulphur Springs and Waterloo Bridge, was well known to me, but I relied confidently upon the forces which I had been assured would be sent from Alexandria, and one heavy division which I had ordered to take post in the woods at Manassas Junction.

I was entirely under the belief that these would be there, and it was not until 1 found my communications intercepted, that 1 was undeceived. I knew that this movement was no raid, and that it was made by not less than 25,000 men. By this time the army corps of Heintzelman, about 10,000 strong, had reached Warrenton Junction. One division of it, I think, on the very day of attack. But they came without artillery, with only forty rounds of ammunition to the man, without wagons, and even the field and general officers without horses.

Fitz-John Porter also arrived at Bealton Station, near Rappahannock river, with one of his divisions, 4500 strong ; whilst his other division was still at Barnett's and Kelley's fords. I directed that corps, about 8000 strong, to concentrate immediately at Warrenton Junction, where Heintzelman already was. This was accomplished on the evening of the 26th. As soon as it became known to me that Jackson was on the railroad, it became apparent that the Upper Rappahannock was no longer tenable.

I could not send a sufficient body of men to meet Jackson, and at the same time attempt to confront the main body of the enemy. I accordingly at once evacuated Warrenton and Warrenton Junction, directing McDowell with his own corps and Sigel's, and the division at Reynolds, to march rapidly by the turnpike to Gainesville, so as to intercept any reinforcements coming to the enemy by the way of Thoroughfare Gap, and instructing Gen. Reno with his command, and Kearney with one division of Heintzelman's, to march on Greenwich, so as to support McDowell in case of necessity.

With Hooker's division of Heintzelman's corps, I moved along the railroad upon Manassas Junction, near Kettle Run. Hooker came upon the advance of Ewell's rebel division on the afternoon of the 27th. A severe action took place, which terminated at dark, Ewell being driven from the field with the loss of his camp and three hundred killed and wounded. The unfortunate oversight of not having more than forty rounds of ammunition became at once alarming. At nightfall Hooker had but about five rounds to the man left. As soon as I learned this, I sent back orders to Gen. Fitz-John Porter to march back with his corps at 1 o'clock that night, so as to be with Gen. Hooker at daylight next morning.

The distance was nine miles, and he received the dispatch at 9.50 o'clock, but did not reach the ground until after ten o'clock the next morning. He can probably explain better than I can the reason for this delay. Fortunately, General Hooker had handled the enemy so severely the evening before, and the movement of McDowell had began to be so apparent, that the enemy, fearful of being surrounded, had retired precipitately from Manassas Junction; directing his retreat through Centreville, as Reno, McDowell and Kearney had made the road through Gainesville impracticable.

I immediately pushed forward to Manassas and thence to Centreville, which place was occupied by Kearney that night, only a few hours after the enemy had left it. Gen. Reno had reached Manassas Junction, and General Fitz-John Porter was immediately ordered from Broad Run, where he had stopped. McDowell's movement, conducted with speed and vigor, had been completely successful ; the enemy being intercepted at Gainesville, and part of his forces driven back through Thoroughfare Gap.

With King's division and Sigel's corps, McDowell continued to march along the turnpike towards Centreville, leaving General Ricketts, with his division, in observation of Thoroughfare Gap. Late in the evening, on the 28th, McDowell advanced Gibbon's brigade near the front of the enemy retiring from Centreville, and about six miles from that place. A very sharp skirmish here took place, ended by the darkness, in which the brigade of Gen. Gibbon behaved very handsomely, and suffered heavy loss. Gen. Sigel was near at hand with his corps, but did not join the action.

I instructed Gen. Kearney to move forward at early dawn of day, toward Gainesville, to be followed closely by Hooker and Reno, and engage the enemy thus placed between McDowell and Sigel ; Heintzelman and Reno on the east, and Fitz-John Porter on the south. I also instructed Gen. Porter, with his own corps, and King's division, which had, for some reason, fallen back from the Warrenton turnpike towards Manassas Junction, to move at daylight in the morning upon Gainesville, along the Manassas Gap railroad, until they communicated closely with the forces under Gen. Heintzelman and Sigel, cautioning them not to go further than was necessary to effect this junction, as we might be forced to retire behind Bull Run that night, for subsistence, if nothing else.

Gen. Heintzelman marched early from

Centreville towards Gainesville, closely followed by Reno. Meantime, shortly after daylight, Sykes' and Reynolds' divisions of McDowell's corps became engaged with the enemy, who was brought to a stand. Heintzelman and Reno soon after came up, when the entire line became actively engaged. Porter marched as directed, followed by King's division, which was, by this time, joined by Rickett's division, which had been forced back from Thoroughfare Gap by the heavy forces of the enemy advancing to the support of Jackson.

As soon as I found that the enemy had been brought to a halt, and was being vigorously attacked along the Warrenton turnpike, I sent orders to Gen. McDowell to advance rapidly on our left and attack the enemy on his flank, extending his right to meet Reynolds' left, and to Gen. Porter to keep his right well closed on McDowell's left, and to attack the enemy in flank and rear, while he was pushed in front. This would have made the line of battle of McDowell and Porter at right angles to that of the other forces engaged. This action raged furiously all day, McDowell, although previously in rear of Porter, bringing his whole corps on the field in the afternoon, and taking a conspicuous part in the operations of the day.

To my surprise and disappointment I received, late in the afternoon, from Gen. Porter, a note saying that his advance had met the enemy on the flank, in some force, and that he was retiring on Manassas Junction, without engaging the enemy or coming to the assistance of our other forces, although they were engaged in a furious action, only two miles distant and in full hearing of him. A portion of his forces fell back toward Manassas, while he remained, as he afterwards informed me, where he was, looking on the enemy during the afternoon of Friday and part of the same night, passing down in plain view to reinforce the troops under Jackson, without an effort to prevent it or assist us.

One of his brigades, under Gen. Griffin, got round to Centreville, and remained there during the whole of the next day's battle, without coming on the field, though in full view of the battle which was raging; while Gen. Griffin himself spent the day in making ill-natured strictures upon the general commanding, in the presence of a promiscuous assemblage. Darkness closed the action on Friday, the enemy being driven back from his position by Heintzelman's and Reno's corps, and by a furious attack along the turnpike by King's division and McDowell's corps, the enemy leaving his dead and wounded on the battlefield.

I do not hesitate to say that if the corps of Porter had attacked the enemy in flank on the afternoon of Friday, as he had my written orders to do, we should have crushed the enemy before the forces under Lee could have joined

them. Why he did not do so I cannot understand. Our men, much worn down by hard service and continued fighting, for many previous days and nights, and very short of provisions, rested on their arms. Our horses had not had forage for ten days.

I had telegraphed and written frequently for rations and forage to be sent us; but on Saturday morning, before the action was resumed, I received a letter from Gen. Franklin, written the day previous from Alexandria, stating that he had been directed by Gen. McClellan to inform me that rations and forage for my command would be loaded into cars and available wagons as soon as I would forward a cavalry escort to Alexandria to bring them up. All hope of being able to maintain my position, whether victorious or not, vanished with this information.

My cavalry was utterly broken down by long and constant service in the face of the enemy, and, bad as they were, could not be spared from the front, even if there had been time to go back thirty miles to Alexandria and await the loading of the trains. I at once understood that we must, if possible, finish whatever we had to do that day, or night would find us behind Bull Run, if we wished to save men and animals from starvation. The enemy's large reinforcements having reached him on Friday afternoon and night, he begun to mass on his right, for the purpose of crushing our left and occupying the road leading to Centreville, in our rear.

His heaviest assault was made about five o'clock in the afternoon. When, after overwhelming Gen. Fitz-John Porter's forces, and driving him back on the centre and left, mass after mass of the enemy's forces were pushed against our left. A terrific contest, with great slaughter, was carried on for several hours, our men behaving with firmness and gallantry, under the immediate command of Gen. McDowell. When night closed our left was forced back about half a mile, but still remained firm and unbroken, while the right held its ground.

Gen. Franklin, with his corps, arrived after dark at Centreville, six miles in our rear; whilst Gen. Sumner was four miles behind Franklin. I could have brought up these corps in the morning in time to have renewed the action, but men and horses were completely exhausted for the want of sufficient food. I accordingly retired to Centreville that night, in perfect order. Neither on Sunday or Monday did the enemy make any advance upon us. On Monday I sent to the army corps commanders for their effective strength, which, all told, fell short of 60,000 men.

The enemy, during Monday, again began to move slowly around to our right, for the purpose of possessing Fairfax Courthouse, and thus turning our rear. A portion of Sumner's division had been left there, and I sent General

Hooker, on Monday afternoon, to take command and post himself at or in front of Germantown; at the same time directing McDowell to take position along the turnpike from Centreville to Fairfax Courthouse, about ten miles west of the latter place. Heintzelman was directed to post himself in the rear and support of Reno, who was pushed north of the road at a point about three miles east of Centreville, and to cover the road.

It was my purpose in the course of the night to mass my command on the right, in the direction of Germantown, where I felt convinced the next attack of the enemy would be made. Late in the afternoon on Monday the enemy made his demonstration upon Germantown, but was met by Hooker at that place, and by Reno, reinforced by Kearney, further west. The battle was very severe, though of short duration, the enemy being driven back one mile, with heavy loss, leaving his dead and wounded. In this short action we lost two of our most valuable and distinguished officers, Generals Kearney and Stevens.

By morning the whole of my command was massed behind difficult creeks, between Flint Hill and the Warrenton turnpike, with the advance under Hooker in front of Germantown. With the exception of Gen. Sumner, the commanders of the army of the Potomac had continued to inform me that their commands had been demoralized ever since they had left Harrison's Landing; that they had no spirit and no disposition to fight.

This latter statement their conduct in the various actions fully contradicted. But the straggling in those corps was distressing. I received orders on Tuesday afternoon to retire to the entrenchments near Washington, which was accordingly done, in good order and not the slightest loss. Gen. Banks, who had been left with the railroad trains, cut off at Bristow, by the burning of the bridge, was ordered to join me on Monday at Centreville, which he did on the afternoon of that day.

This brief summary will explain sufficiently in detail the entire operations of the forces under my command, during sixteen days of continuous fighting by day and marching by night, to confront a powerful enemy with greatly inferior numbers. To fight him by day without the loss of the army; to delay and embarrass his movements, and to force him, by persistent resistance, to adopt long and circuitous routes to his destination, are the duties which have been imposed upon me.

They are, of all military operations, the most difficult and the most harassing, both to a commander and to his troops. How far we have been successful, I leave to the judgment of my countrymen. The armies of Virginia and the Potomac have been united in the presence and against the efforts of a wary and vigorous enemy, in greatly superior force, with no loss for which they did not exact full retribution.

Among the officers whom I feel bound to mention with especial gratitude for their most hearty, cordial and untiring zeal and energy, are Generals Hooker, Kearney, McDowell, Banks, Reno, Heintzelman, and many others of inferior rank, whom I shall take great pleasure in bringing to the notice of the government. The troops have exhibited wonderful patience and courage, and I cannot say too much for them.   JOHN POPE,
                              Major General Commanding.

On Sept. 4th, Gen. Pope was assigned to the command of the Department of the Northwest, consisting of Minnesota, Iowa and Wisconsin, and after a brief sojourn with his family in Cincinnati, proceeded to his new field, arriving at St. Paul and establishing his headquarters there, Sept. 16th, 1862.

In passing through Chicago, Gen. Pope was serenaded, when he made his appearance on the balcony of the hotel, and, after the most vociferous applause from the assembled thousands, spoke as follows:

"My friends—I am glad to see you to-night. I am glad to be back to breathe again the pure air of the State of Illinois. It has been for many years my home, and I am glad to return to it. God Almighty only knows how sorry I am I ever left it. The State of Illinois has poured forth men to this war in a noble way, that has been attested by the bones of her children who have perished upon the battlefield. I am proud of them; I cannot express to you how proud I feel of the noble conduct of the men of Illinois. It is in keeping with the past history of the State. It was with great regret I left the noble army in the West, which was not long since under my command. They were brave men and gallant soldiers. I wanted no higher position. I asked none, than to be at the head of the gallant army, upon whose banner were engraved the names of New Madrid, Island 10, of Donelson and of Shiloh. I could have wished that I might have been permitted to have remained with them.

"My friends, I could tell a sad story to you to-night, of recent events, but it is wiser and better that I should not tell it. I am a soldier and recognize a soldier's duty. My services and my life are at the disposal of the Government, and God knows how gladly I will render up both in its behalf. I have but little to say to-night. I have no desire to speak of the past. Whatever wrong may have been done me, I make no complaint. This is not the place to correct. My record is before the people. The popular voice is the best judge, and with them I am willing to leave it."

GEN. HURLBUT.

Major Gen. STEPHEN A. HURLBUT was born at Charleston, S. C., November 29, 1815. His father was a Unitarian clergyman, and from him he received his education. He read law in the office of James L. Pettigrew, of Charleston, and practiced in that city for some time. Upon the breaking out of the Florida war, he enlisted in a South Carolina regiment, and was elected Adjutant, in which position he served through the campaign, but was not in any very great battle. In 1845, he removed to Illinois, and engaged in the practice of his profession in Belvidere, Boone county, which is still his home. He was a prominent member of the Constitutional Convention of Illinois in 1847, and has several times represented his county with great ability in the Legislature. He was appointed a Brigadier General by President Lincoln, in May, 1861, and was commandant of the post of Fort Donelson for a time after its capture. When Gen. Grant's army moved up the Tennessee river, Gen. Hurlbut was placed in command of the 4th division, comprising twelve regiments of infantry, six companies of cavalry and three batteries of artillery, and with his division was the first to land at Pittsburgh Landing, and for a week held it alone. His division was posted parallel with the river, one mile and a half inward, the flanks resting on ravines, with a battery of artillery on either flank and in the centre, with a reserve of cavalry and two regiments of infantry, which position it maintained until that fierce battle began. When additional troops came, they were pushed miles further to the front, Gen. Prentiss' division of green troops occupying the extreme front of our army; and if there be any fault of a surprise, it in no manner rested upon Gen. Hurlbut, or the gallant soldiers or officers under his command. The following description, from the pen of one of the General's aids, gives a graphic account of the part taken by him and his division in the desperate battle of Shiloh:

"On Sunday morning, the 6th inst., at about 8½ o'clock, it was first known that Gen. Hurlbut's headquarters that there were any signs of an attack by the enemy upon our lines, and in five minutes more a courier came post haste, stating that Gen. Prentiss was engaging the enemy. Gen. Hurlbut immediately

ordered the long beat in his division, and within ten minutes the whole division was under arms, the General and his staff mounted, and an order to send one brigade to the support of Gen. McClernand, which was despatched, and the two other brigades led in person by Gen. Hurlbut, with six companies of cavalry and two of artillery, to the support of Gen. Prentiss. The column had not advanced above half a mile on the march out before it met the entire division of General Prentiss drifting in upon us in full retreat. * * * * * One battery of Gen. Prentiss' artillery was turned about by Gen. Hurlbut, and given a splendid position to play upon the advancing columns of the enemy, but after one fire, the whole battery, cannoneers and postillions, left guns and horses, and fled in the wildest confusion. The boys of Mann's battery, in Gen. Hurlbut's division, left their battery and spiked the guns so deserted, cut the horses loose, and broke the coupling to the gun carriages. Here we met Gen. Prentiss, a brave officer, who, at the request of Gen. Hurlbut, led up one of his brigades, and Gen. Hurlbut the other, forming a line of battle to stop the advancing foe, while the staff of Gen. Prentiss tried with only partial success to rally his division in a line behind ours, and in our support. Our batteries were soon playing upon the enemy, and theirs upon us, and shot and shell flew thick and fast, the enemy firing from superior rifled guns, and their cannoneers evidently understanding their business well. Mann's battery was served with superior skill, and did most terrible execution. Their columns were soon close enough for musket range, and the enemy boldly advancing, a terrible fire of small arms was opened along the whole line, while the artillery poured grape and canister into their ranks, the enemy stoutly resisting, emboldened by their previous success in driving the division of Gen. Prentiss, after their surprise. Gen. Hurlbut mounted on his grey horse, with shabrack, sash, uniform and trappings, a prominent mark for the enemy's fire, rode backward and forward along the line, entirely heedless of the storm of bullets that he was drawing about himself, encouraging his men and directing their movements. When cautioned that his prominent appearance was drawing the enemy's fire, he only remarked, 'Oh, well, we Generals must take our chances with the boys.' The enemy soon found they had new troops to encounter, and, falling back, planned their attack more skilfully, bringing to their assistance more batteries of artillery. Wherever a new battery opened, there rode Gen. Hurlbut, directing the planting of a new battery to meet its fire. Occasionally, under the fire of some battery, a terrible assault with musketry would come from the enemy upon some supposed weak point of our lines, to be met by the steady, stern resistance of the brave troops under his command, and for five hours Gen. Hurlbut, with those two light brigades, and without support, not only stopped the enemy, flushed with victory, but successfully held him in check, checkmating his generalship, and driving him back wherever he chose to assault our lines, and only fell back at last when the enemy by his superior numbers was enabled to outflank on either side and place him within the range of three fires; and even in the falling back giving him as good as he sent, forming new lines of battle on every position that the ground made favorable, and contesting his advance inch by inch. Gen. Hurlbut formed his last line about 4 o'clock P. M., flanking the large siege guns, planted about half a mile from the river bank, and planting his light artillery and all he could pick up in three different positions, so as to open a cross fire from three ways upon the enemy, he determined to stand by those as his last hope. Scarcely were his preparations ready when the enemy appeared above the brow of the hill, but was quickly driven back by the concentrated fire of those screaming batteries, and each time as he advanced, it was only to retire again under that murderous storm of iron missiles. The gunboats getting the range of the enemy's lines, chimed in with their heavy booming, a music that was joy to our boys, and with their massive shells, sent havoc into the enemy's lines. Night soon closed in upon the scene, and by order of Gen. Grant, Gen. Hurlbut moved forward his line of battle about three hundred feet, into the ravine in front of the batteries, where the order was given to lay upon their arms all night, sending out skirmishers—prepared at any moment to resist an attack by the enemy, while the gunboats kept up their fire with their heavy guns, throwing shells alternately of 12 and 20 second fuse up the ravine and in front of our lines, and effectually keeping the enemy from making any advance. Too much credit cannot be given these iron clad monsters of the river, that send terror into the ranks of the 'secesh' wherever their heavy voices are heard, as well by the loud noise they make, as by the terrible execution they do. During the night, Gen. Lew. Wallace, with his entire division, reinforced us from Crump's Landing, and Gen. Buell crossed over to our assistance. These new troops took the advance in the morning, Gen. Wallace on the right and Gen. Buell on the left, and steadily drove the enemy before them, with the assistance of the troops yet left, by the most desperate and heroic bravery ever evinced by any army. Gen. Hurlbut got his division in fighting trim early after breakfast, and I rode along in front of the lines with him. Many familiar faces had gone since the morning before. Col. Ellis and Maj. Goddard, of the 15th Illinois, killed

dead upon the field, and that gallant regiment, led by Capt. Kelly, only about two hundred strong. The 3d Iowa had all of its field officers killed or wounded, and all its captains killed, wounded, or missing, and less than two hundred strong, were in command of a first lieutenant as ranking officer. An order soon came to Gen. Hurlbut to support McClernand's right, and Gen. Hurlbut put his division in motion, himself at its head, and pushing forward was met by an aid of Gen. McClernand and directed to his left, where the enemy was flanking Gen. McClernand's division, and arrived just in time to save his left flank from being turned. The writer was in the engagement at Fort Donelson, and supposed that he had passed through as terrible a fire as it was possible to do and escape, but he has to confess that the assault of the rebels in their last efforts upon our lines was the most recklessly desperate of which the imagination can conceive. It seemed as if the inspiration of devils was infused into the ranks of both armies. Some of the ground in this vicinity was fought over as often as six times, so desperately determined were each to maintain it. Gen. Hurlbut, as was also Gen. McClernand, was always to be found where the fire was hottest, directing the movements, and lending encouragement by their presence. About this time Gen. Hurlbut's grey horse was shot, and he mounted a bay, and the writer confesses he was glad of it, for the General's sake, for the grey seemed to be a special mark. The enemy's effort seemed specially directed to flanking us, and he was ever attempting it, under the cover of the many hills and ravines; and at one time, within one hour, our line of battle changed front three times. So confident were the enemy of victory on the night previous, when in possession of our tents, that they did not destroy them, being certain to keep them for his own use, and it is a well ascertained fact that Gen. Beauregard had his headquarters that night in the large office tent of Gen. Hurlbut, but save the holes torn by the bullets, it was uninjured, and occupied by Gen. Hurlbut on the following night. Although the enemy stoutly resisted, he was all the time driven back on Monday, and by 4 o'clock P.M., his fire entirely ceased along our whole line, and our cavalry and artillery pursuing him in his flight. Gen. Hurlbut was struck by a spent musket ball on his left arm, but save that received no injury. He had many narrow escapes. The writer saw a rifle shot strike a tree within a few feet of his head, eliciting the remark from him, 'They have our range pretty well.' At another time a shell burst within ten feet of him, but he was not scratched by it. His courage and coolness under fire, and his entire disregard for his personal safety, were remarked by all under him, and by his bravery and skill in this engagement, he has won the love and confidence of the brave troops of his command."

For a long time, Gen. Sherman in command, and Gen. Hurlbut with his division, have been at Memphis. Quite recently, Gen. H., with his troops, moved to reinforce Gen. Grant, and is now leading his "fighting" 4th division near Bolivar, Tennessee.

Gen. Hurlbut was recently promoted to a Major General, his commission to date from Sept. 17, 1862, and given for meritorious service at the battle of Shiloh.

At the battle of the Hatchie, fought Oct. 6, Gen. Hurlbut, being in command of a large Union force, after seven hours' hard fighting, drove the rebels back five miles, capturing 300 prisoners, two full batteries, and nearly 100 stand of small arms.

In a private letter to the author, a correspondent, who is well acquainted with Gen. Hurlbut, and who has been in the "cloud and lightning of battle" with him, says : "He is one of the most worthy men in the service. Not an officer or private in his whole division, that went through the fight in those fierce days of battle at Pittsburgh Landing with him, that doubts his military ability or his courage, or that has not learned to love the General like a brother, and would risk life to defend his reputation from the least reproach."

GEN. PALMER.

Brigadier General JOHN McCAULEY PALMER was born in Christian county, Kentucky, September 13, 1817. His education, which was extremely limited, was derived chiefly, not from teachers and schools, but from books, for which in his early life he displayed a strong love. He removed to Madison county, Illinois, in 1832, and in 1839, settled in Carlinville, his present residence. Here he commenced the study of law, and was admitted to practice early in the year following. He was married, December 20, 1842, to Miss Malinda A. Neeley. In 1847, Mr. Palmer was elected a delegate to the State Constitution Convention, and in 1852 was elected to the State Senate to fill a vacancy caused by the death of Hon. Franklin Witt, and was an active member of that body during the sessions of 1852–3–4. In the autumn of 1854, he was re-elected to the same position for another year. In 1856, he was a delegate from Illinois to the National Republican Convention which convened at Philadelphia, and was one of the electors of the State at large to the Republican Convention which met at Chicago in 1860 and nominated Mr. Lincoln. In January, 1861, Mr. Palmer was appointed by the Governor one of the five commissioners to the Conference Convention which met at Washington, D. C., February 4, 1861, in consequence of the preamble and resolutions adopted by the General Assembly of Virginia. April, 1861, he was unanimously elected to the Colonelcy of the 14th Regiment Illinois Volunteers, and received his commission May 18th. Col. Palmer was with his regiment in Missouri during the summer and autumn of 1861, and was with Gen. Fremont in his expedition to Springfield, Mo. December 13th, he was commissioned Brigadier General of Volunteers, and was attached to Gen. Pope's command at Commerce. He was with that General at the capture of New Madrid and Island No. 10, and accompanied him in his march to Corinth. Being in command of the 1st brigade, 1st division of the army of the Mississippi, he took an active part in the battle of Farmington. He is now with Gen. Grant's army, and still in command of the same brigade, but acting temporarily as commander of the division.

GEN. LOGAN.

Brigadier General JOHN A. LOGAN was born in Jackson county, Illinois, February 9, 1826, near the present town of Murphysboro; the town, however, was not built at that time. His father, Dr. John Logan, was of Irish descent, and emigrated at a very early age from Ireland to this country, and for a time lived in Maryland; removed thence to Ohio; thence to Missouri; and from there to Illinois in the year 1823. His mother, whose maiden name was Elizabeth Jenkins, was from Tennessee, and was the mother of eleven children, of whom there are at this time six living, four sons and two daughters. The subject of this memoir is the eldest. John Alexander Logan, during his earlier years, had few opportunities of acquiring an education, as the country at that time afforded scarcely any schools. His father did what he could toward educating him as well as his other children, in sending them to the neighboring country schools, and occasionally hiring teachers for his family. John went to a school in the north-west part of Jackson county in 1840, to which was given the sounding name of Shiloh College, but which was in reality nothing more than a country academy. His remarkably tenacious memory enabled him to retain all he could learn at these schools.

When the war broke out with Mexico in 1844, although then but nineteen years of age, he volunteered, and was elected Lieutenant in a company commanded by James Hampton, from Jackson county, in the 1st Regiment Illinois Volunteers. With these he faithfully served his time out, acting part of the time as Adjutant of the regiment, and returned home in October, 1848. He then entered upon the study of law under his uncle, Alexander M. Jenkins (formerly Lieutenant Governor of Illinois, and now Judge of the 3d Judicial District), and while thus pursuing his studies, in November, 1849, was elected Clerk of his native county, which office he held till 1850. During the year, he went to Louisville, Ky., to attend the law lectures. In 1851, received his diploma, and immediately on his return home, began the practice of law in connection with his uncle. He rapidly rose in the practice of his profession and popularity. In 1852, having been elected Prosecuting Attorney of the (then) 3d Judicial Circuit, he removed to Benton, Franklin county, Illinois, and in the fall of that year was elected to the Legislature of Illinois, representing the counties of Franklin and Jackson.

On the 27th of November, 1855, he was married in Shawneetown to Miss Mary S. Cunningham, daughter of Capt. John W. Cunningham, formerly Register of the Land Office, Shawneetown, now Clerk of the Court of Williamson county. In May, 1856, he was appointed Presidential Elector for the 9th Congressional District; and at the November election, was re-elected to the Legislature, which seat he filled with ability and credit to himself and constituents. In 1858, he was nominated and elected to Congress, by the Democracy from the 9th Congressional District, over his Republican opponent, by a very large majority. In 1860, he was re-elected to Congress from the same district. In the winter of 1860, while he was in his seat at Washington, by the action of the Legislature, his county (Franklin) was thrown out of his old district (at that time including sixteen counties) and added to one running northward. After his return home, he removed to Marion, Williamson county, that he might still be in his district.

Leaving his seat during the extra session of Congress, July, 1861, he entered the ranks of Col. Richardson's regiment, and displayed great bravery at the disastrous battle of Bull Run. He returned home the last of August, 1861; and on the 3d of September, made a speech to his countrymen in Marion, declaring his intention to enter the service as a "private, or in any manner he could serve his country best in defending and bearing the old blood-stained flag over every foot of soil in the United States." The citizens of his Congressional district readily responded to his call for men to go with him, and on the 18th of September, the 31st Regiment was organized at Cairo and unanimously recommended him for their Colonel, from which date he held his commission. The regiment was attached to Gen. McClernand's brigade, and although only of about six weeks' drill, the heroic part taken by his regiment in the battle of Belmont on the 7th of November, 1861, proves how active he had been in the instruction and discipline of his men. Col. L. had his horse shot under him and his pistol shattered at his side by a shot from the enemy, yet he escaped unhurt. He commanded his regiment through the most trying circumstances in the rear of Fort Henry at the capture of that post, and in command of 200 cavalry, pursued and captured eight of the enemy's guns. Col. L. made several reconnoisances around Fort Donelson preparatory to our forces moving on that point, and during the three days' siege before the enemy's entrenchments, he was constantly engaged. On the morning of the 15th of February, Lt. Col. John H. White unfortunately fell whilst aiding Col. Logan in rallying the men when their ammunition was nearly exhausted, to defend their position to the last, although they were hard pressed by a greatly superior force. Almost simultaneously with the death of Col. White, Col. Logan received a ball, entering in the fore part of the left arm near the point of the shoulder, passing round and out through the shoulder. Still he kept on, and by his intrepidity and daring kept their position until finally reinforcements were received, when he was forced to retire to have his wounds dressed, his men being fearful of the result, he having lost so much blood and near exhaustion. The regiment remained on the field under Capt. John Reese till the last gun was fired. Col. Logan remained prostrate from his wound in the shoulder, lameness from being struck in the hip by two spent balls, and disease contracted by exposure for three weeks (his friends at one time despairing of his recovery),—yet he positively refused to leave his decimated and suffering regiment until they should have to some extent recovered. On the 5th of March, 1862, he was confirmed a Brigadier General, and as soon as able reported to Gen. Grant at Pittsburgh Landing, who assigned to his command the 8th, 18th, 30th and 31st Illinois and 12th Michigan regiments, of which he retained command during the movement at Corinth, and could he have gotten leave, would have entered that place before the enemy could have made good their escape. Being satisfied

7

they were vacating, he insisted in pressing on, but was not allowed by superior officers to go beyond the lines. From this place he commanded the division engaged in rebuilding the railroad to Jackson and Columbus. After the completion of the road, he was placed in command of the forces at Jackson, Tennessee, from which place, under date of August 26th, he sent the following patriotic letter to Hon. O. M. Hatch, Secretary of State, and read at the Illinois Union Convention, September, 1862, declining to become a candidate for Congress for the State at large:

"I have the honor to acknowledge the receipt of your complimentary letter of the 18th inst., asking permission to use my name in connection with that of the Fourteenth Representative in Congress from the State of Illinois.

"In reply, I would most respectfully remind you that a compliance with your request on my part would be a departure from the settled resolutions with which I resumed my sword in defense and for the perpetuity of a Government the likes and blessings of which no other nation or age shall enjoy, if once suffered to be weakened or destroyed.

"In making this reply, I feel that it is unnecessary to enlarge as to what were, are, or may hereafter be, my political views, but would simply state that politics of every grade and character whatsoever are now ignored by me, since I am convinced that the Constitution and life of this Republic—which I shall never cease to adore—are in danger.

"I express all my views and politics when I assert my attachment for the Union. I have no other politics now, and consequently no aspirations for civil place and power.

"No! I am to day a soldier of this Republic, so to remain, changeless and immutable until her last and weakest enemy shall have expired and passed away.

"Ambitious men, who have not a true love for their country at heart, may bring forth crude and bootless questions to agitate the pulse of our troubled nation and thwart the preservation of this Union, but for none of such am I. I have entered the field—to die if needs be—for this Government, and never expect to return to peaceful pursuits until the object of this war of preservation has become a fact established.

"Whatever means it may be necessary to adopt, whatever local interest it may affect or destroy, is no longer an affair of mine. If any locality or section suffers or is wronged in the prosecution of the war, I am sorry for it, but I say it must not be heeded now, for we are at war for the preservation of the Union. Let the evil be rectified when the present breach has been cemented forever.

"If the South by her malignant treachery has imperiled all that made her great and wealthy, and it was to be lost, I would not stretch forth my hand to save her from destruction, if she will not be saved by a restoration of the Union. Since the die of her wretchedness has been cast by her own hands, let the coin of her misery circulate alone in her own dominions, until the peace of Union ameli· ra'cs her forlorn condition.

"By these few words you may readily discern that my political aspirations are things of the past, and I am not the character of man you seek. No legislation in which I might be suffered to take a feeble part, will in my opinion suffice to amend the injury already inflicted upon our country by these remorseless traitors. Their policy for the dissolution of the Government was initiated in blood, and their seditious blood only can suffice to make amends for the evil done. This Government must be preserved for future generations in the same mould in which it was transmitted to us, if it takes the last man and the last dollar of the present generation within its borders to accomplish it.

"For the flattering manner in which you have seen fit to allude to my past services, I return you my sincere thanks; but if it has been my fortune to bleed and suffer for my dear country, it is all but too little compared to what I am willing again and again to endure; and should fate so ordain it, I will esteem it as the Lig'iest privilege a just Dispenser can award, to shed the last drop of blood in my veins for the honor of that flag whose emblems are justice, liberty and truth, and which has been, and as I humbly trust in God ever will be, for the right.

"In conclusion, let me request that your desire to associate my name with the high and honorable position you would confer upon me be at once dismissed, and some more suitable and worthy person substituted. Meanwhile I shall continue to look with unfeigned pride and admiration on the continuance of the present able conduct of our State affairs, and feel that I am sufficiently honored while acknowledged as an humble soldier of our own peerless State."

COL. ATKINS.

SMITH D. ATKINS, Colonel 92d Regiment Illinois Volunteers, was born in Horseheads, Chemung county, New York, June 9th, 1833. His father removed with his family to Illinois in 1848, and settled on a farm in Stephenson co., where the subject of this sketch remained until 1851, when he went to Freeport, and learned the "art preservative of·arts" in the office of the *Prairie Democrat*, then edited by J. O. P. Burnside, now Lt. Col. 71st Illinois Volunteers. He afterwards entered the office of the *Mount Morris Gazette* at $2 per week, working four hours each day, and attending the Mt. Morris Seminary. Here he remained eighteen months, when he associated himself with C. C. Allen, now on Gen. Schofield's staff, and purchased the *Gazette*, removing the material to Savannah, and establishing the *Savannah Gazette*. In the spring of 1854, Mr. Atkins entered the office of Hiram Bright, attorney at Freeport, and began the study of law, and in the autumn of the year following was admitted to the bar. In 1856, he was elected States Attorney, on the Republican ticket, for the 14th Judicial District. April 13th, 1861, while engaged in trying a cause in court, he was asked to write out a muster roll

for volunteers under the three months call, which he did, at the same time signing it as a private. In twenty-four hours the company was full, and Mr. Atkins was elected Captain. They immediately marched to Camp Yates, Springfield, and became Company A of the 11th Regiment, Col. W. H. L. Wallace. At the expiration of the three months, Capt. Atkins, with 38 of his company, re-enlisted for three years. He was with his regiment at Donelson, and acted well his part in that hotly-contested engagement. He was soon after detailed as Adjt. Gen. on Gen. S. A. Hurlbut's staff, and remained in that position until after the battle of Shiloh, when he was compelled by ill health to resign. He was promoted by Gov. Yates, to be Major of the 11th, from Feb. 15th, for meritorious services at the battle of Fort Donelson, but his health would not admit of his accepting the commission, which did not reach him until after he had resigned his Captaincy. His health being restored, he raised a regiment under the call for 300,000 volunteers, and was, on the 4th Sept., chosen Colonel of the 92d Illinois Volunteers, recently stationed at Rockford.

GEN. COOK.

Brigadier General JOHN COOK was born in Belleville, St. Clair co., Ill., June 12, 1825. About 1830, his family removed to Springfield, where he ever since resided, and is well known to every one, either by his fast horses or the fine dogs that follow him to the field. With a sportsman's taste, he has all the skill of a practiced hunter, and never fails to kill his share of the game. He comes of good old Sucker stock, having for a grandfather that Governor Edwards of whom Illinois may well be proud. His father was Daniel C. Cook, who formerly represented this State in Congress, and for whom the county of Cook was named. He is frequently mentioned in Ford's History as one of the most prominent men at an early day. Left an orphan in childhood, and heir to an estate which ensured him an ample fortune through life, it is no wonder that young Cook grew up with rather wayward habits. Boys with such anticipations rarely ruin themselves with study, and Cook was no exception. He entered college at Jacksonville, where he was idolized by the students, and acquired the reputation of being the wildest boy in college; but he did not stay to complete the course. His last year of college life was spent at Kemper College, near St. Louis, Mo. He entered public life in 1855 as Mayor of the city of Springfield. In this position his abilities gained him a considerable reputation as an executive officer. He was afterwards elected Sheriff of Sangamon county, at a time when his party was in considerable minority. Ardently pursuing whatever he undertakes with untiring energy, Mr. Cook engaged in the war against the rebellion with a vigor and spirit that made him a favorite among the volunteers, and from being Captain of the first company, the "Springfield Zouave Greys," which was tendered to the Governor after the President's proclamation, he was chosen to be Colonel of the first regiment (known as the 7th) organized in Illinois, his commission bearing date April 26, 1861. Col. Cook was present at the capture of Fort Donelson, where he led a brigade under Gen. C. F. Smith. For gallantry displayed in that desperate action, he was made Brigadier General, his commission dating from March 22,

1862. In consequence of severe exposure at Donelson, Gen. Cook became seriously ill, and was compelled to return home to recuperate. While in Springfield, Gov. Yates testified his appreciation of Gen. Cook's services by presenting him with a sword, on which occasion the following correspondence took place:

SPRINGFIELD, March 29, 1862.
GEN. JOHN COOK:

DEAR SIR: On behalf of the State of Illinois, I present you this sword, as a memorial of her high appreciation for your distinguished and gallant conduct at the glorious battle of Fort Donelson. It is only justice to you and your brigade, to say that proud honors are yours and theirs, and that you are well worthy the thanks and gratitude of your noble and native State.

I assure you that it affords me more pleasure to be the medium of presenting you this sword, because to my admiration of your gallant bearing as a soldier I can add the assurance of my high estimation of you as a true, noble and generous friend.

I have the honor to be, very respectfully,
RICHARD YATES,
Governor of Illinois.

GOVERNOR: In accepting this sword with its flattering inscription, I will not attempt to give expression to the gratitude and pride with which my heart is warmed by this token of the approbation of my beloved native State, and by your words of kindness and friendship.

I beg to assure you that this testimonial will be regarded by me with the utmost gratification as a not undeserved attestation of your appreciation of the valor and patriotism of the soldiers of Illinois, with whom it has been my fortune to have been associated in some of the trials, toils and dangers that have crowned with success the loyal arms in vindication of that glorious and sacred cause which commands their fervid and exalted devotion—as well as your own, and that of the generous people you represent.

May a speedy termination of this unhappy war, and the return of an honorable and happy peace, enable us all to sheath the sword, never again to draw it through a necessity like this —the most remarkable ever forced upon a faithful, impartial and just government.

Once more I thank you, and, through you, the noble State of Illinois. JOHN COOK.

Contrary to the advice of his physician, the prospect of a battle at Pittsburgh Landing induced him to return to the army, which he joined Sunday morning, April 6th. He was ordered to report to Gen. Prentiss for a command. An unsuccessful search prevented his receiving one, Gen. Prentiss being then a prisoner. During both days he was upon the field, until obliged, from sickness and exhaustion, to leave it, and seek a tent, which for nine days he was unable to leave. Again he returned home, and remained until the last of May, when he was ordered to Washington by the Secretary of War, and assigned a command at Clouds Mills, Virginia. This, however, was more a camp of instruction than anything else, having various brigades at different times under his command, and occasionally as many as eight or ten thousand troops. His health still evidently failing, and being totally unfit for service, he was persuaded, much against his inclination, to listen and abide by the decision of surgeons, who thought him uselessly sacrificing health and life by remaining, and urged his speedy resignation and return home. He followed their advice as far as to return to Springfield, and his health being greatly restored, he received orders Sept. 29th to report for duty to Maj. Gen. Pope, and immediately thereafter proceeded to his new field of operations.

COL. JENKINS.

DAVID P. JENKINS was born on a farm near Mt. Pleasant, Jefferson Co., Ohio, August 25, 1823, of orthodox Quaker parents. He was educated at a Quaker seminary and a high school at Mt. Pleasant. For two years, from the age of 17 to 19, he spent among the pioneers of the West, teaching school and hunting. The religious prejudices of his parents prevented his going to the West Point Military Academy, as he desired. After studying law in the office of the late Hon. Samuel Stokeley, then one of the prominent lawyers and politicians of Ohio, he, in the fall of 1844, went to Cincinnati, and attended law lectures, graduating in March, 1845. He then went to Lafayette, Ind., and began the practice of law. From there, after a brief residence, he returned to Cincinnati, where he remained two years, and then removed to Lasalle, Illinois, in the fall of 1852. While the public works were being constructed in the neighborhood of Lasalle, he raised a company of infantry, for the purpose of suppressing riots which occurred among the laborers.

On the breaking out of the present rebellion, he organized a company of cavalry, but was not accepted. When the Governor appointed field officers for the 1st Cavalry regiment, Col. Marshall, he was appointed Major, to rank from 1st July, 1861, and joined his command that month. He held separate command in the two fights at Lexington, Mo., in Sept., 1861. He was one of the commissioners that negotiated the surrender. He was exchanged the following November, and assumed command of two companies at Bird's Point, Mo., Dec. 1st, 1861. He spent the winter and spring in that part of the State. When Gen. Pope commenced his march on New Madrid, Major Jenkins joined him, and was in command of the only cavalry that advanced on the left wing of the army at that place. He was relieved from duty with Pope's army, and ordered to the command of the 1st battalion of the regiment, then in South Missouri, on the road from Rolla to Batesville, where he served in command of two Government posts on the route of the army supplies to Curtis' army, Northern Arkansas. The regiment was mustered out of service about the middle of July last.

Col. Jenkins is now actively engaged in recruiting and organizing the 14th Regiment Illinois Cavalry, for which he has received authority from the War Department. The 14th will probably be ready to take the field with his regiment by Nov. 15th, 1862.

COL. STEWART.

Col. WARREN STEWART was born in Campbell, Steuben county, N. Y., February 11, 1813. He went to St. Louis in 1835, and from there removed to Texas in 1838. A few years later he returned and settled in Southern Illinois, and now resides at Clear Creek Landing, Alexander county, where he was engaged in purchasing and forwarding produce. Upon the receipt of the news of the attack upon Fort Sumter, he called a meeting of the inhabitants of his vicinity to sustain the Government, and called upon the citizens to come forward and enroll their names. One hundred and thirty signed the roll and were sworn in at the meeting. Propositions were made to Mr. Stewart to join a force to be raised in Missouri to capture the small body of Union troops at Cairo. His reply was, "That he would meet them at the river and contest their passage." At this time Capt. Stewart had been furnished with arms by the Governor for the purpose. On the 3d of August, 1861, Gen. Fremont's attention was called to his activity in defending Girardeau, Mo., before that city was occupied by the U. S. forces, and he urged him to enter the cavalry service, and authorized him to raise a company. On August 10th, he had his company mustered into service, and soon cleared the country of Jeff. Thompson and his rebel band. In September, he was ordered by Gen. Grant to Norfolk, six miles below Bird's Point. At this time, Jeff. Thompson, with 1800 infantry and 700 cavalry, were at Belmont, and Pillow at Columbus, Ky., with 20,000 men. Col. Oglesby was in command at Norfolk with Stewart's cavalry and the 8th and 22d regiments. Capt. Stewart was sent out every day to feel the enemy near Belmont, and had several engagements with them, in all of which he was successful. In one of these engagements he charged in advance of his men and was surrounded by the rebels, but he routed them, piercing two of them through the body with his sabre. He was then ordered to Charleston, and was at Likeston, drove in Thompson's pickets, and having learned his exact position, urged our forces to attack him, but he left the next day for Fredericktown, Missouri. Capt. Stewart was then ordered back to Cape Girardeau to take command of the advance cavalry guard under command of Col. Plummer, with 1200 infantry, 90 cavalry, and a section of Taylor's Chicago Battery, destined for Fredericktown. On the 21st of October, at one o'clock P. M., Capt. Stewart discovered that the bushes did not look natural. He ordered a halt, threw the fences down, and ordered the cavalry from the lane, and then notified Col. Plummer that the enemy were present. While Col. Plummer was ordering the artillery into position, Capt. Stewart advanced and discovered the ambush and miraculously escaped their fire. On reporting to Col. Plummer, Col. P. said to him, "if the enemy are not here in force we are making great fools of ourselves." At this moment they opened fire from a twelve pounder, striking within two feet of them. Capt. Stewart then asked if his doubts were removed; his reply was, "Capt. S. you have an eagle's eye, go to the right with your cavalry and prevent my being flanked." The battle then commenced. The enemy being completely routed, Capt. Stewart followed in pursuit ten miles, scattering their forces and taking many of them prisoners. Col. Plummer, in his report, made honorable mention of his valuable services, and also recommended him in person to Gens. Grant and McClernand. He was then ordered to Cairo and placed in command of a battalion of cavalry under Gen. McClernand, and detailed upon his Staff. On the expedition into Kentucky, in January, 1862, he commanded the advance to the abatis, at Columbus, and drove in the enemy's pickets, and with thirty men took the town of Milburn. He was present at Fort Henry, and on February 8th, approached near the works of Fort Donelson. Between the two posts he, with the late Capt. Carson, alone attacked a large body of rebel cavalry, and held them at bay, by stratagem, until joined by his men, when he made a gallant charge, taking twenty-six prisoners and killing several. At the battle of Fort Donelson on the 12th, 13th, 14th and 15th of February, as Aid to Gen. McClernand, he was continually under fire. In March he was with the troops sent up the Tennessee river. At Shiloh, April 6th, when it became necessary to ascertain the exact position of the enemy, Major Stewart went forward to reconnoitre, fell in with them, and learned their position, and was saluted with a volley from a full regiment. His report enabled Gen. McClernand to place his men in such a position as to entirely defeat the enemy in his effort to flank the 1st division. He led the 13th Missouri Regiment to charge —his horse was shot and ran with him the entire length of the line between the fire of the Union and rebel troops. He was then sent to support a portion of the line which was wavering under the attack of an overwhelming force, when he was struck with a ball which broke his skull and compelled him to leave the field. In May he was with the reserve that advanced upon Corinth. Two days before the evacuation, Gen. McClernand said to him, "I believe the enemy are evacuating; can't you ascertain?" He then went forward and had his pickets advanced, drove the enemy from his front, discovered their works, and found there were no guns or men, thereby confirming Gen. McClernand's surmises. In June he was put in command of the cavalry, and advanced on Jackson, Tennessee, and put to flight the cavalry in that vicinity. In one of his numerous engagements in the heart of Western Tennessee, he attacked and defeated the celebrated Jackson cavalry, when greatly outnumbered by them.

In September, 1862, Major Stewart accompanied Gen. McClernand to Springfield, where he is now engaged in organizing the 16th Regiment of Illinois Cavalry, authority having been given to him by the Government to increase his battalion to a regiment. Col. Stewart, who is Chief of Gen. McClernand's Staff, and has for a long time been his Chief of Cavalry, is considered one of the most dashing officers in the service, and has always been a great favorite in the army.

COL. DAVIS.

He that dies in an earnest pursuit, is like one that is wounded in hot blood, who, for the time, scarce feels the hurt; and therefore a mind fixed and bent upon somewhat that is good, doth avert the dolours of death.   *Bacon.*

Col. John A. Davis, of the 46th Regiment Illinois Volunteers, was born in Crawford county, Pennsylvania, October 25, 1823. Removed, when fourteen years of age, with his father's family, to Stephenson county, Illinois; since which time he has resided upon the same farm on which his father originally settled. He was a member from Stephenson county to the Illinois Legislature during the sessions of 1857 and '59. Mr. Davis enlisted as a private in a company of volunteers raised in his county early in the month of September, 1861. Upon the organization of the company, he was elected Captain; reported his company at Camp Butler, Springfield, September 10, 1861, and was commissioned by Gov. Yates, Colonel of the 46th Regiment, Sept. 12. He was with his regiment at the capture of Fort Donelson; and after Gen. McClernand's division had been driven in during the forenoon of Saturday, Feb. 15th, he was ordered to occupy the same position and support Dresser's battery, which was done with a loss of three men. The last cannon fired by the rebels from Fort Donelson was sighted at Col. Davis' regiment. At the battle of Shiloh, he went into the engagement with Gen. Veatch's brigade of Hurlbut's division at eight o'clock in the morning of Sunday, and was under fire constantly until one o'clock on Monday, when he fell, as was reported, mortally wounded, with a shot through the right lung, having had two horses shot under him, and having had one hundred and ninety-seven men killed and wounded out of six hundred that he led into the battle on Sunday morning. He bore with his own hands the regimental flag from the field, the color-bearer having been shot; and his regiment having lost its support on his right and left, was compelled to retreat on Sunday forenoon.

Some three months ago, a large number of the foremost men in the 3d Congressional District requested the privilege of using his name as a candidate for Congress. Col. Davis' noble reply is familiar to many of my readers. He peremptorily declined the honor, deeming it his duty to return to his regiment. Said he, "I can serve my country better, in following the torn banner of my regiment in the battle-field."

With his right arm still paralyzed from the effects of his wound, he returned and took command of his regiment, as soon as he recovered sufficiently to ride on horseback. On passing through Cairo, his friends remonstrated with him and advised him to return home, and remain until he recovered the use of his right arm, but he answered, "My country needs me, and I can manage my regiment with my left hand."

On returning to his regiment at Bolivar, September 18th, he received a warm welcome from his brave soldiers, and was presented with a magnificent horse, saddle and equipments. On the holsters is a large heart-shaped silver plate, bearing the inscription— "Presented to Col. John A. Davis, by the officers and soldiers of the 46th Regiment of Illinois Volunteers, as a token of respect for his heroism and bravery on the battle-fields of Donelson and Shiloh."

At the severe battle of Corinth, October 4th, he fell mortally wounded, and died a few days afterwards. His remains were borne to his home at Rock Run, Stephenson county, for interment.

" Bury him where the brook shall sing
  His requiem, and returning Spring
    Shall deck his peaceful grave;
  And heaven shall watch, with starry eyes,
  The mound under the starry skies,
    Where sleeps the bravest brave."

COL. DOUGHERTY.

Col. HENRY DOUGHERTY, the subject of this sketch, was born in Wilmington, North Carolina, August 15, 1827. In 1833, his father emigrated to Carlyle, Clinton county, Illinois, where, shortly after their arrival, both parents died, so, when only eight years of age, he was left an orphan to provide for and protect himself. He worked on a farm until he was sixteen years of age, when, having a passion for adventure, he joined a Rocky Mountain fur company, and remained with them one year. On his return to St. Louis, he enlisted as a private in the 1st United States Dragoons, went to Oregon, and joined Col. Kearney's command. In the spring, he proceeded to New Mexico with his company, Capt. Bergain, and served through the whole Mexican campaign, being at various times under command of Generals Scott, Taylor and Harney. He was in nine battles, viz., Kenyardo, Lambotha, Taos, Brasito, Sacramento, Buena Vista, and at the capture of the city of Mexico.

An incident, which occurred at the battle of Taos, will illustrate his character. He was severely wounded in the leg by a rifle-ball, and fell from his horse. Attempting to reach the hospital tent, about four hundred yards distant, his strength failed him and he fainted. Surgeon Simpson found him in this condition, and had him carried to the hospital, dressed his wound, and placed him upon a cot. At this moment another member of the company was brought in badly wounded, and while the surgeon was looking after him, Private Dougherty having recovered somewhat, slipped out at the rear end of the tent, mounted his horse, and galloped into the hottest of the battle. Smarting from his wound, he fought like a madman until the engagement was terminated, destroying several of the enemy. When he returned to the hospital, entirely exhausted, he received a severe reprimand from the surgeon, and when asked why he did so, replied, "The fight was not over yet, and I thought it my duty to go and do my part." It was three weeks before he left his bed.

At the close of the war, he sailed from Vera Cruz to New Orleans, and was wrecked at Brazos-Santiago. He then returned again to New Mexico, and joined Colonel (now Gen.) Sumner's command, against the Navijo and Apache Indians. On receiving his discharge in 1852, he returned to Carlyle. In 1855 he married, continuing to reside in the same place, where he was engaged in business. At the call of the President for volunteers, he raised a company, but failed to get accepted. He then joined Captain Johnson's company, as a private, and at the election of regimental officers, was unanimously elected Colonel of the 22d Regiment. He accompanied Gen. Grant on his expedition to Belmont, Nov. 7, 1861, and took part in that hard engagement, and receiving a severe wound while gallantly leading his regiment. He was taken prisoner by the enemy and confined at Columbus, where he suffered the amputation of a leg. Dec. 6th, by an agreement entered into between Gen. Grant and the commander of the rebel forces at Columbus, Col. Dougherty was exchanged, and reached Cairo in company with his wife the day following. The greatest enthusiasm was exhibited by the troops at Bird's Point and Cairo on the Colonel's return. The 22d is in Gen. Rosecrans' division of Grant's army, and is now stationed near Corinth.

GEN. OGLESBY.

Brig. Gen. RICHARD J. OGLESBY was born in Odham co., Ky., June 24th, 1824. He served as a 1st Lieut. in the 4th Illinois Regiment, Col. Baker, during the Mexican war, and distinguished himself at the battle of Cerro Gordo. Upon his return, he studied law with Judge Robbins, of Springfield, and afterwards attended law lectures at Louisville, Ky. Upon passing his examination, he commenced the practice of the law in Decatur, his present residence. In 1856 he went abroad, visiting Europe and the Holy Land during his absence of a year. On his return, he delivered several most entertaining lectures, in which he described his impressions of the countries he had visited. In 1858, he was the Republican candidate for Congress, but was defeated by his opponent, J. C. Robinson. In 1860, he was elected a member of the State Senate of Illinois, and was a member of that body when the rebellion broke out, in April, 1861. He immediately raised the 8th Regiment, and was unanimously elected Colonel. At the battle of Fort Donelson, Col. Oglesby commanded a brigade, consisting of his own, the 18th, 29th, 30th and 31st Illinois regiments, with two batteries, and several companies of cavalry. For his gallantry on this occasion, he was made a Brigadier General, his commission being dated March 21, 1862. At the battle of Shiloh, Gen. Oglesby commanded a brigade; and in the severe engagement before Corinth, Oct. 4th, 1862, between Gen. Rosecrans and the rebels under Price, Van Dorn and Lovell, he was severely if not mortally wounded.

COL. SHERMAN.

FRANCIS T. SHERMAN, son of Mayor Sherman, of Chicago, and Col. of the 88th Regiment Illinois Volunteers, was born in Newtown, Ct., Dec. 26, 1825. Before he was four years of age, the family removed to Buffalo, N.Y., and in 1834 again removed, and settled in Chicago, where they have ever since resided. He received his education mostly at a school kept by Mr. Collins, a well known teacher of the early day of Chicago. When quite young, Mr. Sherman joined a fire company, and afterwards became foreman Engine Co. No. 4. In April, 1849, he went to California, and resided there for a time, returning to Chicago, Dec. 15, 1850, and resuming business as a manufacturer of brick, under the firm of F. T. & E. Sherman. In 1851, he was married to Miss Eleanor N. Vedder, of Lake county, Illinois. In 1855, he formed a copartnership under the name of Sherman, Bay & Co., and two years later began the manufacture of lime, having formed a partnership with his brother-in-law, W. G. Sherman. In June, 1861, he opened, in connexion with P. B. Roberts (the firm being Roberts & Sherman), the magnificent hotel erected by his father, and known as the Sherman House. March 8th, 1862, Mr. Sherman entered the army as Major of the 12th Illinois Cavalry, and accompanied the regiment to the Potomac in June, 1862. The month following, he was detailed, by order of Gen. Wool, to proceed with a company from Martinsburgh to Front Royal and arrest Mrs. Belle Boyd, a sister of Robert J. Faulkner, who had given signals to the enemy under Jackson, at the time of the attack on Gen. Banks. August 8th, 1862, Major Sherman was appointed, by Gov. Yates, Col. of the 88th, and on the 3d September, he proceeded with his regiment to Louisville, Ky. In the severe battle of Perryville, October 8th, the 88th Regiment were under fire for the first time, and displayed great bravery and steadiness. Col. Sherman was highly complimented by Gen. Greusel for his gallantry on the occasion.

COL. SHERMAN.

APPENDIX.

ILLINOIS.—Headquarters, - - - Springfield.

Governor and Commander-in-Chief,
RICHARD YATES, of Jacksonville..1 Jan., 1861

Adjutant General,
Colonel ALLEN C. FULLER, of Belvidere................................11 Nov., 1861

First Assistant Adjutant General,
Lieut. Colonel JOHN S. LOOMIS, of Quincy............................21 June, 1861

Second Assistant Adjutant General,
Major DANIEL L. GOLD, of Lawrenceville..............................17 Aug., 1861

Quartermaster General,
Colonel JOHN WOOD, of Quincy..10 April, 1861

First Assistant Quartermaster General,
Lieut. Colonel GEORGE V. RUTHERFORD, of Quincy.................9 April, 1862

Second Assistant Quartermaster General,
Major JOHN H. SCHERMERHORN, of Springfield.....................11 June, 1862

Commissary General,
Colonel JOHN WILLIAMS, of Springfield...................................April, 1861

Engineer-in-Chief,
Colonel ABNER YATES, of Jacksonville....................................May, 1862

Governor's Aides-de-Camp,
Colonel SOLOMON M. WILLSON, of Chicago..........................3 May, 1861
"   JOHN MOSES, of Winchester......................................1 Jan., 1862
"   JOS. K. C. FORREST, of Chicago...............................14 May, 1862
Major GEORGE W. WINANS, of Quincy................................13 April, 1862
"   JAMES R. LOOMIS, of Equality..................................1 May, 1862

Medical Examining Board,
Major HOSMER A. JOHNSON, of Chicago..............................14 June, 1861
"   ORLANDO M. BRYAN...14 June, 1861
"   HENRY WING, of Collinsville.....................................14 June, 1861
"   ROBERT ROSKOTEN, of Peoria..................................14 June, 1861
"   DANIEL K. GREEN, of Salem.....................................20 July, 1861
"   A. L. McARTHUR, of Joliet...16 Aug., 1862

War Fund Commissioners,
WILLIAM THOMAS, of Jacksonville..7 May, 1861
CHARLES H. LANPHEAR, of Springfield................................7 May, 1861
JAMES H. WOODWORTH, of Chicago....................................7 May, 1861

APPENDIX.

LIST OF COLONELS OF ILLINOIS REGIMENTS.

INFANTRY.

7 Reg't.	Col. A. J. Babcock.		71 Reg't.	Col. Othneil Gilbert.
8 "	" Frank L. Rhoads.		72 "	" Fred. A. Starring.
9 "	" Augustus Mersey.		73 "	" James F. Jacquess.
10 "	" John Tillson.		74 "	" Jason Marsh.
11 "	" T. E. G. Ransom.		75 "	" George Ryan.
12 "	" Aug. E. Chetlain.		76 "	" A. W. Mack.
13 "	" John B. Wyman.		77 "	" David P. Grier.
14 "	" Cyrus Hall.		78 "	" Wm H. Bennison.
15 "	" Thomas J. Turner.		79 "	" Lyman Guinnip.
16 "	" Robert F. Smith.		80 "	" Thomas J. Allen.
17 "	" Addison S. Norton.		81 "	" James J. Dollins.
18 "	" Michael K. Lawler.		82 "	" Frederick Hecker.
19 "	" Joseph R. Scott.		83 "	" Abner C. Harding.
20 "	" C. Carroll Marsh.		84 "	" Louis H. Waters.
21 "	" J. W. S. Alexander.		85 "	" Robert S. Moore.
22 "	" Henry Dougherty.		86 "	" David D. Irons.
23 "	" James A. Mulligan.		87 "	" John E. Whiting.
24 "	" Geza Mihalotzy.		88 "	" Fran. T. Sherman.
25 "	"		89 "	" John Christopher.
26 "	" John M. Loomis.		90 "	" Timothy O'Meara.
27 "	" F. A. Harrington.		91 "	" Henry M. Day.
28 "	" Amory K. Johnson.		92 "	" Smith D. Atkins.
29 "	" Mason Brayman.		93 "	" Holden Putnam.
30 "	" Elias S. Dennis.		94 "	" Wm. W. Orme.
31 "	" Lindorf Ozburn.		95 "	" Laur'ce S. Church.
32 "	" John Logan.		96 "	" T. E. Champion.
33 "	" Charles E. Hovey.		97 "	" F. S. Rutherford.
34 "	" Edward N. Kirk.		98 "	" J. J. Funkhouser.
35 "	" Gustavus A. Smith.		99 "	" Geo. W. K. Bailey.
36 "	" Nicholas Greusel.		100 "	" F. A. Bartleson.
37 "	" Myron S. Barnes.		101 "	" Charles Fox.
38 "	" William P. Carlin.		102 "	" Wm. M. McMurty.
39 "	" Thos. O. Osborn.		103 "	" Amos C. Babcock.
40 "	" Stephen G. Hicks.		104 "	" A. B. Moore.
41 "	" Isaac C. Pugh.		105 "	" Daniel Dustin.
42 "	" Geo. W. Roberts.		106 "	" Robert B. Latham.
43 "	" A. Engleman.		107 "	" Thomas Snell.
44 "	" Chas. Knobelsdorff.		108 "	" John Warner.
45 "	" John E. Smith.		109 "	" Alex. J. Nimmo.
46 "	" John A. Davis.		110 "	" Thomas S. Casey.
47 "	" John Bryner.		111 "	" James S. Martin.
48 "	" Isham N. Haynie.		112 "	" T. J. Henderson.
49 "	" Wm. R. Morrison.		113 "	" George B. Hoge.
50 "	" Moses M. Bane.		114 "	" James Judy.
51 "	" G. W. Cumming.		115 "	" Jesse H. Moore.
52 "	" Thos. W. Sweeny.		116 "	" Nathan W. Tupper.
53 "	"		117 "	" Robert M. Moore.
54 "	" Thos. W. Harris.		118 "	" John G. Fonda.
55 "	" David Stuart.		119 "	" Thos. J. Kinney.
56 "	"		120 "	" John G. Hardy.
57 "	" S. D. Baldwin.		121 "	" Thos. Duff.
58 "	" W. F. Lynch.		122 "	" J. J. Rinaker.
59 "	" P. Sydney Post.		123 "	" James Munroe.
60 "	" Silas C. Toler.		124 "	" Thos. J. Sloan.
61 "	" Jacob Fry.		125 "	" O. F. Harman.
62 "	" James M. True.		126 "	"
63 "	" Francis Moro.		127 "	" John Van Arman.
64 "	"		128 "	" Jon. Richmond.
65 "	" Daniel Cameron, Jr.		129 "	" G. Price Smith.
67 "	" R. M. Hough.		130 "	" Nathaniel Niles.
68 "	" Elias Stuart.		131 "	" G. W. Neely.
69 "	" Jos. H. Tucker.		132 "	" G. W. McKeig.
70 "	" Owen P. Reeves.		133 "	" R. M. Hundley.

CAVALRY.

1 Reg't.	Col. T. A. Marshall.		10 Reg't.	Col. P. Wickersham.
2 "	" Silas Noble.		11 "	" R. G. Ingersoll.
3 "	" Lafayette McCrillis.		12 "	" Arno Voss.
4 "	" T. L. Dickey.		13 "	" Joseph W. Bell.
5 "	" Hall Wilson.		14 "	" D. P. Jenkins.
6 "	" B. H. Grierson.		15 "	" David Hancock.
7 "	" W. P. Kellogg.		16 "	" Warren Stewart.
8 "	" J. F. Farnsworth.		17 "	" Chr. Thieleman.
9 "	" A. G. Brackett.		18 "	" Horace Capron.

ARTILLERY.

1 Reg't.	Col. J. D. Webster.	2 Reg't. Col Thos. S. Mather.

www.ingramcontent.com/pod-product-compliance
Lightning Source LLC
Chambersburg PA
CBHW031124020726
47495CB00007B/2331